Books by Diana Palmer

Long, Tall Texans

Fearless
Heartless
Dangerous
Merciless
Courageous
Protector
Invincible
Untamed
Defender
Undaunted
Unbridled

Wyoming Men

Wyoming Tough
Wyoming Fierce
Wyoming Bold
Wyoming Strong
Wyoming Rugged
Wyoming Brave

The Morcai Battalion

The Morcai Battalion
The Morcai Battalion: The Recruit
The Morcai Battalion: Invictus
The Morcai Battalion: The Rescue

Visit the Author Profile page at Harlequin.com for more titles.

DIANA PALMER

ANY MAN *of* MINE

HQN™

ISBN-13: 978-1-335-96113-6

Any Man of Mine

CONTENTS

A WAITING GAME

To Mary and Georgia,
with love

CHAPTER ONE

Keena Whitman's day had gone backward from the moment she got out of bed. Two of her best sketches had been destroyed when Faye turned a cup of hot coffee over on them. Naturally, the sample-room staff had been livid when they had to wait for Keena to redo the sketches so that they could make up the rush samples for the salesman. Like all salesmen, he was impatient and made no attempt to disguise his annoyance. She'd missed her lunch, the seamstresses had missed theirs and to top it all off, she'd gotten the specifications wrong on a whole cut of blouses, and they had had to be redone with the buyers incensed at the holdup. By the time Keena was through for the day and back home in her Manhattan apartment, she was smoldering.

She kicked off her high-heeled shoes and threw herself down on the long, plush, blue-velvet couch with a heavy sigh. How long ago it seemed that she'd worked at textile design and dreamed of someday working for a big fashion design house. And now she had her own house and was one of the most famous designers of casual wear in the country.

But the pleasure she should have been feeling simply wasn't there. Something was missing from her life. Something vital. But she didn't even know what. Perhaps it was just the winter weather making her morose. She longed for the freedom and warmth of spring to get her blood flowing again.

She lay on her back and stared at the ceiling. She was slender with short black hair and eyes as green as spring leaves. Her complexion was peachy, her mouth as perfect as a bow. At twenty-seven, she retained the fresh look of innocence, despite her sophistication. At least Nicholas said she did.

Nicholas. She closed her eyes and smiled. How long ago had it been when Nicholas Coleman had offered her the chance to work as an assistant designer in his textile empire? It was well over six years ago.

She'd been utterly green at twenty-one. Fresh out of fashion design school in Atlanta and afraid of the big, dark man behind the desk of Coleman Textiles in his Atlanta skyscraper.

It had taken her a week to get up enough nerve to approach him, but she'd been told that he was receptive to new talent, and that he was a sucker for stray animals and stray people.

Even now she could remember how frightened she'd been, looking across the massive desk at that broad leonine face that looked as if it had never smiled.

"Well, show me what you can do, honey," he'd dared with a cynical smile. "I don't bite."

She'd spread her drawings out on the glass surface of the cluttered desk, her hands trembling, and watched for his reaction. But nothing had shown in his dark face, nor in his dark brown, deep-set eyes. He'd nodded, but that was all. Then he'd leaned back in his swivel chair and stared at her.

"Training?" he'd shot at her.

"The—the fashion design school, here in town," she'd managed to get out. "I...that is, I worked on the third shift at the cotton mill to pay my way through. My father works for a textile mill back home—"

"Where is back home?" he interrupted.

"Ashton," she replied.

He nodded, and waited for her to continue, giving every impression of being interested in her muddled speech.

"So I know a little about it," she murmured. "And I've always wanted to design things. Oh, Mr. Coleman, I know I can do it if someone will just give me the chance. I know I can." Her eyes lit up and she put her whole heart and all her youthful enthusiasm into her words. "I realize there's a lot of competition for design jobs, but if you'll give me a chance, I promise I won't let you down. I'll design the sharpest clothes for the lowest cost you've ever seen. I'll work weekends and holidays, I'll—"

"One month," he said, cutting into her sentence.

He leaned forward and pinned her with his level gaze. "That's how much time you've got to prove to me that you can stand the pace." He threw out a salary that staggered her, and then dismissed her with a curt gesture and went back to his paperwork.

He'd been married then, but his wife of ten years had died shortly thereafter of a massive heart attack. Rumors had flown all over the main plant, where Keena worked, but she ignored them. She didn't believe that an argument had provoked the heart attack, and she told one of the women so. Mr. Coleman, she assured her tersely, wasn't that kind of man. He had too much compassion and, besides, why would he keep a picture of his wife on his desk if he didn't love her?

Somehow the innocent little speech had gotten back to him and the next week, he'd sought her out in the canteen on the pretense of asking how everything was going.

"I'm well on my way to making you fabulously wealthy,"

she assured him with an impish grin as she held her plastic coffee cup between her hands.

"I'm *already* fabulously wealthy," he replied.

She sighed. "In that case, you're in a lot of trouble."

He'd smiled at that—the first time she'd seen him smile since his wife's death. The late Mrs. Coleman had been a beauty—blond and delicate, a perfect foil for his size and darkness. Since her death he'd been strangely lost, and his temper had become legendary. He spent more time at the plant than at his office, and threw himself into the accumulation of other plants to complement it. His holdings and his wealth had mushroomed in the months between, and the pressure was telling on him. His hair was growing silver at the temples; his eyes were boasting dark shadows. His tireless business dealings were becoming the talk of the plant. Mr. Coleman was out to become a billionaire, some said. Mr. Coleman was after a business rival, others said. Mr. Coleman was going to make his empire the biggest in America, if he lived, others commented. But only Keena seemed to see through the relentless businessman to the lonely, grief-stricken man underneath. The other employees might think Mr. Coleman was indestructible, but Keena was certain that he wasn't. She would run into him occasionally in the elevator or in the cafeteria. She recalled one time in particular when his eyes had seemed to seek her out. With his coffee in hand, he strolled over to her table and sat down beside Keena and her friend Margaret as naturally and easily as if the three met for a coffee break every day.

"How's it going, Miss Future Famous Designer?" he asked Keena with an amused glance.

Keena had laughed and given him a flip reply, something about an interview in *Women's Wear Daily*. Hadn't he seen it? Margaret finished her coffee and excused herself quickly.

"Did I say something I shouldn't have?" Nicholas asked, staring after the young woman.

"The company brass makes most employees want to run for cover," Keena explained in a dry tone.

"You aren't running," he observed.

"Ah, yes," she agreed. "But then, I've never had much sense."

He chuckled into his coffee, taking a long sip of it. "The patternmakers sing your praises, by the way. They told me your specs were the first they'd had in five years that were written in English."

"High praise, indeed, and I hope I'm going to get a ten thousand dollar a year raise as an inducement to keep them in a good mood?" She grinned.

"Cheeky, aren't you?" he asked with narrowed eyes.

"It's my dimple," she replied in all seriousness.

He shook his head in mock despair. "Incorrigible."

She looked at him—so businesslike and somber in the vested gray business suit that strained against his massive, muscular frame—and dropped her eyes almost at once.

After that day he'd made a point of having coffee with her once in a while. Infrequently, he'd invited her out for a meal, and they'd talk a great deal. She'd asked him once if he had any family, and he'd replied stiffly that what there was of it wasn't to his liking.

"It still hurts, doesn't it?" she had asked quietly then.

He stared at her, his face closed up. "I beg your pardon?"

She met his eyes with compassion and utter fearlessness. "You miss her."

He seemed to see right into her mind in the long minute that followed, and the hauteur slowly drained out of him.

"I miss her like hell," he admitted finally and with a faint, fleeting smile. "She was the loveliest creature I ever knew, inside and out. Generous to a fault, shy." He sighed heavily, his face darkening. "Some women can tear a man down with every word. But Misty made me feel every inch a man every time she looked at me. We married because it was necessary to keep the businesses in the family. But we grew to love each other desperately." He glanced at her. "Yes, I miss her."

She smiled at him. "You were lucky."

He scowled. "Lucky?"

"Some people go through life without ever touching or being touched emotionally by another human being. To love and be loved in return must be magic," she finished gently. "And you had that for ten years."

His eyes had searched hers before they fell. "I never thought of it that way," he said simply.

"Shouldn't you?" Her voice had been gentle and low. And while he was still thinking about it, she changed the subject completely, telling him about some ridiculous mix-up that had occurred in the cutting room that afternoon.

It was sad that he and Misty hadn't been able to have children, she had always thought. They would have made him less lonely. But she could see that he seemed to find solace in her company, and they had worlds of things in common, from a mutual love of ballet and the theater to classical music and art. She found in him a mentor as much as a friend, a tutor and a protector. Nicholas never made a pass at her himself and was fiercely protective. He scrutinized the few suitors she had over the years and gave her his advice, welcome or not, on the men she went out with. If she had to work late, he escorted her home himself. And when he felt that she was ready, he'd found her a job as an apprentice designer in one of New York's grandest fashion houses. He'd encouraged her, pushed her, bullied and chided her, until she climbed straight to the top, which was quite a climb for the only child of a poor, widowed textile worker in the small Georgia town of Ashton. She didn't like to remember her childhood at all. In fact, Nicholas was the only person she'd ever told about it. But then, Nicholas was like no one else. In a real sense he was the only true friend she'd ever had since she left Ashton. And shortly after she'd come to New York, she was relieved to know that Nicholas maintained an apartment in the city.

The phone rang, and she barely heard it, so deeply was she immersed in memory. She was used to Mandy getting the phone, making coffee, serving meals, but this was Mandy's day off, and it took her five rings to realize it. She dragged herself to the end table and picked up the receiver.

"Hello?" she murmured, stifling a yawn.

"That kind of day, was it?" came a deeply amused voice from the other end of the line. "Get on something pretty and I'll treat you to dinner at The Palace." She felt her spirits revive. "Oh, Nicholas, we haven't gone there in months! And they make the most marvelous chocolate mousse."

"Can you make it in half an hour?" he asked impatiently. "I've got to catch the eleven o'clock plane to Paris, and we won't have much time."

"Has anyone ever told you that people who don't slow down get ulcers?" she asked, exasperated.

"They would have to catch up with me first," he told her. "Half an hour."

She stared at the dead receiver. "Nicholas is an enigma," she muttered as she slipped into a long green velvet gown with a deep V neckline and a side slit. He was every inch the high-powered executive, and he had millions, but he wouldn't delegate any responsibilities. If a deal had to be closed, he'd close it. If there was a labor relations problem at one of his plants, he'd negotiate it. If there was an innovative process being presented, he'd go to see it. He pushed himself relentlessly even now, a habit left over from those first horrible weeks after Misty's death. He wouldn't slow down; he wouldn't take time off. It was as if he was afraid to stop, because if he did, he'd have to think and that wouldn't please him. He had too much that he wanted to forget.

Keena was dressed and waiting when the doorbell rang. She opened the door and mentally caught her breath at the sight of Nicholas in evening clothes, as she always did. With his dark hair and eyes, his bronzed complexion in that leonine face, his towering, wrestler's physique, he was the stuff of which feminine dreams were made. And perhaps if Keena hadn't been so wary of men, so unforgetting of that humiliating adolescent romance and the humiliating incident that had followed it, she might have fallen head over heels in love with him. But she'd seen Nicholas in action, and she knew the effect his dark charm had on women. She'd seen his occasional conquest swoon, fall, succumb and be heartlessly discarded too many times to risk joining that queue herself. Nicholas had found safety in numbers since Misty's death, and he was apparently risking no emotional involvement by confining himself to one woman. Keena preferred the position of being just Nicholas's friend and confidante. It was much safer than being added to the notches on his bedpost.

His own eyes were busy, sliding up and down her body with his usual careless appraisal.

"Delightful," he said with a cool smile. "Shall we go?"

"I'm starved," she told him as they got into the empty elevator and Nicholas pressed the main floor button. "I feel as if I haven't eaten for days."

"You look it, too," he growled, eyeing her from his lounging position against the rail. "Why the hell don't you give up that diet and put some meat on your bones?"

"Look who's talking!" She glared. "It would take a forklift to get you up a hill!"

He moved toward her with a dark look in his eyes under that jutting brow. "Think it's fat, do you?" he taunted. He caught her hands and dragged them to his shoulders. "Feel. Show me any flab."

It was like discovering fine wine where she had expected to taste water. She'd never noticed just how broad Nicholas's chest and shoulders really were, or how the scent of tobacco and expensive cologne clung to him. She'd never noticed how chiseled his mouth was, or how exciting it could be to look into his dark eyes at close range. It had been safer not to notice. But her hands touched him through the smooth fabric of his evening jacket and lingered there when she felt the hard muscles under it.

"Well?" he asked, a strange huskiness in his deep voice as he looked down at her.

"You… I never realized how strong you were," she stammered. She looked up into his eyes and time seemed to stand still for a space of seconds while they looked at each other, discovering facial features, textures, expressions, in an unfamiliar intimacy, in the quiet confines of the elevator.

It took several seconds for them to realize that the elevator had stopped and the door had opened. Self-conscious and a little clumsy, Keena managed to get out a little ahead of him and lead the way to the front of the building where his white Rolls-Royce waited with Jimson at the wheel, staring straight ahead stoically.

"Doesn't Jimson ever get a day off?" she asked Nicholas when they were inside the car with the glass partition up, giving them total privacy.

"Not lately. I've been working twenty-five-hour days," he replied.

"I'll never get used to this car," she sighed, leaning her dark head contentedly back against the leather as he was doing.

"What's wrong with it?" he asked curtly.

"Nothing! It's just that few people ever get to ride around in a Rolls—white, no less." She laughed.

He half turned in the seat, one big arm over the back of it, his eyes gleaming, though his smile had not completely disappeared. "And what's wrong with that?" he asked with deliberate slowness.

She braved his glittering eyes. Why did he look so suddenly predatory to her? So dark and menacing? "Nothing—except that I feel as if I were on display every time I ride in it. That's all."

"You should be on display, Keena." Something in the way he fairly growled her name sent a warm, unfamiliar tingle up her spine.

"Because I'm rich and famous now, you mean, and everyone back in Ashton would hardly recognize *this* Keena Whitman?" She laughed shortly, her words underscored with a note of self-derision.

Her answer hadn't pleased him. It was in the hard lines of his face, the narrowing of his eyes. "No, not at all, though you needn't take that little-Miss-Nobody-from-Ashton tone with me. You know what you are and what you've accomplished. And that you're a very beautiful woman," he said in that hard, matter-of-fact way of his.

If he had been looking at her, then he would have seen the shock register on every feature. Keena was suddenly thankful for the darkness between them and the sudden blare of a horn that had broken Nicholas's steady gaze for just that instant.

"Damn city traffic," he muttered half to himself. When he turned back to her, it was with a faintly puzzled expression. "Surely, you've had men tell you that before, that you're beautiful? Scores of them, I'm afraid." His words broke off abruptly, his gaze dropping to her slender body, outlining it with a masculine approval that was new and frightening.

"Why are you looking at me like that?" she asked in a faint whisper.

His dark, quiet eyes eased back up to meet hers. "I was wondering what it would feel like to make love to you."

CHAPTER TWO

Her toes tingled. She'd never felt such a wild surge of emotion and it came up suddenly, stunning her.

Nicholas began to chuckle, the deep sound of it faintly irritating.

"My God, what an expression," he murmured, leaning back against the seat with a heavy sigh. "I thought that would get your attention."

She glared at him. "Now that you've got it, what are you going to do with it?" she asked grumpily.

He glanced at her. "Get you back to the present. I loathe self-pity. Wait until I'm in Paris. I've got enough problems of my own without your dragging new ones from the past."

"What kind of problems?" she probed.

His lips compressed. "Maria."

Maria was his mistress. Keena had read about the relationship in the gossip columns long before Nicholas had introduced the two of them. It shouldn't have bothered her. He was, at forty, an active, virile man, and it would have been absurd to expect him not to have women. But one evening soon after he'd picked up the volatile brunette, Keena had seen them together in a popular night spot dancing so close that the fabric between them seemed to burn. And she'd begged her escort, a harmless young man who'd only lasted one date, to take her home. She couldn't bear the sight. She'd hated the surge of jealousy, but it had persisted until even now she could hardly bear to hear Maria's name.

"What's wrong?" she asked, trying to sound casual.

"She won't believe it's over," he said curtly. "She's calling me in tears twice a day, moaning over the lonely life I've condemned her to. Lonely, my foot, with two diamond necklaces, a new Porshe and an ermine coat!"

"Maybe she really does miss you," she muttered, able to be generous now that she knew he'd lost interest. She felt strangely relieved.

"She misses the Rolls, honey, not me." He laughed shortly.

"Was it good in bed?" she asked, tongue in cheek, and darted a glance at him.

"The Rolls or me?" he replied, refusing to be ruffled.

"I imagine she misses the warmth," she retorted, grinning at him.

His dark eyes smiled at her. "Do you think I'd be warm?"

"Like a blast furnace, I'd imagine," she said demurely. "Is that why you're going to Paris, to escape Maria?"

"It isn't funny," he said, the smile fading.

"No, I don't suppose it is, to you." She shot him a teasing glance. "But your love life is like one ongoing adventure to me. I really think you should assign the girls numbers or something so you can keep things in order."

"I'm delighted that my private life amuses you so," he said in a chilling voice.

"You could always tease me about mine," she said grandly.

His dark eyes cut around toward her. "You don't have one," he said. "Not a love life, anyway."

Her eyebrows shot up. "What makes you so sure?"

"I keep a sharp eye on you, little one," he said with a somber tone that startled her. "Sharper than you know. You don't sleep around."

She glared at him. "Maybe I should hire a private detective of my own!"

"What do you want to know?" he asked with a wicked grin. "Go ahead, ask me. I'll tell you."

She glared at him again. "I'd just love to ask you something so personal it would embarrass you to the roots of your hair."

"Dream on, honey," he returned with a smile.

She sized up his muscular, imposing physique. "I'll bet you crush them," she murmured absently.

He lifted an eyebrow. "Is there only one position?" he asked in all innocence.

The blush started at her hairline, worked down into her cheeks, seeped into her throat and down into the plunging neckline of her dress. And he sat there and watched her and laughed softly, lazily, as if the sight delighted him.

"Instead of the theater, I'd better start taking you to some X-rated movies," he murmured. "Your education is sadly lacking."

She opened her mouth to speak, but before she could manage a retort, he picked up her hand and pressed her palm to his lips. It was unexpected, and the sensation it caused made her heart turn over wildly. He caught her eyes, holding them in the dim confines of the car until she felt as if she'd never get her breath again.

He drew her forearm against his lips, sliding it past his rough cheek, holding her eyes the whole time, studying her like some rare and beautiful thing he'd captured.

"I use my elbows," he whispered, drawing her imperceptibly closer, his voice caressing, seductive. "And I've never had a single complaint. Would you like me to prove it?"

Her heart was hammering wildly in her trembling body. She stared at him and couldn't look away, and she was suddenly afraid.

"Little coward," he murmured, watching the expressions chase each other in her eyes. "Are you really afraid of me?"

She cleared her throat. "I'm hungry," she lied.

"For me?" he asked humorously.

She tore her hand out of his grasp and edged back into the corner by the door, glaring at him like some fierce little animal.

"You're priceless," he chuckled. "Did you think I was going to make a pass at you in front of Jimson?"

"Jimson is trained not to look," she reminded him, her voice strangely breathless. "And it's not kind of you to make fun of me."

"I can't help it. You rise to the bait so sweetly." He cocked his head at her, his eyes watchful. "Haven't you ever wondered in all these years what kind of lover I'd be?"

She averted her eyes then dropped them. "Yes," she said finally, because she'd never made a habit of lying to him.

"Well," he prodded. "What did you think?"

She glanced at him with unfamiliar shyness. "That you'd be heavy," she grinned.

He laughed softly. "And what else?" he persisted.

She shrugged. "Tender," she said softly. Her eyes met his across the space. "Patient. A little rough."

"Not demanding?" he asked quietly, and there were deep undercurrents in the conversation.

"Are you?" she asked involuntarily.

"It depends on the woman," he replied. "But I can be patient. And tender, when I need to be."

"How…how do you like a woman to be?" she asked breathlessly.

He stared at her, his eyes darkening, his face hardening with emotion, and there was an electricity between them like nothing Keena had ever experienced.

"The Palace, sir." Jimson's pleasant voice interrupted their wordless communication as he stopped the car in front of the exclusive restaurant.

Keena drew in a breath in relief, wondering what had gotten into her to make her ask such an intimate question. *It must be my age*, she thought wildly, waiting for him to come around and open her door.

"I think we're going to have to do some talking when I come back from Paris," he said on the way inside, "I've got something in mind that might benefit us both."

"You want me to design you a wardrobe!" she said with mock enthusiasm. "Something suitably flashy, but elegant, to go with this car. Frankly, I don't think the job's for me, but…"

"Damn you!" He burst out laughing in spite of himself. "Come on and feed me before I take a bite out of you!"

It was impossible not to notice as they made short work of filet mignon and lobster, buttery rolls, a salad and rich red wine that he was paying more attention to Keena than he was to the food.

She stopped in the act of lifting a piece of steak to her mouth, staring across the white linen-covered table at him. "Why are you watching me so closely?" she asked with a faint laugh. "Afraid I'm going to try to walk out with the silver?"

"You remind me of a pixie," he murmured absently. "Mischievous little face, teasing eyes slanted just a bit at the corners, perfect little mouth. You look as if you're out of place in this setting, and I've only just noticed it."

"I'm twenty-seven," she reminded him, "and I'd hardly fit under a leaf in somebody's forest."

"Twenty-seven," he echoed quietly. His dark eyes narrowed. "And you barely seem half that to me."

"It's because you're so old," she told him with mock seriousness. "Entering the golden years, where your bones creak and your eyesight is slowly dimming…"

"Damn you," he growled harshly. "Shut up!" His tone was venomous, so controlled that it seemed to shudder with sudden rage.

It was unexpected, and it silenced Keena immediately. She'd always teased Nicholas, from the beginning, and often about his age. He'd always laughed. But tonight she'd caught him on the raw for the first time, and he wasn't laughing. His face had snapped closed like something untamed. His eyes were the only things in his broad, hard face that seemed alive, and they were blazing with menace. She'd only seen Nicholas this angry once, when one of her coworkers had gotten miffed when she refused his advances. Nicholas had intended to surprise her in the office that day and had come in on them unexpectedly. Keena was sure that she could have subdued the young man without any help. But Nicholas, summing up the situation with a glance, had not stopped to ask for an invitation to rescue her. She'd learned later that he'd broken the young man's jaw. And ever since she'd carefully avoided antagonizing him.

Until now. And it hadn't been deliberate. "Nicholas, I was only teasing," she said softly.

That didn't calm him a bit. He picked up his wineglass with a grip that threatened to snap the slender stem and drained it in one huge gulp.

"Nicholas, please," she whispered, shivering a little in the face of his white-hot anger. "Don't be angry with me."

He set the wineglass down with slow, deliberate movements before he pinned her with his eyes. "I'm forty, not eighty, and all the parts still work. If you don't believe that, ask Maria," he added icily.

She chewed on her lower lip. She hadn't meant to pull the lion's tail, but he was reacting in a way she'd never expected. Amazingly, she felt tears prick at her eyes and that was new, too. She hadn't cried for years. But she felt tears damming up in her eyes now.

She put her napkin down very gently, avoiding Nicholas's blazing eyes. "Uh, if you don't mind, I've an early start tomorrow," she managed in a shadow of her normal tone.

"Would you like dessert?" he asked with glacial courtesy.

She stared at him with a brave but trembling arch in her chin. "Only if I get to pour it over your head," she managed with dripping sweetness.

For an instant, amusement vied with anger in his face, but it was quickly subdued. "Let's go, then," he said.

She preceded him out of the restaurant after he'd paid the check, walking quickly, her slender legs rippling the sensuous velvet of her dress, her head held as regally as a princess's.

"Careful you don't sprain your neck," he chided.

"Your temper's more in danger of a sprain than my neck is," she countered coolly. "If you'd rather brood for a while, I can get a cab back to my apartment," she added. "I've had a pretty rotten day so far, and tonight isn't making up for it."

"Stop it," he growled, nodding to Jimson as they reached the car. He opened the door for Keena as Jimson got in under the wheel and cranked the engine.

"I didn't start it," she returned, avoiding his hand as she got into the seat that he was holding the door open to. She moved as far away from him as possible when he got in beside her and closed the door.

"Don't pout, for God's sake," he shot at her with a hard glare.

She returned the glare with interest. It was the first major argument they'd had, and it was beginning to set records for antagonism.

"I'll pout if I damn please!" she flared up, hunched in her corner. "Why don't you go find Maria if you want a sparring partner? I didn't try to lure you into my bed and then refuse to let you go when you were tired of me."

"You wouldn't know what to do with me if you got me into your bed," he returned with malice.

She started to make a smart remark back, but she was suddenly too tired to make the effort. It had been a perfectly horrible day; and it was just getting worse. Now her only friend was furious with her, and she wanted to wail.

They rode in a tense silence until Jimson pulled up at the curb in front of her apartment house and sat looking straight ahead while Keena reached for the doorknob.

But a big, warm hand got there first, holding hers where it rested on the handle.

"Not like this," he said heavily, his tone strained. "I can't leave for Europe tomorrow with a sword between us."

"Why not?" she countered, not looking at him. "I've seen you walk away from worse—and laugh."

"Not you," he said quietly. "*Never* you."

The tone of his voice more than the words calmed her. She turned slowly and looked up at him. He was closer than she'd realized, his dark eyes only inches away, the warmth and fragrance of his big body permeating her, drowning her in sensation.

"I don't think you're old," she whispered unsteadily, affected by him as she'd never been before. "I've never paid any attention to the age difference. It never mattered."

His dark eyes searched hers with a scrutiny that made her nervous. "Tease me about my size, or my money, or my temper. But leave birthdays out of it from now on."

She swallowed. "All right, Nicholas."

He removed his hand from hers as if it burned him. "I'll see you when I get back. It may take two weeks to close this deal, so don't expect me before the middle of February."

Two weeks without him. The bleak winter was going to move even slower until he returned, and she was just realizing how empty her life was going to be without those unexpected visits and phone calls. He'd been away from the city for long periods before and it hadn't bothered her. But suddenly it did, and she looked up at him with a curious frown above her pale green eyes.

"You look strange," he remarked.

"We haven't argued in a long time. In fact, I don't really think we ever did," she said gently, her eyes troubled.

"Perhaps we're more aware of each other now," he said, his voice unusually quiet as he looked down into her eyes.

"Aware?" she whispered.

His breath came hard and quick as he looked down at her soft mouth with an intensity that made her heart race. It was as if he was kissing it, and her lips parted involuntarily, her eyes half-closed at the intensity of the gaze.

"I can almost feel your mouth under mine. Do you know that?" he murmured in a voice like deep velvet. "Your lips trembling, your breasts swelling against me…"

"Nicholas!" she burst out, half gasping, half angry, at the intimacy of it.

"If Jimson wasn't sitting up front trying not to see us, I'd give you a damned sight more than words to remember me by," he growled harshly. "I'd wrestle you down on the seat and teach you things about your body you've never dreamed it could feel. And you want it," he added with a level gaze that made her knees melt. "Don't you?"

Her body was trembling madly. She gaped at him, hating her own reactions, hating him for sensing them.

"You're my friend," she choked.

"I'm going to be your lover," he replied curtly. "Think about that while I'm gone."

She got out of the car quickly, almost tripping in her haste while Nicholas sat there and watched her with unholy amusement, his eyes glittering with triumph. He knew how he affected her. He had too much experience, damn him, not to know.

"Maybe I won't be here when you get back," she cried with a pitiful attempt at self-preservation, at pride.

"You'll be here," he said, and closed the door.

"You'll be lucky," she muttered as the elegant taillights of the Rolls disappeared into the night. She didn't realize how prophetic the words were. The next morning her father's doctor called to tell her that her only surviving relative had been found dead in his bed. Her father was gone.

The funeral had been harrowing, and Keena was grateful when it was over at last, when her father's few well-meaning friends had gone and the house was finally peaceful.

She thumbed through the documents on his desk with a faint smile. It had been so like him to leave everything neat, in order. It was almost as if he'd expected the massive coronary that had taken his life.

The will was just as straightforward as Alan Whitman had always been. It left the house to Keena, along with pitifully few possessions. It saddened her that the entire estate barely amounted to the profits her business realized in one day.

She got up from the desk and stood at the window. Her father had never allowed her to give him any money to provide him with even a new car. He and his daughter had been close, but like her he valued his independence. He wanted nothing that he hadn't earned himself, although he was pleased with her success and frequently told her so.

She looked through the window at the narrow road that ran by the front of the house to the small town beyond. How many of her old classmates would know her now? she wondered. In adolescence she'd been a gangly, painfully shy girl with clothes that always seemed to hang on her, and an eternal slump. Most of the other students had laughed at her, boys and girls alike, and had made fun of the way she dressed, the walk that they said had the grace of a pelican running. She was as out of place in the small town as a sparrow would have been in a den of hawks. Alan Whitman had moved here from Miami, settling in this pleasant section of south Georgia with a mind toward starting his own business. But illness had slowed him down, diminished his resources, and he'd had a daughter to support. So he'd taken a job at the local textile mill, just until he could get on his financial feet again. But he'd been trapped by house payments and car payments and doctor bills into keeping the hated job, and he'd found all too soon that there was no way out. He was stuck.

His spirit was all but broken by the long hours, and there was no laughter in the big house he'd spent his life savings on. He had dozens of get-rich-quick schemes that fell through quickly. He spent his life looking for the rainbow, but all he found was the pants line of the manufacturing company.

Keena sighed bitterly at the irony of life. Her father had gotten poor making clothes, while she'd gotten rich. Even now she looked the part of the wealthy career woman in her chic designer jeans and wide-sleeved silk blouse. The emeralds on her ears and her wrist were real, not the paste ones she'd loved to wear as a poor teenager.

How long ago it all seemed now, those brief, secret meetings with him in the woods, the first few kisses that led a naive Keena to an apartment owned by one of James's friends. Tall, dark-headed, with vivid blue eyes under thick black lashes, James Harris had been the darling of the social set, a young attorney with promise. Keena had known that it was disastrous to care about him, but her heart had ignored her mind and gone end over end every time it saw him. She couldn't begin to look at another boy, or even Larry Harris, who worshipped her.

If only she'd realized that he had never had any intention of marrying her. She'd been too blinded by her own feelings to realize that James was keeping his relationship with her a secret from everyone. He'd never even stopped by the house to see her, or pick her up there for one of their few dates, and he was careful to stay away from public places. They spent long hours in his car at the local lover's lane, necking, until one night when the kisses grew suddenly longer and slower and deeper, and he suggested that they go to his friend's apartment to have a snack before he took her home. They both knew why they were going, and it had nothing to do with food. Keena, young and naive and with her first passion for a man in full bloom, went trustingly.

She was expecting all the fiery passion and tenderness of every romantic novel she had read. But James, for a supposedly practiced lover, was carelessly intent on his own satisfaction. He hadn't even bothered with taking time to study the softly curving young body he'd taken so quickly and roughly.

"Get your clothes on fast," he'd said the minute he was

through, leaving Keena confused, frustrated and ashamed of
her easy capitulation. He didn't even look at her as he dressed.
"Hurry!" he'd called over his shoulder. "Jack could come in
any minute. He told me I could only have the apartment for
an hour."

She'd dressed hurriedly, tears streaming from her eyes, her
body feeling bruised, violated. She'd expected a loving word
or two, but there had been none of that.

She'd followed him to the door, and he'd taken her back to
the end of her driveway, careful to stop the car in the privacy
of the alley so that no one would recognize it.

"Sorry I had to be so quick," he'd said with a half smile.
"Next time it will be better. I'll find another place."

There wasn't going to be a next time, and she'd told him
so, her voice shaking with disappointment.

"Well, what did you expect, rose petals and fireworks?"
he'd burst out. "I thought you cared about me."

"I did," she'd wept.

"I don't want any part of your fears, Keena. There are too
many willing girls." And he'd driven away.

Keena had sweated out the next few weeks, and she hadn't
relaxed until she knew she wasn't pregnant. But her love for
James hadn't eased. She watched for him; she listened for the
phone. But he didn't even try to get in touch with her. In
desperation she accepted his brother Larry's invitation to a
party at the Harris home, hoping for just a sight of James, a
sign that he wasn't really through with her. It had just been
an argument, after all. He'd talked about marriage, about an
engagement. Perhaps he was giving her time to think. Of
course, that was why he hadn't called. And all that gossip
about James and Cherrie was just that—gossip. So what that
Cherrie was the daughter of a prominent local attorney, and a
voluptuous blonde? It was Keena whom James really cared for.

She accepted Larry's invitation, wondering if he knew how she felt about his brother, if that might account for that odd, vague pity she often read in his eyes. In later years she'd wondered, because Larry had seemed to wait deliberately until she was in earshot to talk to James the night of the party.

She'd worn a dress of white crepe, which she'd made from material bought with money she earned working in the local grocery store at the checkout counter. Even then she'd had a flair for fashion, creating her own design. The dress had caused a mild sensation, even on a mill worker's daughter. But James had only spared her a sharp glance when she'd walked in on Larry's arm. He hadn't asked her to dance or greeted her. Neither had his father or mother, in fact, unless those cold smiles and curt nods could be classified as such.

She'd been only a few feet away when she heard Larry ask James, "Doesn't Keena look like a dream tonight?"

"I hadn't noticed," came the terse reply. "Why in hell did you have to invite her here tonight? Mother may play Lady Bountiful to the workers, but she won't care much for her son dating one," James reminded him with a short, cold laugh. "Keena's father is, after all, just one of our spreaders. He isn't even an executive."

"He's nice," Larry had defended.

"My God, maybe he is, but he's as dull as a winter day, just like his skinny daughter. She's plain and stupid, and she's practically flat-chested to boot. Believe me, it was like making love to a man..."

She'd felt Larry's shock, even at a distance. "Making love?" he breathed.

Keena hadn't stayed to hear any more. With her eyes full of tears and her makeup running down her white face, she'd left the house and walked every step of the way home in the dark without thinking about danger. And those cold, hurting

words had stayed with her ever since. They'd been indirectly
responsible for her success, because her hatred for James Harris
and her thirst for revenge had carried her through the lean,
hard times that had led up to her enrollment in the fashion
design school. All she'd wanted in life from that terrible night
forward was to become something more than a mill worker's
daughter—an outsider. And she had.

There was a discreet tap on the door before Mandy came in
like a small, dark-haired whirlwind, her dark eyes sparkling.

"Brought you some coffee," she said, placing a tray on the
coffee table. A plate of doughnuts rested temptingly beside
it. "Come on, you've got to eat something."

Keena grimaced at her housekeeper. "I don't want food,"
she said. "Just coffee. You be a love and eat the doughnuts."

"You'll blow away," the older woman warned. "Why
bother to bring me down here with you if you aren't going
to let me cook?"

"It gets lonely here," she replied. She gazed around her at
the towering near-ruin of a house. It must have been a show-
place years before her father bought it, but lack of care and
deterioration had taken their toll on it. Without some sub-
stantial repairs, it was going to fall in.

"Did you reach the construction people?" Keena asked as
she stirred cream into a cup of steaming coffee.

"Yes," Mandy replied, looking disapproving. "Look, it's
none of my business, but why are you going to funnel good
money into this white mausoleum?"

Keena ran a lazy hand over the faded, worn brocade of the
antique sofa. "I'll need to have the furniture redone, as well.
See if you can find an upholsterer while you're at it."

"How long are we going to be here?" Mandy asked curiously.

"A few weeks." She laughed at Mandy's obvious shock. "I

need a break. I can run the company from here. Ann can call me if she needs help. And meanwhile, I'll play with mending this pitiful house."

"I wish I knew what you were up to," Mandy sighed.

"It's a kind of game," Keena explained with a smile.

"And is Nicholas going to play, too?"

Keena glared at her. She didn't want to think about Nicholas right now. "He's a friend, nothing more. Just because we go out once in a while…"

"Twice a week, every week, and he protects you like a mother hen," Mandy corrected.

Keena shifted uneasily. "Nick's like a brother. He feels responsible for me."

"Some brother," Mandy scoffed. "You should have noticed the way he was watching you at that Christmas party we gave. He started scowling every time another man came near you. He'll be along, Miss Independence, or I miss my guess. No way is Nicholas going to let you spend several weeks down here without doing something about it."

"What do you expect him to do, come and drag me back home?" Keena asked curtly.

"I wouldn't put it past him," came the equally brusque reply.

"You," Keena told her with a mock scowl, "are a professional busybody."

Mandy grinned. "Thanks. About time you paid me a compliment or two for these gray hairs you've given me."

Keena laughed, studying the little salt-and-pepper head. "Not so gray," she returned.

"You going to see that Harris man?" Mandy asked suddenly with narrowed eyes.

Keena met that gaze levelly. "Maybe."

"Good thing, too. Get him out of your system once and

for all." She wiped her hands on her apron. "Memories are dangerous, you know. They're always better than reality."

"That's why I came back to face them," Keena admitted.

She stretched hugely and got up from the sofa. "We've been getting some interested glances since I had the corral and stable fences repaired and bought that mare." She smiled. "I think I'll go for a ride."

"Didn't you tell me once that this property joins the Harrises'?" Mandy asked.

"In back," Keena agreed. "I used to rent a horse to ride. I saved all my money just to catch a glimpse of James Harris in the woods. Maybe I'll get lucky today," she added with a smile and a wink.

It was chilly in the woods, and Keena was glad of her jodhpurs and boots, the thick cashmere sweater she put on over her silk blouse, the warm fur-lined gloves on her hands and the thick tweed hacking jacket. She'd never been able to afford a decent kit in her youth, so it was something of a thrill to be able to wear it now. It almost made up for those rides she'd gone on with Jenny Harris, James's sister, in worn jeans and a denim jacket that Jenny was too sweet to make fun of.

She paused by a small stream, her eyes closed, taking in the cold, sweet peace of the woods, the sound of water running between the banks, the sudden snapping of twigs nearby.

Her eyes flew open as another horse and rider came into view. A big black horse with a slender man astride him, a dark-haired man with blue eyes and an unsmiling face. He was wearing a tweed jacket, too, over a turtleneck sweater. The hands on the reins were long-fingered, and a cigarette dangled in one of them.

"You're trespassing," the man said. "This is private property."

She lifted an eyebrow at him, ignoring the wild beat of her heart as she felt the years between her last sight of him fall away.

"The property line is two paces behind you," she replied coolly. "And if you care to look, there's a metal survey stake— quite a new one. I had the property lines resurveyed two days ago."

His eyes narrowed as he lowered them to her slender body, past her high, firm breasts to her small waist and flaring hips, clearly outlined by her tailored riding gear.

"Keena?" he asked as if the thought was incredulous. His eyes came back up to her lovely, high-cheekboned face framed by black hair that feathered around it, her pale green eyes like clear pools under her thick lashes.

She allowed herself a smile. "That's my name."

"My God, you've changed," he murmured. His eyes went to her wrist, and he smiled faintly. "Except for that habit of wearing gaudy costume jewelry. I'm glad something about you hasn't changed."

She wanted to hit him with the riding crop, but that would have been more in character in her adolescence than it was now. She'd learned control, if nothing else.

"Old habits die hard," she replied with a bitter smile.

"How true," he murmured. "I was sorry to hear about your father. He was a good worker. There's a small insurance policy, of course. You might check with the personnel office about that. You got the flowers we sent? A potted plant, I think…"

"They were very nice, thanks," she replied.

"Are you still living in Atlanta?" he asked politely.

"New York," she corrected.

He made a distasteful face. "Nasty place. Pollution and all that. I prefer Ashton."

She stared at him, letting the memory merge with the reality. He'd changed. Not just in age, but in every other way. He looked older, less imposing, less authoritative.

"How's Jenny?" she asked quietly.

"Doing very well, thanks. She lives with her husband and son in Greenville. Larry's married," he added pointedly. "He lives in Charleston."

"I heard that you and Cherrie married," she said.

His face drew up. "She and I were divorced two years back," he said coldly.

She shrugged. "It happens."

He was staring at her again, his eyes thoughtful. "I can't get over the change. You're different."

"I'm older," she replied.

"Married?" he asked, openly curious.

She shook her head. "I have a career."

"In textiles?" he asked with a faint smile.

She paused. "In a matter of speaking, yes."

He laughed shortly. "Sewing, I suppose."

"That, too." She patted the mare's mane. "I've got to get back. Nice seeing you," she said with a parting smile.

"I'll drop by before you leave for home," he said unexpectedly.

She gave him her best smile. "That would be nice," she managed huskily. "But you needn't rush. I'll be here for several more weeks."

His eyebrows shot up. "Can you spare that long from your job?"

"I have a wonderful, understanding boss," she returned. "See you."

And think about that, she laughed to herself as she let the mare have her head on the way back to the stable.

What Ashton needed, she decided, was a party. A big, lavish, New York, society-type party, so that she could show her dear old friends how much the gangly textile worker's daughter had changed. Just thinking about it brightened her dark mood. Before she got back to the house, she was already planning her strategy, from redecorating and renovation, to the caterers. This was going to be an absolute delight.

It was like having a houseful of relatives come to stay when the carpenters and decorators descended on them. Keena couldn't move without bumping into a ladder or a pile of lumber.

"They're multiplying," Mandy moaned one morning, watching two carpenters hard at work trying to replace a portion of the kitchen ceiling. "And how can I cook?"

"Make two plates full of sandwiches." Keena laughed. "Maybe if we feed them enough, they'll work faster. And don't spare the coffee."

"You're the boss," Mandy sighed, shaking her head as she moved toward the cupboard.

"Hey, lady, somebody's at the door!" one of the electricians called, pausing with a length of cord in one hand.

She squeezed past a painter on a ladder, her jeans and pale blue T-shirt making her look younger than her years, clinging outrageously to her long, graceful legs and the soft, full curves of her body. Her hair was curling softly around her face, and some of the strain of big business had fallen away despite the grief this trip had started with. She felt younger, more relaxed and more feminine.

"Hey, guys, there's a Rolls-Royce out there!" one of the carpenters whispered to his friends, stunned.

Keena paused with her hand on the doorknob. It couldn't be James Harris, even though that was whom she'd expected after their confrontation two days ago. The Harrises had money, but not enough to run a Rolls. She knew only one man with that kind of careless wealth, and she hadn't dreamed—despite Mandy's prediction—that he'd come here.

She twisted the crystal doorknob and pulled the wide door open. The man standing there towered over her, as broad as a wrestler, all hard muscle and determination, with a craggy face and dark eyes that were devouring every inch of her.

"So here you are," he growled, his voice reminiscent of the last time she'd seen him, and remembering it made her flush slightly. "I've had a hell of a time finding you. Mrs. Barnes said you called the apartment to see if I'd come home, but all you told her was that you were going home to Georgia."

"And you couldn't remember where that was?" she asked with a sweet smile.

"It's a damned big state," he replied curtly, staring past her at the gaping workmen who were openly curious about the newcomer in the gray suit. "I had to hunt through your old personnel file to find out your hometown. I couldn't remember it."

"You didn't think to call my office?" she asked.

"I got back only yesterday," he said under his breath. "Sunday, madam, and your people don't work on Sunday."

She drew in a steadying breath. Seeing him again was causing her heart to do acrobatics. "My father died," she said quietly.

"I'm sorry," he said curtly. "Was it quick?"

She nodded. "Very." She looked up at him with sad eyes, and wished she could have run to him when they'd called to tell her. His arms would have felt so good, and she could have cried in them. "Did you think I was in hiding?" she added with a mirthless laugh.

"Hide, here?" He glared at the workmen. "You'd have hell trying with this crowd. It looks like a damned construction site in here."

"Would you like to come in?" she asked.

"My insurance company wouldn't like it," he said bluntly, with a wary eye on the two carpenters up on ladders just inside the open door.

"Well, we could sit in the porch swing," she suggested, gesturing toward it.

His eyes followed hers. Two boards were missing in strategic places. His dark eyes danced and just for an instant she caught a glimpse of something different in them.

"Not unless you want to sit on my lap and give your audience something to stare at," he replied. "Besides that, it's blasting cold out here, and you aren't dressed for it." He caught her arm. "We'll sit in the car and talk for a minute."

"Lecherous thing," she murmured, following him to the car quickly to get out of the biting cold. "You'll probably lock me in and try to seduce me."

"There's an idea," he agreed, putting her in the passenger side of the Rolls. "Slide over."

She made room for him, feeling swallowed as he slid one huge arm around her and gave her the benefit of his warmth against the faint chill of the car.

"Some idea," she murmured. "You've never even made a real pass at me."

He leaned down, his face suddenly closer than it had ever been before, so close that she could see the tiny lines at the corners of his eyes, the thickness of his eyelashes, the faint shadow around his firm, chiseled mouth. An expensive fragrance, a familiar fragrance, clung to his big, warm body.

"You never wanted it before," he reminded her. His eyes went to her mouth, pale without lipstick, and her heart rocked at the sensuous look in his glittering eyes. "Not until the night I left for Paris. But this is as good a time as any to satisfy your curiosity, little Miss Purity. Let me show you how I kiss."

He leaned closer, brushing his parted lips against hers before she had time to protest. The tenderness of the action paralyzed her, and in a trance, she watched his mouth touch and lift and brush against hers in a silence that was suddenly sparkling and alive with new sensations, new awareness.

His strong white teeth nipped softly at her lips, tugging them deftly apart as his tongue tasted, slowly, the inner curve of her upper lip.

She gasped at the contact, her eyes looking straight into his, seeing shadows that had never been there before.

"You taste of coffee," he said in a deep, sensuous tone.

"I...had it...for breakfast." Was that her voice, that high-pitched, husky stammer? She felt as rigid as a board, tense, waiting for something with a hunger that was as shocking as the look on Nicholas's face.

"I think I'll have you for breakfast," he murmured, and she watched his mouth open slightly as it fitted itself expertly to her soft, tremulous lips. "Open your mouth," he whispered against the silken softness. "Don't make me force you."

"Nicholas?" His name came out as a gasp when she felt his big, warm hands cupping her face, barely aware of his body half covering hers, crushing her back against the soft leather in a warm, breathless embrace.

He didn't answer her. His mouth was hard and warm and faintly cruel as it moved with slow deliberation deeper and deeper into hers. Her heart felt as if it were on a merry-go-round. She was spinning, flying.

"Oh," she whispered, shaken, into the hard mouth laying claim to her lips.

His tongue went into her mouth, teasing, withdrawing, causing sensations she'd only dreamed about before. Something devastating was happening to her.

One of his big, warm hands left her cheek and eased down

to the soft cotton fabric over her breast. He took the weight
of it into his cupped palm, savoring its softness, testing its
firmness, and she gasped at the newness of his touch, drawing back to look into his dark eyes.

"You don't wear a bra, do you?" he asked in a slow, tender
voice. "You don't need one, either. Your breasts are so soft,
Keena, firm and soft and warm under my hands."

"Nick..." she gasped, drowning in the sure touch of his
fingers, probing, caressing.

She caught his hand and stilled it, half-frightened.

"Please, don't," she whispered. "Nick..."

"I like the way you say my name," he murmured deeply.
"Say it again."

She felt like a fish out of water, floundering. She couldn't
get her breath at all, and her mouth throbbed with both his
possession of it and her own hunger to have him do it again.
She lowered her eyes to his white shirt.

"Shy of me?" he asked softly. "After all these years?"

She looked up at him warily. "We've never made love before," she whispered unsteadily, keenly aware of his fingers
still resting lightly on her breast.

"I wouldn't call this making love," he corrected quietly,
studying her wild eyes. "Why don't you want me to touch
you?"

She blushed furiously, hating her foolishness, her lack of
sophistication, hating his mocking laughter.

"You liked it, didn't you?" he asked, removing his hand to
ruffle her dark hair.

"I've got to go back inside," she ground out.

"Not yet. When was the funeral?"

"A week ago."

He scowled. "And you're still here?" His eyes narrowed.
"Why?"

Her lips compressed stubbornly. She wasn't going to be talked out of this, not now. She told him why she was staying, in no uncertain terms, tacking on, "And the first guest I'm inviting to the party is James Harris."

His dark eyes seemed to burst with flame as he stared down at her.

He knew that Keena had loved James Harris and that he had hurt her badly because Keena had cried her heart out on his shoulder one night after too many whiskey sours on an empty stomach—one of those rare occasions when she drank hard liquor. But he'd never learned exactly what Harris had done to her to cause her so much pain. All he knew was that he'd never let James Harris hurt her again.

"You're crazy as hell if you think I'm going to let that creep get his hands on you," he said in a cutting voice.

"And just what do you think you're going to do about it, Nicholas?" she demanded with more courage than she felt. The long, searching kiss and the touch of his big hands had knocked half the fight out of her.

He moved away from her, got out of the car and stood back to let her get out of the car. "I fight with no holds barred," he reminded her with a strange, cool smile. "And I've put in a lot of years on you. I'm not about to stand by and watch you put your pretty neck into a noose."

"It's my neck," she murmured.

He tilted her chin up and bent down to her, brushing his mouth slowly, softly, against hers with something like possession in his dark eyes. He watched her helpless reaction with a smile. "I told you before I left for Paris that one day I was going to be your lover. That day's closer than you think, sweetheart, and you're hungrier for me than I'd imagined. Ripe, ready to be picked."

"I'm not an apple," she ground out.

"No, you're a peach," he corrected with a last, soft kiss. "A sweet, juicy little peach that I could eat. But first, I'm going to have to knock you out of the tree."

She glared at him as he went around the elegant hood of the Rolls and got in under the steering wheel. "You'd better get a big stick, Nicholas Coleman!" she cried.

He only laughed. "No, honey, you had. I'll be back."

And before she could fire a retort, he drove off in a cloud of dust, leaving her standing there in the cold.

CHAPTER THREE

Mandy glanced up from the rolls she was making in the kitchen as Keena walked through.

"Flames," she murmured, muffling a grin.

"What?" Keena asked absently, unaware of the picture she made with her hair mussed from Nick's big fingers, her eyes wild, her lips swollen and red.

"Coming from you," Mandy commented drily. She started laying the rolls into a pan. "Seen Nick, have you?"

"Seen him?" she burst out. "You should have heard…" She flushed. "On second thought, you shouldn't have heard him. But he's absolutely unreasonable!"

"How?"

"He doesn't want me to stay here, for one thing," she muttered darkly, her lovely eyes narrowing. She folded her arms across her throbbing chest and leaned back against the counter. "As if he had any right, any right at all, to order me around. The nerve, talking about knocking me out of trees and getting sticks…"

"You feel all right?" Mandy asked pleasantly.

"No. Yes. I don't know."

"That's what I've always liked most about you—your definite answers." Mandy grinned.

Keena, not even half hearing her housekeeper, turned in a daze and walked under the ladder where two painters were busy on the walls and ceiling of the dining room. She was confused as she'd never been, as shy as a girl when she thought about seeing Nicholas again after that ardent kiss. He'd touched her…

She sighed, walking aimlessly up the stairs with dreams in her eyes. In all those years, not a single pass, not a touch out of the way, but overnight her whole relationship with Nick was different, exciting. He'd been her friend, but now what was he? She was going to have to rethink her entire relationship with him after today.

Funny, she hadn't really taken him seriously the night he left for Paris, when he'd said that he was going to be her lover. Reflecting on it, she'd decided that he'd been teasing. But today was no joke. The tenderness of the mouth he'd kissed so thoroughly was very real, and her chest tingled from the long, hard contact with his big body, from the touch of his experienced hands.

Part of her, a small, vague part, was afraid of Nicholas. He wasn't the kind of man to do anything halfheartedly. He wouldn't stop at acquiring her for his bed. He'd want nothing less than possession. Keena liked her independence; she wasn't sure she was ready to give it up. In that, she must have been like her mother, who died giving her birth. Alan Whitman had always spoken fondly of his late wife's bullheaded independence. Keena was like that herself. She'd been on her own for so long, an achiever without props. Oh, there had been men; charming, attractive companions that she had always managed to keep at a safe distance—no ties, no commitments.

She'd let them know that it would be on her terms, or not at all. No, she wasn't at all sure she could manage a full-time man in her life, especially a man like Nick, in an intimate relationship. She had no doubts at all after today that he'd be everything her body would ever want. But what about the rest of her? Would he try to take her over the way he took over businesses? And if she let herself be drawn into his life, would she ever be able to break away before it was too late? She was afraid to let him close enough to find out. Perhaps it was just as well that he'd gone back to New York. But it wasn't like Nicholas to give up without a struggle. She had a feeling she hadn't heard the last of it, either.

"How old were you when you left here?" Mandy asked several days later when Keena was driving her through town in the rented car, pointing out the small high school, the public library and the modest shopping center near the house.

"Eighteen," Keena said, veiling the memories that the admission dredged up. They weren't pleasant ones, for the most part.

"You must have missed it." Mandy smiled, watching two young boys ride their bicycles along the sidewalk, bundled up from head to toe against the February chill. "It's a lovely little town."

"Lovely," came the absent reply.

The older woman glanced at her. "You're quiet lately. Brooding because Nick hasn't come back?" she probed drily.

Keena's face toasted. "Of course not!"

"Don't run over the curb, love. You'll crease the tires," Mandy pointed out.

Keena steered the car back onto the road, hating that momentary, telling lapse. "Why should I care that he comes storming down here, threatens me and then vanishes into the woodwork? It's no worry of mine!"

"Oh, that's obvious."

"Besides, it's my life," Keena added firmly, shifting uneasily behind the wheel. "I can do what pleases me."

"Sure you can."

"If I want to decorate the house and give a party, it's my own business."

"That's right, dear."

"And anyway, if he cares so much, why hasn't he called?" Keena's green eyes flashed. "He could have spared time for a phone call."

"He's a busy man."

"I'm busy, too," Keena pouted. She sighed, the action gently rustling the blue striped scarf at her neck that complemented her navy pantsuit and white silk blouse. "He's just sour because I'm not at his beck and call down here."

"He's jealous of James Harris, you mean," Mandy remarked with a secret smile.

"There's nothing to be jealous of. James hasn't called. He hasn't come by the house…" That rankled, too. She'd been a very young eighteen when she'd overheard that bitter speech of James's, when she'd realized just how fully she'd been taken in by his teasing and flirting. She'd been too naive to realize the cruel game he was playing until it was too late. Part of her hadn't grown past that day. And that part, the hurting part, wanted to bring the tall, blue-eyed lawyer to his knees. It was something inside her that she didn't fully understand, but it was too strong to ignore. Nicholas might tolerate the thirst for revenge, but he wouldn't tolerate its presence around him. He didn't need it. Nick was above that sort of pettiness. But Keena didn't find it petty, and she needed to see James Harris humbled, as she had once been. Now successful, full of confidence she'd never had as a teenager, she was desirable. And she wanted James to find her so, to satisfy a craving that had never completely died. She had to prove to herself that she could have him if she really wanted him. And no one, not even Nick, was going to stop her.

She'd just worked up her nerve to call James and invite him over for a meal when she drove up in front of her house to find him waiting for her. Her heart jumped wildly at the sight of him in an expensive tweed coat with a sweater-vest and dark trousers. He looked sophisticated, handsome and not a day older than he had nine years ago.

"Speak of the devil," Mandy murmured, rushing out of the car and up the steps before Keena had time to reply.

"So there you are." James grinned, hopping down the steps as he used to, athletic and trim. "I thought you might invite me in for coffee if I showed up at your door. Quite a crowd of workmen you've got there," he added, nodding toward the carpenters at work on the outside of the house.

"We're adopting them. They're orphans," she told him with a straight face.

He threw back his head and laughed. It didn't sound genuine somehow, but Keena laughed with him. "Uh, Jones said you'd borrowed quite a lot of money to accomplish this," he added shrewdly.

She only smiled. She could have paid cash for the renovation, but it had done her good to borrow the money from Abraham Jones at James's bank, leaving that priceless emerald bracelet as collateral. She'd expected it to get back to James. Now he was curious, and that was just what she'd wanted.

"That bracelet," he murmured, looking at her with his head cocked to one side in that old, familiar pose. "It was real, wasn't it?"

"Quite," she agreed with a wry smile.

"A present?" he probed.

"No."

He frowned, really puzzled now. "I can't figure you out," he admitted finally.

She smiled up at him, turning on every trace of charm in her slender body. "Can't you really, James?" she asked softly.

Something kindled in his blue eyes, something new and pleasant. He moved toward her, removing his hands from his pockets to take her gently by the shoulders and study her lazily.

"You've changed so," he remarked gently. "You were pretty before. But now…"

"Now, James?" she prodded, breathless.

He opened his mouth to speak just as the soft purr of an approaching engine broke into the silence between them.

Keena turned her head in time to see Nicholas bring the white Rolls to a gentle stop and get out, carrying a big leather suitcase in one hand and an attaché case in the other. He was dressed in an expensive tweed suit that flattered his massive physique, emphasizing his broad chest, flat stomach and powerful, muscular legs. He not only looked rich, he also looked imposing. His eyes punctuated the threat in the graceful way he moved, the way he looked at James, the way a hunter might glance toward a kitten on his way to shoot bear.

"I hope you've got a room ready," Nicholas told Keena without breaking stride, "I'm in a hell of a tangle with my London office."

She stared after him, her mouth slightly open.

"Who's he?" James asked coolly.

Keena looked up at him helplessly. For one wild second she wondered if he might believe Nicholas was her insurance agent. But with a sigh, a shrug and an apologetic smile, she dismissed the thought.

"Nicholas," she replied instead. "Uh, I've got to go, James, but do ring me later on."

"Oh…of course," he stammered. It was the first time Keena had ever seen him at a loss for words, as if he couldn't believe any woman would willingly part with his company.

She turned and walked quickly up the steps with blood in her eyes. Now what was Nicholas up to? And where did he plan to stay?

She caught up with him at the foot of the staircase, oblivious to the stares of the two fascinated painters on ladders in the hall.

"Where do you think you're going?" she demanded.

"To my room," he said impatiently.

"You don't have one," she pointed out.

"Yet," he admitted, taking another step.

"This is my house," she told him, her voice rising shrilly. "You can't just move in like this, without even asking!"

"Think you can stop me?" he asked politely, gazing at her with that level, devastating stare that made her want to back away slowly.

"I'm not alone and defenseless," she reminded him, turning to the nearest painter, a rugged-looking individual about Nicholas's age.

"That's right, lady," the painter agreed, pausing with his brush raised to give Nicholas his best threatening look.

Nicholas lifted his hard, broad face and stared up at the man unblinkingly. "I hope your insurance is current," he remarked politely.

The painter turned back to his work and began painting with a vengeance. "Like I said, lady, I'd give the poor tired man a room," he murmured sheepishly.

Keena glared at him before she transferred her irritated stare to the other painter, who pulled his cap low over his eyes and began to whistle softly.

Nicholas grinned at her before he turned and started up the staircase again.

She followed along behind him, her temper exploding like silent fireworks inside her taut body, watching helplessly while he peeked into the first room he came to, then the second, before he finally settled on the third. It was, as he had guessed, unoccupied, with bed linen neatly piled at the foot of the large, four-poster bed.

"This will do," he murmured, glaring around him at the antique furniture. He set the suitcase down and went to the window. "Nice view. Does it have a bathroom?"

"In between this bedroom and the other one," Keena said. "But that needn't concern you. You aren't staying."

He turned around and let his eyes roam over her taut figure. "God, you're pretty when you want to bite. Come over here and put up your fists, you little firecracker," he taunted in a deep, velvety voice.

"What are you doing here?" she challenged, feeling the ground slowly being cut from under her feet.

He shrugged. "What does it look like? I'm moving in."

"For how long?" she demanded fiercely.

"For as long as it takes to bring you to your senses," he replied calmly. His dark eyes searched her flushed face. "You can't go back, honey," he added quietly. "I won't let you."

Her color deepened. "I don't know what you mean."

"Yes, you do." He moved forward, one corner of his firm, chiseled mouth going up as he noticed her involuntary step backward. "Don't panic. I'm not going to throw you on the bed. Not now, anyway. I've got work to do. Is there a study?"

"Downstairs," she managed through her fury. "But it's full of painters."

"So is the rest of the house. Are they leaving, or are you adopting them?"

"They'll be gone tomorrow," she replied. "Nicholas, you can't stay here," she added, trying to reason with him. "It's a small town. People will go wild gossiping. They'll think you're my lover!"

"They might be right," he said, moving forward again. "Come here."

"Nicholas!" She backed right up to the closed door.

He trapped her there with his big arms on either side of her head, his eyes dancing with devilish amusement, the shimmering depths secretive, mysterious. "Shy?" he murmured. "You were flirting with Harris for all you were worth. Why not try it with me?"

"Because I don't want to be fitted with a straitjacket, and how did you know it was James?" she asked nervously. The deliciously expensive scent of his cologne settled around her like a sensuous mist, and she tried not to be so aware of the size and strength of his body, the heat of it warming her in the faint chill of the room.

"I recognized the sickening adoration in your eyes, little fox," he murmured. His dark eyes pinned hers. "You may think you can pick up where you left off all those years ago, but you're going to find that it's not possible."

"It's my life, Nicholas," she reminded him.

"So it is," he agreed. "But I'm not going to let that anemic snob cut you up a second time."

She tried to get closer to the door, but the cold wood wouldn't give under her shoulder blades.

"I do appreciate the thought," she said. "But how are you going to spare the time?" She didn't like the look in his eyes.

It was frankly predatory. "As you're so fond of telling me, you're a busy man."

His eyes glittered with amusement. "All work and no play…" he murmured, bending.

She watched his face come closer with a nervous sense of inevitability. *No wonder he'd gotten so far in business*, she thought dimly as his mouth brushed lightly against her forehead. He was unstoppable, like a runaway locomotive.

"You'll go through that door in a minute," he murmured lazily. "Why don't you move toward me instead?"

"You're making me nervous," she choked. Her lovely eyes had a faintly haunted look; her black hair was brushed with fiery lights in the glare of the window.

"Is that what it is?" he murmured. He moved, holding her eyes while he eased the full weight of his flat stomach and powerful thighs down against her as he guided her slender body down on the bed. She felt the warm, heavy crush with a sense of awe. She'd never been so close to him before, felt so overwhelmed by him. The kiss they'd shared in the Rolls, as ardent as it was, couldn't compare with the sensations this was causing. She'd never dreamed that she could drown in her awareness like this.

His powerful arms bent, and his chest gently flattened her soft breasts. His watchful eyes never left hers, reading signs in them like a Native American after tracks.

She began to tremble under the contact. He had to feel it, too.

"Nick…" she whispered brokenly.

"Fire and kindling," he whispered deeply, shifting his powerful body sensuously against hers. "We make flames when we touch like this."

A wave of intolerable sensation washed the length of her trapped body. Her hands, pressed helplessly against the warm front of his white shirt, began to move slowly, caressingly, against the smooth, hard muscles.

"Nick," she moaned, her eyes half-closed, her body suddenly, involuntarily, answering his. She pressed closer, molding her body to fit the hard, sensuous contours of his. Her fingers curled under the top button of his shirt.

"Unbutton it, Keena," he murmured deeply, searching her eyes in the blazing, throbbing silence that stretched like a blanket around them. "Touch me."

Her eyes wandered in his while she took the pearly button out of the buttonhole and lightly touched the warm, hair-covered flesh underneath it. She felt the powerful muscles contract beneath her hands.

"You…feel like…warm stone," she whispered unsteadily, burying her fingers in the thick curling hair on his chest.

"I feel like a damned blazing inferno," he breathed, shifting his chest to enlarge the pattern of her caressing fingers. "My God, I've never wanted a woman's hands on me so much!"

She flinched at the sound of another voice merging with his, shattering like brittle glass as the spell was suddenly broken.

"Keena, I've got lunch!" Mandy was calling from the hallway.

A tiny sound burst from her tightly held lips, her eyes telling him how she felt about the intrusion.

His breath was coming as roughly as hers. "There'll be another time," he said tautly.

She managed a slow nod. He levered his body away from hers and moved to open the door.

"What are we having?" he asked Mandy, as composed as ever, one big hand unobtrusively closing the buttons Keena's searching fingers had loosed.

Mandy grinned at him, her hands buried in a dishcloth. "Your favorite," she said drily, hiding a smile when she caught a glimpse of Keena's flushed face and wild eyes. "Beef Stroganoff, homemade rolls, a potato casserole and fresh apple pie."

"Remind me to pry you away from Keena," he told her with a lazy wink.

"Can't split the set," came the murmured reply.

He chuckled. "I'm working on that."

Keena, a little more recovered now, moved around him and followed Mandy down the hall on rubbery legs without looking back. She couldn't meet Nicholas's mocking, confident gaze.

James called later in the day to invite Keena to supper that night, his voice faintly caressing on the other end of the line.

"If your houseguest doesn't mind, of course," he added waspishly.

Keena's hand clenched on the receiver. "My...houseguest doesn't tell me what to do." She crossed her fingers involuntarily. "Nicholas is only a friend."

"If you say so. Does six o'clock suit you?" he added, a purr in his pleasant voice. "I thought we'd dine at the Magnolia Room."

She remembered the exclusive restaurant well. She'd ridden the bus past it on her way to Atlanta at the age of eighteen, when she'd left Ashton behind. She'd been crying, and through her tears she'd strained for a sight of James as the bus passed his favorite eating place.

"I'd like that," she murmured.

"See you at six, then."

She stared at the receiver when he hung up, wondering how she was going to explain it to Nicholas. She had a feeling it wasn't going to improve his mood.

★ ★ ★

Nicholas set up shop in the study and tied up the phone for the rest of the day. Keena could hear him growling through the closed door, and she was careful to keep out of his way. So were the painters, she noticed. Everyone walked wide around the study except Mandy, who darted in and out with coffee and pastries.

"Do you have to encourage him?" Keena asked once, only to be met by an innocent stare and raised eyebrows.

She went downstairs just five minutes before James was due to arrive, wearing a gown that she'd originally designed for a well-known actress—and then decided that something a little flashier would suit her client better. It was a green— more olive than emerald—deep, soft velvet with short puffed sleeves, an empire waist and a low neckline that relied on a hint of cleavage for its charm. The color mirrored that of her eyes, adding to the flush of her lips and cheeks, and the highlights in her freshly washed, curling short hair, an effect achieved with a blow-dryer to make the ends turn toward her face. She eyed herself critically in the hall mirror. If this dress didn't set James on his ear, nothing would.

"Bewitching," Nicholas murmured from the doorway of the study.

She turned around, glaring at him. He was wearing his tweed slacks, but he'd discarded the jacket, and his silk tie hung loose across his chest, the top few buttons of his shirt undone. It was one of the few times she'd seen him when he didn't look impeccable and businesslike. His dark, shaggy mane was faintly rumpled and a forgotten cigarette smoldered in one big hand. Her fingers itched to touch him.

"Going somewhere?" he asked pleasantly.

She swallowed and straightened her elegant figure. "Out. With James," she added defiantly.

One dark eyebrow curled upward. "Oh?"

She stiffened at that mocking reply. Only Nicholas could mingle distaste, contempt and reprisal in a single sound.

"He asked me out to dinner," she elaborated.

He studied the wisps of gray smoke that came between them. "I hope you don't plan on being out late," he remarked. "Waiting up for people makes me cranky."

"I'm twenty-seven," she reminded him. "Nobody waits up for me anymore, not even Mandy."

"Well, honey, I'll have to do something about that, won't I?" he asked with a mocking smile.

"Mandy will fix you something to eat," she replied.

"So she told me."

"There's James," she murmured, her ears picking up the sound of an approaching car.

He shouldered away from the door facing. "Have fun. While you can."

He went back into the study and closed the door.

The restaurant was the very best Ashton had to offer, spacious, elegant, with a hint of grandeur that would have taken Keena's breath away nine years ago. As it was, she murmured suitably as James seated her. But the sophisticated woman she'd become wasn't overly impressed, despite the company she was keeping.

James stared at her across the table when the waiter had brought the menus, frowning thoughtfully, his blue eyes approving.

"What a change," he murmured softly, turning on the old charm she remembered so well.

A tiny thrill shot down her spine, but it was hardly the surge of pleasure she'd once imagined it would be to see that particular look in James's eyes. It was disappointing. She'd halfway expected the earth to move.

She shifted restlessly in her chair. Nicholas had upset her in more ways than one. What in the world was she going to do about him? By tomorrow his presence in her house would be the subject of early-morning gossip over half the coffee cups in town. Not that she minded gossip ordinarily, but she had plans, and Nicholas was going to upset them all if she didn't find some way to pry him out of her guest room.

"Did I say something wrong?" James asked, his tone one of concern.

She mentally pinched herself. "Of course not." She created just the right smile and reached out boldly to touch his long-fingered hand. "I'm having a marvelous time. Remember when this restaurant first opened? Mayor Henderson cut the ribbon, and the lieutenant governor was the first guest..."

"He was a friend of Max's," he recalled, referring to the restaurant's owner, Max Kells.

And not in my league back then, she thought drily. "Tell me, how is Max?"

He shrugged. "Fine, I suppose. I've been too busy lately to socialize much." James stared at her thoughtfully across the table, breaking the gaze only long enough to give the waiter their order.

"You really have changed." He repeated himself. "Velvet gowns, sophisticated, worldly. Do you really work in textiles?"

"I started out there," she admitted. "But not on the floor. I'm a fashion designer now. My casual line sells to some of the most exclusive stores in the country—and abroad."

"So it isn't your...houseguest's money that's keeping you up?" he asked with careless bluntness.

It would be an obvious conclusion for someone who didn't

know about her unusual relationship with Nicholas, but it brought back James's cruelty of years past with full force.

"No," she replied coolly. "Nicholas doesn't keep me."

"Nicholas?" he fished.

"Coleman," she provided. Her long, well-manicured fingers toyed with her crystal water glass. "Of Coleman Textiles," she added.

Both his eyebrows arched toward the ceiling. "Exalted company," he murmured.

"Isn't it?" she replied with a smile. Nicholas's vast holdings were hardly fair comparison for James's small company, which he ran along with his modest law practice. In fact, Nicholas could have bought it all out of what he'd term petty cash, and James knew it.

"Is he your lover?" James persisted with an interest that seemed casual, but that Keena knew wasn't. His fingers were idly rearranging his silverware, his blue eyes glancing at hers restlessly.

She only smiled. "How have things been with you?" she replied, ignoring the question.

He shrugged, acknowledging the slight with that tiny gesture. "With the factory? Well, it could be worse. With me?" he added with a soft laugh. "Life can be lonely."

"Can it?" she asked absently. "I don't have time for loneliness. I'm much too busy."

"Are you staying for good, Keena?" he asked suddenly.

She met his eyes. Along with the cruelty, memories came back of the few good times, of James laughing, teasing her, of the first time he'd kissed her, of long walks in the woods. And then inevitably she recalled that last evening, her initiation into womanhood at his careless hands...

"Goodness, Keena, I've missed you," he said gently, reaching for her hand. Smiling, he caressed it slowly.

Don't fall for it, she told herself firmly. *Don't listen.* But the pull of the past was strong, and James was handsome, and she was falling ever so gently under his spell. More by the minute.

"I've…missed you, too," she replied hesitantly.

The waiter, standing patiently with his tray, finally caught James's eye and began to serve the oysters Rockefeller that James had ordered along with a magnificent salad, filet of sole and dainty little croissants with butter.

James cleared his throat, his long face betraying his obvious interest in Keena to an outsider. Keena looked up from her salad, her eyes wary as they searched his intent face. He was looking at her in a new and exciting way. She smiled at him. The evening was suddenly full of promise.

"After we leave here," James murmured sensuously, "how would you like to drive over to the lake?"

That had been one of their favorite haunts years ago when he took her out. Her eyes involuntarily sought his mouth. He had nice lips. Almost too soft to be a man's, and she remembered the faintly chaste feel of them. She wondered if he'd learned to be more patient with women. Involuntarily, her mind went back to the way Nicholas had kissed her in the Rolls, and she flushed suddenly.

James, thinking the blush was due to the question he'd asked her about the moonlight drive along the lake, smiled confidently.

"How about it?" he murmured over his wineglass.

"Uh—" she began.

"Excuse me, sir," the waiter interrupted delicately, "there's a call for you."

James muttered under his breath as he got to his feet. "Excuse me, darling?" he asked possessively.

Darling! "Of course," she murmured breathlessly.

Her eyes followed him to the phone at the desk. She studied

his long, elegant back while he spoke into the receiver, made a sharp gesture and hung up. His face was troubled when he came back to the table.

"We'll have to leave, I'm afraid," he muttered, pausing long enough to take one last sip of wine before he helped Keena out of her chair. "I can't tell you how sorry I am. I'll drop you off on my way to the plant."

"What's wrong?" she asked.

"There's been some problem at the plant," he sighed. "Strange, I don't remember my night watchman having a cold, but I suppose the line could have been bad."

She thought about that on the way out. "Did he have an unusually deep voice, you mean?" she asked with dawning curiosity.

"Deeper than normal," he replied absently. He paused to pay the check. "That company has been nothing but a headache to me since the day my father died. There are times when I wish…" He shrugged. "Never mind. Maybe it's fate. An albatross around my neck to curse me." He smiled down at her. "And maybe a beautiful fairy can break the spell."

She smiled back as she followed him out to his car. All the way home she thought about that strange phone call. She didn't mention her suspicions to James, but she had a sneaking hunch that he wasn't going to find any trouble at his plant at all.

James pulled up at the steps behind the elegant Rolls-Royce.

"How about tomorrow night? Oh, damn, no, I've got a business meeting with a client in Atlanta. Thursday, for dinner?" he asked with flattering eagerness.

"I'd like that," she agreed.

"Sorry about this," he murmured, leaning toward her. But

a second before he could kiss her, the front porch light blazed on and James drew back abruptly.

He cleared his throat. "Well, good night," he said reluctantly.

"Good night," Keena replied, forcing herself not to explode with the rage she was feeling. When she got inside that house, she was going to shoot Nicholas Coleman!

"Is he staying more than a day?" James added, nodding toward the Rolls with a distasteful look.

"No," she said firmly. She got out of the car and waved him off. When she turned toward the house, there was fury in every slender line of her body.

She took the steps two at a time and blazed through the front door, her dark hair curling softly around her face like a halo, her green eyes glittering with anger.

Mandy turned from the door into her own quarters at the foot of the staircase, her eyebrows risen. "Home so early?" she asked.

Keena glared at her. "Did Nicholas make any phone calls tonight?"

"He always makes a lot of phone calls," Mandy replied smoothly, "I'm sorry about the porch light," she added sheepishly. "I thought I heard a car, and it didn't occur to me that it would be you so soon..."

Keena waved the apology off. "Where's Nicholas?"

"Upstairs, I guess. I heard water running a minute or so ago."

"Getting ready for bed, no doubt," Keena growled, tossing her coat and purse onto a chair in the hall before she stalked up the staircase. "He is not getting away with this. I will not have my life controlled by that...that tyrant!"

Mandy only grinned as she went into her room.

Keena marched up the steps to the room Nicholas had

commandeered and, without thinking, threw open the door and walked in.

The first thing that caught her eye was Nicholas. He was standing in front of his chest of drawers combing his dark, still-damp hair into place. The second thing that caught her eye was the fact that he didn't have a stitch of clothing on his powerful, dark, hair-covered body.

CHAPTER FOUR

Keena froze just inside the door she'd slammed behind her, gaping at him involuntarily.

He lifted a dark eyebrow, as unconscious of his nudity as a stag in the forest. "Do come in," he murmured with a half smile. He laid down the comb and picked up his electric razor. "That bathroom stays fogged up forever," he commented. He lifted the humming razor to his chin. "I have to do this twice a day or I wouldn't be able to get it off with sandpaper. Sit down and tell me about your date."

"Uh…" she began, her breath catching in her throat. She wasn't totally innocent. But the looks of a man had never quite affected her this way, and she couldn't tear her eyes away from Nicholas. It had never occurred to her that a man could be called beautiful, but he was, his big, muscular body, perfectly sculpted, without a single curve or angle in excess.

He glanced at her, patient amusement on his face. "If I'm not embarrassed, why should you be?" he asked. "Sit down. You're perfectly safe."

She moved numbly to a chair against the wall and eased

down into it. "I…just wanted to ask you a question," she stammered.

He shifted, raising one cheek toward the mirror as he drew the shaver over it. "What?"

"Did…did you call the restaurant and tell James there was a problem at his company?" she asked point-blank.

The shaver hummed in midair as he turned and stared at her. "What restaurant did you go to?" he asked politely.

She fought a losing battle to keep her eyes on his face, and he laughed softly at the color that blazed in her softly rouged cheeks.

"You blush delightfully, did you know? Surely, you must have guessed at some point in our relationship that I was a man."

She nodded. "But…I…that is…"

"My God, you're repressed," he sighed. "I really will have to take you to a blue movie."

She let a smile peek from her lips. "I don't need to go anymore," she murmured.

He chuckled, turning back to the mirror. He drew the razor across his square jaw and under his chin. "You should be properly flattered that I haven't grabbed for a robe," he said with a mischievous glance as he finished and turned off the razor, running a hand over the newly shaven areas to check for missed spots. "At my age, I'm damned particular about being seen like this."

"Even by women?" she blurted out.

He looked across the room at her, a long, intense look that made her pulse race. "It depends on the woman," he replied.

"You…don't mind me," she murmured, confused.

"No."

Involuntarily, her eyes roved over his body, lingering curiously, memorizing, trembling inwardly at the sheer sensuality of it, the blatant power in those bronze, hair-covered muscles.

"So, do you approve?" he asked very quietly.

She averted her eyes suddenly, embarrassed by her fascination with the sight of him. "I'm sorry. I didn't mean to stare."

"And I've already told you, I don't mind." He moved toward her, a slow movement she caught out of the corner of her eye. Uncharacteristically, she jumped and rose from the chair with a start, tension in the soft lines of her body.

He stopped, froze in place, and she'd never seen that particular look on a man's face before—desire shadowed with smothered anger.

"If it's that much of a damned trauma, go to bed," he said harshly, turning back to the chest of drawers. He took a short terry-cloth robe from a drawer and shouldered into its thick brown softness, jerking the sash together with sharp, deft movements.

"I'm sorry," she said, wary of his gunpowder temper. "Nicholas, I didn't mean to do that. I…well, I…damn it, what did you expect? This isn't exactly our usual style of conversing."

"Forget it." He picked up the comb and ran it through his hair, his face still dark and taut.

She stood there, helpless, her hands twisting the elegant velvet of her long skirt. "Nick…" she murmured pleadingly.

"Go to bed, Keena," he repeated, his voice rigid.

"How can I, when you're furious with me?" she burst out. "I panicked. All right! For heaven's sake, I'm lucky I didn't go right out the window!"

That seemed to calm him. One corner of his mouth turned up. He chuckled softly. "You're on the second story," he reminded her.

"That first step would be a doozy, wouldn't it?" she teased.

He lifted his shoulders. "I overreacted. I'm damned touchy."

She was just beginning to realize what he meant. She knew men were sensitive about such things, but the degree of Nick's sensitivity hadn't occurred to her until now.

"About what?" she asked gently. "Nicholas, you must know that you're magnificent."

He darted a glance at her. "Compared to whom?"

She glared at him. "You might be surprised," she said haughtily.

"Liar." He laid down the comb and stuck his big hands into the pockets of the robe. "You may not be a vestal virgin, honey, but I'm damned sure that you haven't much of a scrapbook to compare me with. Was it always in the dark?" he added with a veil of humor over a rather harsh curiosity.

She knew what he was asking, but she wasn't about to give him the satisfaction of an answer. He didn't know all of the truth about herself and James, and she was reluctant to tell him how foolish she had been.

"You never did answer me," she said, changing the subject. "And you haven't asked why I'm home so early."

He blinked. "Would you like to run that by me one more time?"

She sighed. "Don't you want to know why I'm not still out with James?"

"Harris wouldn't be stupid enough to take you along to the plant if there was trouble," he replied drily.

"Aha!" she burst out. "You did make that phone call!"

"I was bored," he said with a careless shrug. "There isn't a lot to do here." He glanced around the room. "I could paint the door facings, I suppose."

"You could go back to New York," she suggested.

"I'm taking a vacation. I work hard."

"I realize that, but couldn't you take your vacation in Acapulco or Martinique or Paris?"

"I like it here," he said.

"Nicholas!" She stomped her small foot. "Have you thought about the gossip it's going to cause if you stay here? James is already upset."

"Is he?" he purred. "How disappointing."

"You're fouling up all my plans," she grumbled, her eyes spitting fire at him.

"You're not doing mine a hell of a lot of good, either," he replied, his broad face harder than she'd seen it in weeks.

"I am not, repeat *not*, going back to New York until I've renovated this house and given my party," she pouted. "Put that in your pipe and smoke it!"

"I don't smoke a pipe," he pointed out.

She shifted restlessly. "What do you want?" she moaned. "What are you trying to do, Nicholas?"

"Maybe I'm trying to get you to stop running from me. Have you ever thought about that?" he asked thoughtfully.

She gaped at him. "But I've never run from you," she protested.

He searched her face with slow, darkening eyes. "Honey, you've done little else since the day we met. You'll let me just so close before you start backing away."

"Do I?"

He turned away, reaching for his cigarettes and lighter. He lit up before he turned back, blowing out a thin cloud of smoke. "What are you afraid of, Keena? Is sex such an ordeal for you that you've given it up, or are you afraid that I'd be too rough with you? Despite the way you seem to have a knack for making my temper boil, Keena, believe me, I'm not an impatient lover."

"I'm not…not afraid of you like that," she replied. The

conversation was getting rapidly out of hand. "Don't rush me, Nicholas."

"Rush you? For God's sake!" he ground out, his dark eyes splintering. "It's been six years!"

"The world is full of women," she growled, feeling a surge of sheer fury as she remembered his mistress. "If all you need is to satisfy a passing urge, I'm sure you could pick up someone in town."

He looked as if she'd slapped him in the face, and for just an instant he tensed as if he was considering retaliation. She tensed, too, ready to run at the first movement of that tall, overpowering form. But all at once the tension seemed to drain out of him. He turned around and moved to the bed, pausing to pick up the white alarm clock and set it.

"We've been friends for a long time," he said quietly. "I thought you knew me well enough to realize that I could *never* think of you that way."

She felt shame like a fog surrounding her, and she had the grace to flush. "I didn't mean that," she told him. "Nick, I don't know what's wrong with me tonight. I haven't meant half of what I've said. I just… I think I'm rattled, that's all," she finished, and ran a smoothing hand over her hair. "Don't hate me."

"That's not likely." He unfastened the robe and threw it on a chair, throwing back the covers to ease himself under them. The sheet and coverlet covered him to the waist, leaving his broad, hair-rough chest and muscular arms bare. "Turn out the light on your way out, will you, honey?" He yawned. "God, I'm tired."

She studied him lying there, so strong and imposing, and she wanted more than anything to climb into bed with him and be held and soothed and comforted. It had been a horrible day, and the time she'd been away from him had dragged on forever. And now here he was, and all she could do was scream at him. James Harris, the party, revenge, all of it took a backseat to the things she'd said to Nicholas tonight, and she hated herself for every single one of them.

"Nick…" she whispered, her lips trembling, her eyes misting with unshed tears.

He studied her sad little face across the room, and suddenly held out his arms. "Come here, little fox," he said deeply.

She all but ran to him, hurting with all the pent-up emotions of a lifetime, like a little wounded thing seeking a gentle hand.

He pulled her down beside him, with the cover between them, and held her close and warm in his bare arms. Under her moist cheek she could feel the crisp dark hair and warm muscles. She could smell soap and cologne mingling with the scent of the man himself and she'd never felt so safe, so utterly safe.

"I've been horrible, haven't I?" she whimpered softly. Her small fist collided gently with his chest. "Oh, Nick, what's the matter with me?" she wailed.

"The shell's cracking loose, that's all," he murmured comfortingly, one big hand idly caressing on her back through the softness of the velvet.

"Shell?"

"The one you've worn around you for the past six years," he explained. "There have been men in your life, but even if you've been with them physically, you've managed somehow to remain untouched emotionally."

She opened her eyes and stared across his broad chest to the chair against the wall. "Nick…"

"Hmmm?" he murmured.

She licked her lips, hesitating over the question.

He tugged at a short lock of hair. "There's nothing you can't ask me. What is it?"

"Would it matter if I'd been with other men?"

"To me?" he asked casually. "No. Why?"

She couldn't explain the question to herself, much less to him. It had been important to know the answer, despite the fact that there had been only one man in her life in any intimate sense.

"You're very quiet all of a sudden," he commented, his voice tender in the silence of the room.

She raised her head and propped herself up beside him, her fingers idly tracing patterns in the rough hair on his chest.

"I can't figure you out," she replied gently. Her eyes searched his, looking but not finding anything out of the ordinary in them. Only a slight dilation of the pupils disclosed any emotion at all.

"What do you want to know?" he asked.

"Nick, do you want me?" She put it into words, whispered it as if it was something secret.

His fingers caught hers and stilled them on his chest, warming them. "What a hell of a question!" He chuckled softly, sounding more like the friend he'd always been than like a lover.

"Do you?" she persisted, frowning.

He drew in a deep, slow breath. "I'd rather not go into that right now," he told her. "It's late, and I'm bone tired."

"Too tired to answer a single question?" she teased, half-irritated.

He lifted an eyebrow. "Miss Whitman," he said deeply, "I could answer that particular question without a single word, and in a way that would shock your uninitiated soul." He chuckled wickedly at the starburst of color that drowned out her peaches-and-cream complexion. "I see you understand me. Now, if you're through with inane questions, would you like to leave me in peace and let me get some sleep? The feel of you is, quite frankly, disturbing me."

She couldn't smother a laugh. "Complaints, complaints," she teased delightedly, pleased for some hidden reason that he felt more than comradeship for her, that she could disturb *him*.

"Would you like to take off your dress and discuss it?" he asked with narrowing eyes.

"Why would I have to take off my dress?" she asked in mock innocence as she got to her feet and smoothed the wrinkled velvet down over her full hips.

"You're tempting fate, foxy lady," he murmured as he rolled over onto his back and stared up at her.

Her eyes searched his with all the brief humor gone out of them. "Would it be so terrible if I let you make love to me?" she asked quietly.

"For a woman who backs away from me constantly, you're suddenly damned brave," he murmured.

She stared down at her feet. "I'm confused."

"I know that. But confusion is no good foundation for a love affair," he said bluntly. "Get Harris out of your system before you make me any offers, Keena," he added with a faintly dangerous note in his voice. "It's all or nothing with me—in everything."

She didn't know whether to be insulted or flattered, and her own boldness shocked her. She'd never been that forward with any man.

"You don't understand about James," she began quietly.

"No?" He studied her slender figure with a practiced eye. "I understand you better than you think. You don't have to prove anything to anyone, Keena. You've made your mark in the world. But something in you needs to see the past acknowledge that success. And for the past, we might as well say James Harris." He flexed his shoulders against the pillow. "Play your games, honey. But don't expect any cooperation from me. I won't be a stand-in for another man."

"How dare you!" she hissed.

"Do you want me?" he asked curtly.

She opened her mouth to speak, but the words trapped themselves in her throat. Want him? Of course she wanted him, but the question was, how?

"When you can answer me without any hesitation, we'll have a nice long talk," he said gently. "Now get out of here and let me sleep."

"With pleasure," she ground out, storming to the door.

"Keena!"

She stared at the doorknob in her hand. "Yes?"

"Have you ever considered that maybe the only reason you think you want Harris is because you couldn't get him?"

She opened the door quietly, but she slammed it furiously behind her.

Mandy seemed to sense something at breakfast the next morning. The house was uncannily quiet before the arrival of the painters, who had promised to be through by today, and Keena and Nicholas were quiet, as well.

She glanced at him once and read patient, faint amusement in his dark eyes as they dropped deliberately to the soft swell of her breasts under the yellow sweater she was wearing with her hacking jacket and jodhpurs.

Mandy went to get the coffeepot for refills when they finished the scrambled eggs, country ham and homemade biscuits, and Nicholas laughed softly at the expression on Keena's face.

He leaned back in his chair like a well-fed lion. His shaggy mane of dark hair was slightly ruffled; his eyes were a little bloodshot. But in a red shirt that emphasized his darkness and the dark slacks that hugged, lovingly, every powerful line of his legs, she was hard-pressed to find fault with him.

"You've barely said two words to me this morning," he observed, relaxing in the chair like a man who'd found a new hobby and was preparing to enjoy it to the fullest.

"What would you like?" she asked with sweet politeness, "the Gettysburg Address or a soliloquy from *Hamlet*?"

"How about a chorus of 'I Love You, Truly'?" he murmured.

She fought the color but lost to its quick invasion of her face.

"I didn't," she replied tightly.

"Didn't what?"

"Love you, truly—or *otherwise*."

"Have you become too blasé for love, little fox?" he asked quietly.

She toyed with her empty cup. "Love is just a synonym for infatuation," she said bitterly. "I had my heart stepped on enough to last me a lifetime. I suppose I expected too much from men."

"Such as?"

"Loyalty," she replied. "Courtesy, kindness, consideration…"

"Buy a dog," he suggested.

She glared at him. "You have no poetry in your soul."

"Perhaps not. I'm a realist."

"What do you expect from your women?" she tossed back.

Something flared in his dark eyes at the undisguised sarcasm in her tone. He slammed his napkin down onto the table and stood up.

"Raw sex, of course," he said with biting sarcasm. "When I want it, however the hell I want it."

She glared up at him with her lower lip faintly tremulous. She didn't really want to argue with him, but lately they set each other off with every other sentence. It was new and disturbing to fight with Nicholas. She wasn't at all sure she liked it. She missed the old, easy relationship with its comforting aspects. There was nothing comforting about the icy stranger beside the table. He looked more than a little dangerous.

Mandy came through the door with the coffeepot before Keena could get the words off her tongue, and her sharp eyes didn't miss much.

"Isn't it a little early in the morning for war games?" she asked the taciturn man, with a grin.

"Tell Madame Attila," Nicholas growled, turning on his heel to leave the room.

Keena stood up, her face stormy, her eyes stinging with sudden tears. "I'm going for a ride," she said tightly. "I'll be back later."

Mandy looked after them, then at the coffeepot. She shrugged and poured herself a cup before she sank down in the chair and leaned back to drink it.

The woods were lovely and quiet, except for the whisper of the pines high above, and Keena felt the rage burn out of her in the peace of it all. Nicholas had only been baiting her, but she was still shaking from the encounter. He could look so fierce when he was angry, and she was hurt by the way he'd glared at her. She never should have taunted him, but she couldn't help herself.

She settled lower in the saddle, finding peace in the creak of the rich saddle leather, the measured thud of the horse's hooves on the hard pine-straw-covered forest floor. It was a glorious day, all blue and fluffy, with sculptured clouds and a cutting February wind. The little brown mare wasn't a pure-

bred, but Keena liked her. She was gaited, barely four years
old, with a touch of mischief mixed in with her gentle na-
ture. It was fun riding her. She thought about Nicholas riding a horse and laughed involuntarily, momentarily forgetting
the argument. She could visualize him only on some towering black stallion.

He'd looked ridiculous on anything less.

A noise nearby startled her. She pulled back on the reins
and turned in time to see James riding through an opening
in the thick underbrush. She smiled, delighted at the unexpected meeting.

He looked trendy in his hacking jacket and jodhpurs, his
booted feet firm in the stirrups and an Irish walking hat atop
his head. His blue eyes twinkled merrily.

"I called the house," he told her, reining in beside her on
the wide trail. "Mandy said I'd find you here."

"Did she?" she murmured, and her eyes flirted with his.
She felt reckless this morning.

"With a little persuasion," he admitted. He studied her
slender figure approvingly. "You look good."

"Thanks. So do you." She peeked at him from under her
lashes. "Did you settle your problem last night?"

His face clouded. "It was a crank call," he grumbled. "I
went rushing over there only to find that my night watchman
was as surprised as I was. He hadn't made the call. Can you
imagine anyone with such a bad sense of humor?"

"Oh, no," she agreed readily. It cost her an effort not to
burst out laughing. She shouldn't have been amused, but
Nicholas could be such a devil…

"No harm done, I suppose," he sighed. His eyes twinkled.
"Care to ride along with me for a bit? I've got a meeting later
in the morning, but I'd enjoy the company. I'm going down
to the river and back."

"I'd love to," she agreed, letting the mare fall into step beside his gelding.

She couldn't help but remember how many times in her youth she'd haunted these woods for just a glimpse of James on his horse. Her heart had been such a fragile thing in those long-ago days, and she'd wanted so badly to give it to him. But she was older now, wary of emotions. She enjoyed James's company, but she didn't want to risk getting involved with him again. She knew from painful experience how devastating that could be. She wasn't really tempted, she realized, to give James any second chances.

Involuntarily, her mind went back to Nicholas, to the way she'd seen him last night, and her mind went into chaos. She'd never seen anything as devastating as Nicholas without clothes. Her dreams had been wild ones, adding to her irritable mood this morning when she'd made that unforgiveable remark about his women. But when she thought about women, she thought about Maria, and the certainty that she'd seen Nicholas in every way there was only made her more furious. She just couldn't bear the thought of him touching any other woman.

"You're very quiet." James interrupted her thoughts as they reached the banks of the wide, softly running river.

"It's peaceful here," she replied. "I'm not used to peace. I live at a breakneck pace these days."

He saw an opening and took it. "You must be very successful."

She nodded. "I design for an exclusive clientele in addition to my leisure line."

"Do you have your own manufacturing company, as well?" he persisted.

"Nicholas and I have an arrangement about that," she replied. "I contract my big cuts out to him, although I have a small cutting room and sample sewers. Nicholas owns a number of textile mills and manufacturing companies," she added.

"I know. Do you, uh, suppose he might be interested in acquiring another one?" he asked, suddenly serious as his blue eyes met hers.

She studied him warily. "Thinking of selling yours?" she asked.

"I'm playing around with the idea," he admitted. "Could you, uh, mention it to Coleman?"

If we ever speak again, she thought silently, but she smiled halfheartedly. Was this what he'd been up to all along with his sudden interest in her? She felt used, and not a little let down. It was old times again.

"Yes, I could mention it to him." She laughed shortly. "Shall I have him call you?"

"Please." His face lit up like a blazing candle. He got down from his mount and reached up to lift Keena down beside him, his chest lightly touching hers. "You're a lovely thing," he murmured.

"Useful, too," she commented drily. He was so easy to see through. Nothing like Nicholas, who was a closed book.

He grimaced. "It sounded that way, I suppose," he admitted. His eyes searched hers. "But I am…interested in you."

"Why shouldn't you be?" she asked, slinging a bitter smile up at him. "After all, I'm rich, halfway famous and I have useful contacts."

He scowled. She puzzled him. She was nothing like what he'd expected. He'd imagined he could wind her around his little finger, but it was she who was doing the winding, and he didn't like it.

"You're twisting my words," he said coolly. "I didn't mean it that way."

"No?" she purred with faint hostility. *Damn all men everywhere.* "How did you mean it, then, James, dear?"

"You little cat..." He bent suddenly to take her mouth.

His mouth was firm and warm, and he was making no concessions at all. It was a lover's kiss that the eighteen-year-old girl who'd worshipped him would have swooned from. But Keena was years older, and she had Nicholas's ardor for comparison. James was practiced, that much was obvious. He knew how to use his experience, exploring her mouth to the fullest. But Keena wasn't giving him the response he expected. It made him rough, until she pushed at his chest.

He drew back, breathing heavily, his emotions obviously on the verge of loss of control. His fingers bit into her upper arms.

"You don't give an inch, do you?" he asked curtly, glaring down at her.

"What did you expect me to do, swoon?" she asked half-angrily. "I'm hardly eighteen anymore."

"Good God, I know that," he ground out, lowering his eyes to her high breasts. "I've always wanted you, even nine years ago."

"Wanted, yes," she agreed. "But desire, without any deeper emotion to give it meaning, is rather empty."

He relaxed his grip a little. "I don't know very much about deep emotions," he admitted quietly. "I like women. I like variety. I don't really care for emotional involvement. Not at all."

"Neither do I," she replied, and that seemed to irritate him as if he had nothing to give, but still expected to receive in full measure.

"You might change your mind," he murmured. He bent again. "Let's try that again."

She let him kiss her, but the earthshaking passion she'd once felt for him had been reduced to a faint tremor of remembrance that worked its way down her body and seemed to drain out of her. That irritated her, and she clung closer, trying to force it.

He wrapped her up against him, gentle now, very ardent, but behind the practiced lover there was only remembered bitterness. Her heart, expecting a banquet, had come away with crumbs.

He moved away finally, his eyes dancing. "Not bad," he murmured. "We'll have to practice more, though."

She let him keep his illusions with a smile and a tiny shrug that could have meant anything. "I have to get back," she said.

"Have dinner with me tomorrow night, as we planned?" he asked, and for an instant there really was something new in his voice. "I wish I didn't have this meeting in Atlanta today…"

"Tomorrow will give me something to look forward to," she told him.

She'd wanted to let him sweat for a few days, to build his interest and then… But she was just beginning to sense that there might be a man under that mask James wore, and she was curious about what was really behind it. But Nick wasn't going to like it. She knew that before she waved goodbye to James and headed back toward the house.

There were so many everyday problems in her life lately. She sighed. Nicholas, being suddenly possessive and irritable and impossible, and James, just turning into a person she might really like.

Nicholas was the biggest puzzle she faced. He'd never been overly concerned about her, except that he kept a watchful eye over her dates to make sure she wasn't in danger from them. But about James he was being positively unreasonable. What did he want? Not her body, she remembered with embarrassment, or he wouldn't have hesitated to take what she'd offered him so blatantly last night. His rejection had hurt more than she'd realized at the time. She could disturb him all right, but not to any overpowering extent. And there was no moral reason for him to hold back since she had been so willing. What kind of game was he playing? Was he just being protective, not wanting to see James hurt her?

By the time she got back to the house, the only thing she was sure of was that she wished she'd never come back to Georgia. If only her father were still alive, to listen to her problems, to advise her. She missed him so. At least her battle with Nicholas had helped her over the grief. It was hard to be sad when your temper was being constantly pushed to the boiling point.

She walked into the house only to find Nicholas pacing the hall. He whirled when he saw her.

"So there you are," he growled. "Come in here."

She puffed up proudly, glaring at the broad back going into the study. "Nicholas..."

"We don't have a lot of time," he returned, his face solemn, and she felt a surge of apprehension as she followed him quickly into the room.

"What is it?" she asked.

He rammed his hands in his pockets. With his back to the light coming in through the window, he had a faintly ominous shadow around him.

"There's no easy way to say it," he said quietly. "There's been a fire at your office, Keena. Almost everything you'd done for your fall line has been destroyed."

CHAPTER FIVE

Her mind seemed to go numb at the words. She stared at him. "A fire?" she echoed.

"That's right. Do you want to sit down?"

She shook her head. Her eyes went wild. "But I've still got orders to fill," she burst out. "The last of the summer line is still being sewn, and we'd just received the cloth for the fall-and-winter line and the samples were ready for the boutiques!"

"Don't panic!" he shot at her. "Now, just calm down. How long will it take you to replace the specs and the spring collection designs?"

She felt herself trembling. She moved jerkily, uncertainly. "I... I'm not sure. They, uh, they had some innovations..."

He moved toward her, easing her down on the sofa. He knelt in front of her and drew her head onto his shoulder. His big fingers soothed the back of her neck gently.

"I'm here," he said quietly. "It's all right. I'm here. There's nothing to be afraid of."

Tears trickled from her closed eyes, hot and salty, flowing down into the corner of her mouth. All that work, gone! How many of those designs would she be able to remember? Why hadn't she moved the portfolio of the spring fashions to her apartment? Why hadn't she left them in the office at Nicholas's plant? And what about the bulk orders on the fall line that the cutting room had just received the fabric for? Bolts of cloth, expensive cloth, all gone. And the summer boutique orders that had just been completed? Were they gone, as well?

Her fingers crept around his neck and she clung to him, comforted by his very size.

"Why?" she whimpered.

"There's always a reason, honey," he replied quietly. "I've learned that, if nothing else. Just chalk it up to fate and go on from there."

"How can I go on?" she wailed. "With what?"

"Sheer grit, if that's what it takes."

"Hold me tight," she whispered, inching closer.

"Much closer than this, and I'll crack a rib," he said with a whisper of humor in his deep voice. He got to his feet, melting her body into the hard contours of his until she felt the imprint of him all the way to her toes.

"Oh, Nick, I'm so glad you're here," she whispered.

"You weren't when you went out the door," he recalled.

"Not now," she pleaded. "Don't. Let's not fight. I'm not up to it."

He rocked her against him, soothing her. "What is it about my women that sets you off, Keena?" he asked in a deep, soft tone. "That wasn't the first time you made some offhanded remark about them."

This was getting dangerous. She shrugged. "Did I? I haven't done it intentionally."

"Perhaps you didn't realize it," he replied.

She looked up into his eyes through the mist of tears, and it was as if she'd never really seen him before. Her eyes traced the broad, hard lines of his face, his straight nose, his deep-set dark eyes, the sensuous line of his mouth, his jaw square as a tracker after signs of his quarry. Her eyes met his again suddenly, and a wild, explosive chill ran through her, a tingle of pleasure that was devastating.

"Your legs are trembling," he murmured quietly.

They were. Rubbery, unsupportive, and she was too shocked by her new discovery to explain it.

"Did he kiss you?" he asked suddenly, with hard, narrowed eyes.

She nodded, her gaze locked into his.

His cool eyes went to her soft mouth. "Was it good?" he persisted.

Her breath caught just under her breasts and refused to submerge. "It…was pleasant," she corrected.

"Is that what you feel when I kiss you—pleasant?" he whispered as his dark head bent.

"Nick…the fire…" she managed weakly.

"People should always do wild things in times of disaster, honey," he murmured as his mouth broke against hers. "Didn't you know? Put your arms around my waist and hold on."

She obeyed him without a murmur, her mouth accepting his, inviting his tongue, his teeth, feeling his body intimately against hers with a wild surge of pleasure that made her moan.

"Volcanic," he whispered into her open mouth. "My God, you quake all over when I take your mouth. Feel me, Keena. Feel the tensing that happens when I hold you. Is it like this with him? Is he even capable of passion?"

Her short nails were digging madly into his muscular back; her body was pressing as close as it could get to his, savoring the rough, warm contact with those steely muscles. She barely heard him, her mouth accepting his, begging for more,

drowning in the sweet, hard crush of it, the intimate thrusting of his tongue, the nip of his strong white teeth.

His hands ran up her sides, almost but not quite intimate
in their exploration. "Answer me," he murmured gruffly.

"I go…crazy…when you kiss me," she whispered brokenly,
her eyes riveted to his hard mouth. "Nick, don't stop."

"It's now or never, little fox," he murmured, dropping one
last hard kiss on her mouth before he raised his head with a
sharp, rough sigh. His eyes were stormy, his chest rising and
falling as unevenly as hers.

She hit his chest with her hand, feeling the softness of the
red fabric under her fingers. "Nick!"

"I can't take you on the floor," he whispered, mischief in
his dark eyes.

Her face blossomed with color and she hid it against him.

"Business first, little one," he murmured, holding her gently. "I've got to fly up to New York today. You might as well
come with me in the jet."

"You brought it here?" she murmured dazedly.

"Where in hell would I park it, in the rose garden?" he
asked with a short laugh. "I had Mark Segars fly it down this
morning. It's waiting at the airport."

"I'd better pack, then," she murmured, dreading the trip,
dreading the sight of her elegant office all black and charred,
all the burned remains of that gorgeous fabric. "Nick, did
they salvage anything?"

"Ann grabbed up a handful of sketches just before the curtains caught," he replied. "And a few samples. But by the time
the firemen got there, it was far too late. They managed to
save the rest of the building, but your office, the cutting room
and the shipping room are gone, along with every scrap of
fabric in the place."

She nodded. This must be how it felt to lose an arm—this

lonely, empty feeling in the pit of her stomach. But the arm she'd lost was her livelihood, and she had to find some way to replace it. Thank God she could still count on Nicholas. She looked up at him helplessly.

"Go on," he said, nudging her toward the door. "It will be all right. Trust me."

"Haven't I always?" she asked gently.

He nodded. "Too much sometimes," he said drily, watching her eyes fall quickly.

She hurried out the door.

Two hours later they were well on the way to New York in Nicholas's private jet. She sat lost in her worries, her hand clinging like glue to Nicholas's big, warm one. He seemed to like that contact, because he didn't make a move to break it, even when he smoked or drank his coffee. His own fingers were comforting, but vaguely caressing as if he enjoyed having her cling to him. Funny, she thought through the nightmare of reality, he didn't seem the kind of man who'd enjoy a clinging woman.

"I hope Mandy can manage while I'm gone," she murmured. "I hated leaving her behind."

"She'll have everything organized by the time you get back," he told her.

"I know." She leaned her head against his broad shoulder. "Oh, Nick, I'm so glad you're with me. I don't think I could face it alone."

"I like looking after you, Miss Independence," he murmured against her hair. "When you let me, that is. I wish to God you'd let me know about your father."

"You were busy," she sighed.

"I'm never, not now or ever, too busy when you need me,"

he said shortly. "Will you jot down a memo to that effect and promise to read it at least twice a week?"

She smiled wearily. "I'll try." She peeked up at him. "Nick, why are you so good to me?" she asked seriously. "You always have been, and I know it isn't because you feel paternal or because you want me."

He searched her eyes quietly. "I want you, all right," he replied in a deep, slow tone. "And you damned well know it."

She swallowed. "Not to the exclusion of everything else."

"Are you sure about that?" he asked.

Her eyes went down to the gray-and-burgundy patterned tie and his white silk shirt. "You always manage to push me away in time," she said under her breath, feeling the rejection all over again.

"With good reason," he reminded her.

She jerked her eyes up to his. "James?" she asked with a bitter smile.

His eyes searched hers. "Not entirely."

She shifted and let her face slide down against his soft, warm shirtfront once more. "You're worse than any clam, Nicholas."

"With you, I have to be. Go to sleep, tired little girl. I'll take care of you."

He would, too. She felt her eyes mist over before she let the drowsiness and emotional turmoil lapse into sleep. It had been a long time since anyone had cared enough to worry about her.

They stopped by Keena's apartment, Jimson effortlessly steering the Rolls through the rush-hour traffic to the Manhattan high-rise apartment complex she called home.

She felt like a stranger in the elegant confines, replete with white curtains and carpeting and chrome and blue-velvet upholstered furniture. It seemed artificial, somehow, after the big, rambling old house in Ashton and the small-town atmosphere there.

"What's the matter?" Nicholas asked, sensitive to her changed mood.

"Culture shock," she murmured.

He laughed softly. "From rural peace to urban panic in the space of a couple of hours?" He shook his head. "It's a little worse for me when I come back to this country after a few weeks abroad. Especially on the return trip from the Bahamas. It's the only place on earth where I can really slow down, and then I come home and get slapped in the face with frantic haste."

"I can't picture you ever slowing down," she commented, her eyes ranging all over him. Dressed in a becoming blue business suit, he looked alarmingly conventional for a man who wrote the rules as he went along. It was vaguely unfair, like a wolf wearing wool.

"You're staring, honey," he said quietly.

She drew her eyes away. "Sorry."

"Undressing me mentally?" he murmured wickedly.

She flushed wildly. "Shame on you!"

"You should have committed me to memory, considering the way you studied me that night," he reminded her. "My God, talk about eyes like saucers…"

"Nicholas!" she burst out.

"I can't help it," he replied with a strange smile in his dark eyes. "You blush beautifully."

She stared back into his eyes as if her own were linked to them by a silken cord. He seemed to hold her without moving, to possess her mind as they stared quietly into each other's eyes, and she recalled vividly the feel of his mouth covering hers, the warmth and strength of his body against her. A tin-

gle of pure pleasure made its way through her, and her lips
parted on a hungry sigh.

"My God, I want you," he whispered roughly. "We'd better get out of here before I give in to the urge to do something about it."

"That would be a first," she managed, the hunger blatant
in her eyes.

"I'm trying to give you time, you little fool," he ground
out. "Besides," he laughed shortly, "we can hardly leave Jimson sitting downstairs with the engine running for the next
two hours, can we?" he added. "He'd have carbon monoxide poisoning, and where in hell would I find someone to
replace him?"

She drew her lips into a nervous smile. Always the humor
returned in time to prevent him from letting her inside that
hard shell he kept around himself. And she was too shaken
to argue.

"What a unique way to go—in a Rolls." She laughed.

"Think of the insurance claims," he replied. "And the loss
of Jimson would send me into mourning."

"You might tell him that," she replied as they started toward the door. "It would make his day."

"Oh, I tell him often enough," he said. He opened the
door for her.

She paused just outside it and turned to look up at him.
"Nicholas, if I can't meet my commitments, I'll have to close
down," she said, letting all her secret fears out into the open.

He reached down and smoothed one broad-tipped finger
along her cheekbone. "You won't close down. I'll see to that.
Come on, love, let's go and see the damage."

Love. She let him guide her down the hall while a peculiar
sensation tickled like a feather around her midriff. Strange
how much pleasure the careless endearment gave. Equally

strange how quickly she forgot James Harris, pushed every-thing to the back of her mind but Nicholas's firm grasp on her arm as he led her to the elevator. At the moment he seemed to comprise her whole world.

Ann Thomson, Keena's dark-haired assistant, was trying to sort out what was left of Keena's designs and spec sheets in the small sample-room office when Keena and Nicholas arrived.

"Oh, you're here!" Ann cried, running to meet her em-ployer. Her slightness made Keena seem like a giant by com-parison. "Darling, what a terrible homecoming," she groaned, embracing the taller woman, "I'm so sorry!"

Keena bit hard on her lip and tried not to cry. "There, there," she murmured, drawing back with a quick swallow and a shake of her head to distribute the tears under her eye-lids and keep them from spilling over. "It won't be easy, but we'll pull through. It's just a temporary setback, that's all."

"But all that work," Ann sighed. "All that lovely cloth. And this is all Faye and I managed to salvage." She gestured toward the desk, where a pitiful few sketches, belts, buttons, tops and one skirt were spread in disarray. The heavy smell of smoke lingered in the air beyond the charred walls, ceiling and floor, and the ashes of the long cutting tables, the huge bales of rolled fabric.

"Cheer up," Nicholas said from behind her, looking im-perturbable with his hands in his pockets, his confident ex-pression. "You can borrow any of my people or facilities. And don't worry about this place," he added, dismissing the ruins with a sweep of his big hand. "I'll have the contractors over here first thing in the morning. If you need an office, the two of you can borrow one of mine."

"I can manage here," Ann said, wrinkling her nose, "smoky smell and all." She looked around the sewing room with its

two production sewing machines and its racks and desk and
drafting table. "Faye and the girls have gone home, but they're
coming back first thing in the morning. The worst of it was
the cutting room."

"Tell me what fabrics you need and where you buy," Nicholas told Ann. "And I'll have it here by noon tomorrow if I
have to buy you the mill that makes it."

"Oh, if you could!" Ann enthused.

"I'll work from my apartment," Keena told them. "Nicholas, if I give you the specs for the small cuts—the ones we
did here—could you get me twenty dozen of the dresses and
skirts before the end of the week, or would that cripple your
own production?"

"I'll manage. Why only twenty dozen?"

"Because they're new styles. I want to send them to a few
exclusive boutiques I sell to and see how they go before I risk
putting them into mass production. I can give them a trial
run before I commit myself to other buyers."

He grinned. "Good economics. You learned early, didn't
you?"

She nodded. "I learned all I know from you," she reminded
him. "And you're no novice at it."

"Or at a few other things," he added with a faint gleam in
his dark, deep-set eyes.

She laughed under her breath. "How about the cutting-
room staff?" she asked the room in general. "Here it is winter, and they're out of work…"

"I'll give them jobs until you get back into full production here," Nicholas said, making mincemeat of the problems
as quickly as she thought them up. "It's almost March, too.
Spring's a breath away."

She smiled at that, feeling some of the worry evaporate.

"Now, if there are no other small mountains nagging at

your mind, can we go?" he asked. "I've got businesses of my own to groan over."

"I guess that's about all," she sighed. She turned away from the charred cutting room. "Oh, why?" she moaned. "Why now?"

"The firemen said it was the wiring." Ann shrugged. "Anyway, darling, when was there ever a convenient disaster?"

"True, true." Keena gathered up one of her barely used sketchpads and clutched it to her breast. "When Faye comes in, ask her to get me up those prices we discussed when I began work on the spring line, will you, on notions and such? And you know where to find me if you need me."

Ann nodded. She wiped away a tear. "If only I'd been here…"

Keena put her arm around her. "I could stand to lose the plant easier than I could bear losing you," she said. "And we were lucky that it was no worse than it is."

Ann shrugged her thin shoulders. "I suppose so. And we are insured."

"Which reminds me…" Keena began.

"I'll take care of it," Nicholas said, impatient now as if the whole thing was beginning to wear on him. "Come on, honey, let's go."

"Yes, Your Lordship," Keena said, batting her long eyelashes at him.

He narrowed his eyes at her. "Impertinent little thing," he muttered.

"Why, Nicholas, don't blame me. After all, you taught me everything I know," she cooed, waving to Ann as they went out the door.

"Not yet, I haven't." He chuckled.

She tossed him a mischievous smile. "Are you going to?"

"We'll talk about it one of these days," he said. They walked toward the Rolls, feeling the cold wind as the smell of smoke was replaced by that of carbon monoxide from passing traffic. "Right now I've got some knots of my own to untangle. I'll drop you at your apartment on the way to my office."

"Nick, thank you," she said with genuine emotion in her voice as they reached the car. "Maybe I can pay you back someday."

"You owe me nothing, Keena," he said tautly. "Let's go."

He was, she thought, the most confusing man in the world. She was never going to figure him out.

The next week turned into a merry-go-round of days that melted into nights, their dividing line, the presence of either light or darkness outside. Working around the clock, Keena hardly ate, nibbling on fruit and cookies and drinking pots of black coffee. Hour after hour she struggled to fit her memory to the pages of specs that littered the sofa, the coffee table and the floor, along with figures on the cost of all sorts of accessories, trims and fabrics.

No one bothered her, as if her coworkers knew that her creativity hit its high peak when she was alone. Only Nicholas invaded her privacy from time to time, bringing in the various Chinese specialties he knew she loved, and other tempting things to stimulate her failing appetite. One morning he showed up at seven o'clock with a full breakfast, which his own excellent chef had prepared, and woke her from a sound sleep on the soft shag carpet to feed her every spoonful himself. He'd charmed her landlady into letting him in with a pass key, and Keena hadn't even been able to work up any indignation over the invasion. It was such a thoughtful act.

"I'm not a baby," she mumbled as Nicholas popped a fresh strawberry into her mouth.

He only smiled, studying her flushed face, her dreamy eyes and tousled hair with an approving eye.

"No," he agreed. "But I think you deserve a little pampering all the same. Eat."

She opened her mouth again and the taste of a warm, flaky croissant joined the last traces of the strawberry.

"Good?" he asked.

She smiled, nodding up at him from her lounging position. "You're so kind to me, Nicholas."

"I have ulterior motives," he assured her, handing her a cup of coffee laced with cream. "I plan to seduce you one night soon, and I'm plying you with good food to get you in the mood."

"How are you going to seduce me if I know about it in advance?" she asked.

His eyes traveled down the olive silk dressing gown fastened around her slender waist, with just a hint of lace from her nightgown peeking out of the low neckline and the parting at the hem. "Oh, I thought I'd wait until you were half-asleep and wrestle you down on the rug."

"I'm already on the rug," she pointed out, lying back after she'd replaced her coffee cup on the low table. She smiled. "But I'm much too full to give you my best."

He stretched out beside her, casually dressed for once in a white turtleneck sweater and dark slacks. He looked younger, much more relaxed than usual. She could feel the heat from his body, and her eyes went to his mouth. She ached to have him touch her, kiss her. But he crossed his arms behind his dark, shaggy head and closed his eyes with a musing smile, ignoring her.

"That makes two of us," he murmured. "I ate before I left the house."

She rolled over on her side and studied his profile. "Nicholas, where are you from?" she asked suddenly.

The question seemed to stun him, because it was a full minute before he answered her. "Charleston," he said finally.

"You don't have a Charleston accent," she remarked.

"So I've been told."

"You lived in Atlanta when we met," she reminded *him*.

"And you never asked if it had always been home. Why the sudden interest?"

She didn't know. She laughed softly. "I was just curious, that's all."

"I keep an apartment in Atlanta now, just as I keep one in Manhattan. But my family goes back to the Revolutionary War in Charleston. One of my ancestors was part of Francis Marion's band, in fact. There's a plantation, complete with huge live oaks, Spanish moss and the Ashley River running through it all. Rice was the cash crop before the Civil War."

She studied his relaxed face. "Did…did you and your wife live there?"

"Misty loved it," he agreed. "I moved my office to Atlanta after her death. The memories were eating me alive, so I stayed away."

"You were at the office a good bit after that," she recalled.

He smiled, with his eyes still closed. "Until the day I met you, green as grass and shaking with nervous confidence." He chuckled. "When Misty died, there wasn't a person alive I could talk to about it. Everyone was afraid to mention her name around me. Except you."

"You were driving yourself to death," she said with a sigh. "I figured it was because of grief. Do you still miss her, Nicholas?"

He turned his head and looked at her. "Sometimes. At odd times. Not as much as I used to. You've helped the scars heal."

"I have?" she asked gently.

"You brighten up dark corners in my life," he mused, "when you aren't setting fire to my temper."

She shifted, curling up next to him like a tired kitten next

to a warm fire. She settled against his broad chest, fed and
safe and comfortable, her cheek on his shoulder, her fingers
pressed against the softness of his cashmere sweater. "Talk
to me," she murmured. "Tell me about your family. Is there
anyone left in Charleston?"

"Nobody worth mentioning. My parents are long dead.
Keena, don't do that," he added curtly, stilling the idle fingers making patterns on his chest.

She could feel the effect her nearness was having on him
by the sudden rise and fall of his chest. It gave her a sense of
power, along with a surge of pure pleasure.

"Killjoy," she murmured. The pressure of the last few days,
the lack of food and sleep, were telling on her. She nuzzled
closer with a sigh. "Nicholas, I'll have everything caught up
tomorrow. I'm going back to Ashton."

He drew in a deep breath, and she felt the muscles under
her head stiffen. "For what—Harris?" he growled.

"For me," she returned. She sat up, brushing the hair from
her eyes. "Don't ask me to turn around now," she said coolly.
"I've made up my mind, and I won't change it."

He glared up at her. "How long do you think I can stay
away from my office before things start crumbling around
my vice presidents?" he asked curtly.

"You don't need to go with me," she replied, equally curt.

"Like hell I don't. I'm not handing you over to him," he
told her bluntly.

"What if I want to be handed over?" she demanded. She
jerked the robe closer around her tense body. "You don't
own me."

His eyes sketched every soft curve of her body before they
returned to touch on her delicate facial features. "I feel responsible for you," he said finally.

That hurt. Inexplicably, it was a stinging blow.

"Why?" she asked bitterly and with tremulous lips. "Because I could see through the high-powered executive to the man all those years ago? Because I listened when no one else was brave enough to come near you? Thanks for the compliment, *Mr.* Coleman, but don't bother feeling any obligation toward me. I'm quite capable of taking care of myself."

"How do you plan to go about it?" he asked with cold courtesy. "By seducing that second-rate attorney in Ashton?"

Her eyes exploded. "He's not second-rate," she flashed.

He got to his feet with a lithe, graceful movement, and turned away to light a cigarette. "Are you going to marry him?" he asked curtly, glaring at her through a cloud of smoke while he searched the living room for the ashtray she kept for him.

"If I do, what business is it of yours?" she retorted, wounded and wanting to wound.

He stopped in the action of reaching down to flick an ash into the big square ceramic ashtray, his eyes cutting into hers even at the distance. He straightened, towering over the furniture, big and dark and threatening.

"Push just a little harder," he warned in that soft, deep tone that hinted at a hurricane force of anger brewing inside him, "and you'll find out what business of mine it is."

"I'm fairly trembling, Nicholas," she threw at him. She felt reckless as she rarely had in her life, so stung by his opinion of her that she was willing to risk anything, everything. "Is this how you handle your women—with threats?"

The explosion burst into his dark eyes without warning. He tossed his barely touched cigarette into the ashtray and headed straight toward her, retribution in his taut face, in his pantherish stride, in the set of his square jaw.

CHAPTER SIX

Her heart lashed against her ribs, but she stood her ground as he moved toward her.

"I'm not afraid of you," she said with bravado, although she felt like crashing through the nearest wall to get away from him.

He didn't bother to answer her. One big arm shot out to jerk her against him while the other went under her knees. He turned, carrying her as if she weighed no more than a sack of groceries, and started down the hall.

"Nicholas—" she began nervously.

"Shut up." He shouldered open the door to her bedroom and strode across the deep blue carpet to toss her onto the rainbow-colored quilt that graced the queen-size bed. He stood beside the bed just long enough to peel off the sweater, baring his broad, hair-matted chest, before he came down alongside her.

She tried to get up, but his hands caught her wrists and pressed them down into the soft coverlet over her head. He held her there until her sudden, panicky struggles finally ceased from sheer exhaustion, and she lay breathless, helpless, looking up at him with bright green eyes full of apprehension.

"Not so brave now, are you, little fox?" he asked in a rough, angry tone. His hands slid up to lock her fingers into his, still holding them down on the quilt. His body shifted, so that his chest crushed into her soft breasts and flattened them against it. "Come on, honey, fight me. This is what you've been working up to ever since that night I left for Paris."

She licked her dry lips nervously. "I don't understand."

"Young girls throw rocks at boys, some of them pick fights by calling them names, but it all leads to some kind of physical confrontation," he replied, his eyes stormy even though his voice was calm enough. "You've been trying to goad me into your bed for days. All right, I'm here. Now what are you going to do with me?"

Her lower lip trembled. "You're out of your mind if you think that's what I want," she replied shakily. "Of all the conceited…"

He leaned closer, his dark eyes filling the room, his breath warm on her face, his sensuous mouth close enough to brush hers when he spoke. The heat from his body scorched her, and the weight of it was new and pleasant. More than that. Delicious.

He rolled over on his back abruptly, carrying her with him so that he took the weight of her slender body. His hands drew hers to his broad, warm chest, pressing them against the hard, hair-covered muscles while he searched her eyes at unnerving closeness.

"Don't mutter insults at me," he whispered deeply. "Besides, this is really all your idea, anyway. I'm only following up on your lead, little fox."

His touch was intoxicating. She'd wanted this for a long time; he was right about that. Her hands had itched to run over the muscles of his brawny chest, to test the thickness and crispness of the hair that covered it. But she didn't want to be taken in anger, and she couldn't stand the idea that his feelings were the result of some misplaced sense of responsibility.

"My lead, my eye! If and when I *ever* want you to make love to me—"

His eyes darkened, his jaws tautened. "Right now," he cut in, "I'd settle for turning you over my knee and paddling your charming derrière. My God, you're in an unpleasant mood this morning."

"How do you expect me to be, when you—" She broke off, lowering her eyes to his chest.

"When I what?" he asked quietly. "Come on, don't stop now. When I what?"

"You don't have to...to feel *responsible* for me," she said in a tight, wounded tone.

His chest rose and fell slowly. "So that's it." He brushed back the unruly hair from her cheeks. "Don't you like being cared about?"

Her eyes glanced off his and fell again. "I'm not your property. I... I don't like being thought of as an obligation—a..." She bit her lip as the tears threatened again.

His big, warm fingers caressed her throat idly. "I do what pleases me, Keena," he murmured softly. "That includes taking care of you when you need it. I do nothing out of a sense of obligation. Especially not with you."

She lifted her eyes back to his and searched them, finding nothing more than a patient kind of amusement. "You sounded as if you did. As if you...you only came around because you felt you had to."

"I come around," he replied, "because I feel at ease with you. Because I can talk to you. In my position—with my money—it's damned hard to trust people. Hasn't that ever occurred to you?"

She studied his nose, focusing on a spot that looked as if someone had broken it once. Unthinking, she reached out and traced the small flaw in its imposing lines.

"I never thought about it, about your money, I mean," she admitted. "Nick, how did your nose get broken?"

"In the navy," he replied. "A slight disagreement over a disciplinary action. Why don't you think about it?"

She shrugged, shifting over him so that her legs were beside his, not being supported by them. "You've been rich ever since I've known you," she explained.

"That's true enough." He studied her face quietly. "You never asked me for anything, even when I knew for a fact that you could just barely pay your rent."

Her eyes opened wide. "How?"

"I was curious about you."

She shifted restlessly. "What else did you find out?"

One corner of his chiseled mouth went up. "That you were too trusting for your own good. I've sweated blood over you, little fox, especially with a couple of your men friends who weren't exactly what I'd call gentlemen."

She laughed. "You did a thorough job of discouraging one in particular," she murmured humorously, remembering the coworker whose jaw Nicholas had broken.

He sighed wearily. "I owe three of these gray hairs to you."

"Which ones?" She tugged at one silver hair among the dark, curling ones on his broad chest. "This one?"

"Among others." His fingers bit into the small of her back. "Keena, I want to make love to you."

Her eyes flickered against the wildness that was smoldering in his. She seemed to stop breathing, the tension thinned so between them.

"You…you didn't the other night," she whispered uncertainly.

"You were afraid of me," he replied. "I just started toward you before I put on the robe, and you were ready to tear down a door getting away." His eyes searched hers. "You don't look much calmer right now, love," he added gently. "If you could have seen your face when I brought you in here…"

She swallowed. "You were so angry."

"What did you expect? I don't like having other men rammed down my throat," he said curtly. "Especially James Harris."

She half smiled. "And I didn't like being told that I was an obligation."

He linked his hands behind her, flexing his powerful shoulders with the motion. "Which still doesn't answer me. I want you."

Her eyes dropped to the massive chest supporting her. She wanted him, too, but she wasn't blinded by passion; she was too aware of consequences, of motives. She was confused—utterly confused. How had this all happened between them?

He caught her chin and tilted her flickering eyes up to his. "I won't let you get pregnant. Is that what you're afraid of?"

The flush went from her hairline down to her throat in a slow, vivid flood, and he watched it with a dark scowl.

"What kind of men have you been with?" he asked with a rough chuckle. "Didn't you ever talk about sex, for God's sake?"

"Not a lot, no," she managed to blurt out.

"On the other hand," he murmured, easing her down onto her back, "why talk about it at all?" His mouth brushed lazily across hers, a shimmer of exquisite sensation that he repeated again and again while his warm hands moved against

her back, slipping her robe from her shoulders and then easing down the straps of her gown.

"Nick…" she whispered shakily under his warm, hard
mouth as its expert pressure increased sensuously.

His hands eased up to her rib cage, his thumbs rubbing
slowly, gently, at the sides of her breasts in a growing pattern
that made her body rise toward him pleadingly.

"I've held back until I ache like an adolescent," he whispered against her throat. "My God, I've tried to give you
enough time, but I'm running out of it." And this time he
meant business. There was no light, teasing pressure in it now.
He kissed her with practiced skill, exploring every inch of
her mouth with his lips, his tongue, his teeth.

His warm hands were on her breasts now, the gown somehow lowered to her waist, his fingers making incredible sensations flow through her taut body as they caressed her.

"Oh, Nick," she gasped, looking straight into his dark eyes
as he lifted his head to look down at her.

His chest rose and fell heavily, and there was a faint damp-
ness on the skin her fingers were pressed against. His eyes
lowered to the high, bare curves of her breasts and he studied
her as if he'd never seen a woman's body before, something
thrilling in the bold intensity of his gaze.

"Nicholas," she whispered.

"What, love?" he asked softly.

Her hands reached up to touch his broad face, to trace the
hard lines that never seemed to relax, even now. "I… I want
to be…closer," she managed shakily.

His mouth gently crushed hers. "Do you?" he murmured.
"How close, like this?" He eased his massive body over hers
until it relaxed onto hers from breast to hip, his arms taking
the bulk of his formidable weight.

"No," she whispered under his seeking mouth. "All…all of

you, Nicholas," she murmured, gasping as she felt the crush of his body pressing her down into the mattress, making silvery waves of emotion surge through her slenderness. Her soft, bare breasts flattened under the rough, hard crush of his chest, and she could feel the pattern of the dark, curling hair on it tickling as her arms reached up to hold *him* closer than she'd ever been to another living soul. She wanted desperately to please him, to give and give and go on giving until he burned with the same fires he was kindling in her.

"I want…to please you," she whispered into his rough, hungry mouth.

"You are pleasing me," he ground out. His mouth broke hers open, invading it intimately, hungrily. "God, your breasts are soft…"

She moved sensuously under him, feeling the crisp, dark hair on his massive chest make new and wild sensations run through her slender body.

"Am I too heavy?" he murmured against her eager mouth.

"No," she whispered achingly. Her eyes looked straight up into his as her tongue traced patterns along the chiseled line of his upper lip.

He watched her, his eyes dark and full of secrets, his chest throbbing against her breasts, his breath flaring through his nostrils.

"Do you always watch your women like this?" she asked unsteadily, pausing to run her fingers along the long, broad curve of his muscular back.

"Only when I've wanted them like hell for years," he replied. He pressed against her deliberately, making her feel the proof of his desire like a brand against her hips. "Do you feel how much?"

She caught her breath at the sensation, her legs going boneless, admitting the full weight of his body between them so that not one part of their bodies were separated.

He bent and kissed her again, thoroughly this time, the way he had that first day in the Rolls, with a thrusting, demanding pressure that made her body arch into his—that ripped a moan of pure pleasure from her throat.

She heard a soft, triumphant laugh and opened her eyes lazily, feeling a hundred tiny tremors raking her yielded body as his hands eased the rest of the gown away from her. The room was cool enough that she missed his warmth when he raised himself up to throw the gown over the side of the bed.

His dark eyes ate every inch of her, running up the long, smooth curve of her legs to the curve of her hips, the deep indentation at her waist, the thrust of her breasts. She had the strangest feeling that she would have minded that scrutiny from any other man. Even years back, James Harris had been too intent on possession to pay much attention to her young body. He'd been in a hurry and the result had been a blur of discomfort, embarrassment and no pleasure at all for Keena.

But this was different. Nicholas was special to her in ways she'd never discovered until just lately. And to him she wasn't merely a body or a one-night stand. She was something quite different; she could see it in the dark, appreciative gaze he drew over her.

He bent and pressed his mouth to her soft, warm stomach, working his way up to her breasts, his hands smoothing her flesh, touching her in new ways, learning the sweet contours of her body while his lips and tongue and teeth fostered a riot of sensation that left her breasts tingling, her body hungry and writhing under the expert arousal.

Her fingers were tangled in his shaggy mane of hair, her eyes half wild as he rose to see the expression on her flushed face.

"You don't know how to give it back, do you?" he asked in a strange, husky tone, his powerful body pulsing with desire.

She touched his mouth with her fingers, fascinated by it, by the pleasure it gave. "Give what back?" she whispered. "I want you, Nick," she added softly. "You must know that by now."

"You aren't a virgin," he said, but it was a question.

She bit her lip. "No."

"Damn it, don't look like that," he ground out, turning her averted face back to his. "I told you once that it didn't matter to me, and I meant it. But you don't act like an experienced woman. How careful am I going to have to be?"

She sighed weakly. "The first time…the only time…was with James," she admitted tightly. "It was uncomfortable, and hurried—" her voice broke off.

"Go on," he urged.

"I thought I'd die of shame when I found out that he hadn't any plans to marry me. He'd only wanted me, and he told his brother that it had been like…like making love to a man."

Nicholas didn't say anything. Not a word. He stared down at her with eyes she couldn't read in a face gone as hard as granite. Now he knew the agony that Harris had inflicted on her.

"Don't hate me…" she pleaded tearfully.

"Hate you? For God's sake!" he blurted out. He bent and crushed his mouth down on hers. "Does it feel as if I hate you, you little fool?"

Tears rolled down her cheeks. She clung to him, even as he sat up, drawing her across his lap to hold, to comfort. His big arms were warm and as pleasure-able in a sense as they had been in passion. She nuzzled her face against his throat, drinking in the scent of him, the feel of him.

"Nick?" she whispered.

"What, honey?"

She drew away and looked up at him. "Love me," she whispered.

He brushed a strand of hair away from the corner of her mouth, studying her lips with a hungry intensity, but he didn't make a move toward her.

"How do you feel about Harris now?" he asked, his dark eyes darting up to catch the surprise in hers.

"Now?" she echoed. "I…well, I don't know," she blurted out.

"Don't you think," he said gently, "that you'd better find out before you and I go any further?"

She searched his eyes, looking for answers that she couldn't find. It was like tracking a lion who didn't want to be found.

"Don't you want me?" she asked.

He took her hand and pressed it deliberately against his flat stomach, watching the color run into her face as she touched him.

One dark eyebrow went up and he smiled faintly. "I want you," he said. "But I'm not going to do a thing about it until you've put him back in the past where he belongs. You were a girl, Keena," he added seriously. "You thought he was sincere, and he wasn't. But there was no harm done. It's something that happened long ago." He lowered his dark head and brushed his mouth slowly, sensuously, against hers, smiling against it when it parted and pleaded for something harder. "It doesn't have a damned thing to do with you and me."

She kissed him back in the same teasing, arousing manner. "Nick…" she pleaded.

He nipped her lower lip delicately. "Why did he say it was like making love to a man?" he murmured, deliberately making her face that specter. "Were you that thin?"

"Flat-chested," she corrected, her voice faintly bitter.

Nicholas drew back and looked down at her taut, firm

breasts, his lips curving sensuously as he traced their soft curves. "You?" he chuckled.

"Oh, Nick," she breathed, her voice, her eyes, full of emotion as she reached up and clung to him, her cheek against his broad, strong chest, secure in the arms that held her, the hands that caressed her bare back.

"I hate to break this up," he murmured, "but even at my age, I can't sit with a gorgeous nude brunette in my lap for very long without doing something about it. Suppose you put your clothes on and I'll pour some coffee."

"I'd rather wrestle you down in the bed," she whispered. "If you'd just teach me how to seduce you…"

There was pure delight in his laughter, and more than that in the slow, warm embrace that followed it. "At my earliest opportunity," he promised.

She eased reluctantly out of his arms, off his lap, feeling strangely comfortable with him as she gathered up her gown and robe.

"Clothes," he said, dragging his sweater on as he went out the door, pausing to glance back at her with a musing smile. "You're far too tempting like that, even with a robe over you."

"You're very flattering, you know," she murmured from the safety of the robe while she searched for her slacks and blouse in the closet.

"No, love," he said quietly. "I meant every word."

He closed the door behind him, leaving her to dress.

Five minutes later she joined him on the sofa, wearing a black silk blouse over a pair of beige suede jeans, her hair in place, her face made up, her eyes full of Nicholas.

He whistled softly. "What an eyeful," he murmured approvingly. He handed her a cup of black coffee as she curled up near the arm of the couch before he leaned back with his own cup held in one huge hand.

"You told me once that you liked black-and-beige combinations best," she said without thinking.

"On you, yes." He sipped his coffee, watching her over the rim of his cup. "I can still taste you," he murmured, his eyes dark with passion, smiling when she averted her eyes. "Miss Sophistication," he chuckled. "I thought you were a woman of the world, even at the beginning. I was mad as hell at you about that crack you made the night I went to Paris." He lifted an eyebrow at her shocked expression. "I was out for revenge. I'd seen the way you looked at me in the elevator. I wondered how far I could get," he said, amusement in his tone. "It was a game. Nothing more than that. And then—"

The phone rang before he could finish, and Keena went to answer it with her pride around her knees. A game. A cruel game of which he should be ashamed as she was ashamed. To think that she let him look at her, touch her, that intimately.

"Hello?" she asked numbly.

"Nicholas Coleman, please," came a cultured masculine voice from the other end of the line.

She held out the receiver without meeting his eyes. "For you," she said quietly.

She sat back down with her coffee, as wooden inside as the floor, feeling nothing at all. She vaguely heard Nicholas's deep, measured voice, now sharp, now questioning, for several minutes before he hung up the phone and turned back to her.

"Where was I?" he murmured darkly.

"Leaving," she replied, her eyes cold as they met his. "Goodbye."

"I wanted to explain something to you," he said quietly.

"I'm very busy. If I'm going to leave for Ashton in the morning, I've got a lot of work to do," she said tightly.

His eyes narrowed. "You're not going back alone," he warned.

"Why bother?" she asked haughtily. "The game's over, Nicholas. I'm not playing anymore."

"Neither am I, honey," he said softly, smiling faintly at her. "Not anymore."

She watched him go with a leaden feeling in her stomach.

"Thanks for breakfast," she managed politely.

He turned at the door, studying her slender, graceful body wistfully. "How would you like to see the plantation on the way to Ashton?"

The question stunned her. "Go to Charleston, you mean?"

He nodded. "We could spend a few hours there. I'd like to show it to you."

Would he really, or did he just want to visit his ghost and have her there to make it bearable for him? She wasn't sure of her footing with Nicholas anymore. She was more than a little frightened of him now.

"Keena, I won't try to take you to bed again," he said gently. "That's over."

She studied him for a moment before she nodded. "All right."

"I'll send Jimson for you at seven," he added, going out the door. "I want to get an early start."

"All right. I'll be ready."

A highly polished black Lincoln was waiting for them at the Charleston airport, with Jimson standing tall and dignified beside it.

"You think of everything," Keena murmured as they got into the spacious backseat.

"I have to, honey," he replied. "Jimson, go through town

before we start home. I want to show Miss Whitman some of the city."

"Yes, sir," Jimson replied. "Where would you like to start, sir?"

"Turn down Meeting Street and down Broad," he replied, "then onto Church as far as St. Philip's and the Pirate House. That's about all we'll have time for this trip."

"There are a number of interesting homes on East Bay and Tradd streets, sir," Jimson reminded him.

"Time, Jimson," he sighed, leaning back. "Time."

"Yes, sir," came the quiet reply.

Keena looked across the seat at him, her eyes hesitant, wary. But his eyes were closed, and there were deep new lines cut into his broad, hard face, and deep shadows under his eyes. She'd seen Nicholas in all sorts of conditions, but never this worn.

"Have you slept at all?" she asked softly.

"Not a lot, no," he replied. His eyes opened and looked straight into hers, searching them. "Did you, Keena?"

She looked away, her face rigid. "I never realized there were so many palm trees in this section of the state," she murmured, studying the old houses along the way as they began to get into city traffic. "How old is Charleston, anyway?"

"It was founded in 1670," Nicholas said, following her gaze to the fascinating examples of architecture—the Charleston double house, the Greek Revival style, the plantation house, and just about every other architectural style from a period of almost two centuries. "But the French Huguenots who settled here around fifteen years after that left the most lasting impression on the city. My ancestors, the St. Juliens, founded Manteau Gris."

"I'm sorry?" she murmured as the French flew right over her head.

"The plantation house. It means 'gray cloak,' but we cling to the old name," he replied. "The name comes from the Spanish moss—which is, by the way, neither Spanish nor moss—hanging from the huge live oaks along the river. The first house was built in 1769. It burned during the Revolutionary War, and all but the flooring and some of the timbers were destroyed. It was rebuilt, then it was burned again during the Civil War." He laughed softly. "Only a little of the original cedar remains. It was rebuilt that last time of Bermuda stone overlaid with stucco, and given a gray wash. It has heart pine flooring and some imposing woodwork, including a winding staircase that the staff keep polished to a glass sheen."

"You love it, don't you?" she asked, already seeing the rambling country house in her mind.

"Very much. The older I get, the more aware I am of my roots. Look," he said, sitting up to point out the window at her side. "That's St. Michael's Episcopal Church. It's the oldest church building in the city."

"How lovely," she murmured, her eyes on the tall spire as they passed the white structure.

"And down that way is what we call 'South of Broad.' It's the old section of the city. Restaurants serve our famous she-crab soup, made from the roe of the crab, along with roasted oysters and tiny Iceland lobsters in a special sauce. I'll have to take you there one day. There's too much to see to spend less than half a day browsing."

"I'd like that," she said quietly, drinking in the sights and sounds with a smile. "Nick, what about Fort Sumter?" she asked, "and the Battery?"

"We'll go back that way," he assured her as Jimson made a right turn followed scant minutes later by a left turn. Two cross streets later, Nicholas had Jimson slow down.

"The church is St. Philip's Episcopal," he told her. "But this

Bermuda stone house is known as Pirate House, and I used to haunt it when I was a boy." His dark eyes sparkled with merriment. "Rumor has it that pirates used to meet with respectable Charleston merchants here to barter."

"There were pirates in Charleston?" she exclaimed. "I thought they only sailed the West Indies."

"Stede Bonnet was one of the worst," he told her. "He was hanged in 1718 and his body was buried in the marshes near the Battery. There was a female pirate, too, a beautiful woman named Anne Bonney, the illegitimate daughter of an Irish merchant. She married a pirate named James Bonney, whom she later deserted in Nassau for another privateer named Calico Jack Rackham."

Keena, all big green eyes, prodded him. "And?"

"The ship was taken in Jamaica in 1720 and the crew brought to justice." He chuckled softly at the dismay in her face. "Maybe they got away," he murmured, and laughed again when she brightened.

"I'd love to go inside," she sighed as they passed the house.

"All apartments now," he replied. "But I may be able to arrange something the next time we come here. Back around by East Bay and the Battery, Jimson," he told the driver.

"Yes, sir."

Fort Sumter looked so peaceful sitting out in the harbor, and Keena eyed it wistfully as they passed it and drove along the Battery back into the city.

"It's hard to believe that wars were ever fought here," she told Nicholas.

"Charleston has had its share of problems over the years," he returned. "It was captured by the British in 1780, and fought valiantly during the Civil War. It's withstood hurricanes and an earthquake, but it's still standing. Stubborn, proud and as eloquent as any Southern statesman. I suppose that's why I have such a high regard for it."

"Do they have tours of these houses?" Keena asked.

He nodded. "Every spring. We're a few weeks too early."

Keena's first glimpse of Manteau Gris was enough to make her fall in love with it. The towering gray stone house sat far back off the road amid a nest of huge live oaks dripping with Spanish moss, along with magnolia trees, pine trees and shrubs that must have been magnificent in bloom. There was a gray split-rail fence all the way around the grassy front lawn, with its circular driveway, and several small, attractive outbuildings, one of which was a gazebo.

"It's magnificent," Keena breathed reverently.

"That runs in the family," he murmured, catching her eye to remind her of the last, very embarrassing time she'd used that word.

"Who looks after it for you?" she asked.

"The housekeeper and her husband—the Collinses. They've been with the family since I was a teenager."

She studied his hard, unyielding face. "I can't imagine you as a teenager," she murmured.

"Can't you?"

"I'll bet you were born an adult," she replied with a faint smile.

"I had to be," he replied matter-of-factly. "My parents were never here. Mrs. Collins damned near raised me."

"Where were your parents?" she asked softly.

"In Cannes. Switzerland. Rome. Paris. Anywhere except here. They shared a common allergy—me."

She saw through that toughness and cynicism for just an instant to a lonely, wounded little boy, a dark-haired child who spent his free time sitting near the harbor, watching the ships come and go and dreaming of pirates.

Her fingers reached out and very hesitantly touched the back of the broad, dark hand resting on the seat beside him.

He stiffened at the light contact and drew back, his eyes daring her to pity him as they cut across toward her.

She shifted, pretending an interest in the flat face of the house with its imposing woodwork and long front portico and steps, wide and cool-looking, and she wondered how that coral would feel under hot, bare feet in the summertime.

"It's a house meant for children," she murmured without thinking.

He jerked open the door as Jimson lulled the engine to a full stop and got out, leaving Jimson to open the door for Keena. It was only then that she realized how much of what she'd said must have hurt him.

She recalled belatedly that he and his first wife couldn't have children at all. She'd never bothered to ask why, whose problem it was. It had never occurred to her that it would have hurt a man like Nicholas, who was so very much a man, not to be able to have sons or daughters of his own.

Although she was still smarting from his treatment of her the day before, she'd never meant to deliberately hurt him. And if his stiff back was any measure of the wounding, it was going to take a truckload of finesse to make a balm. He looked more imposing, more unapproachable, than she'd ever seen him. And for the first time she wanted to get close to him in a more than physical way. She wanted to be a part of his life.

CHAPTER SEVEN

Keena stood very still and silent as that single thought penetrated. She wanted to be a part of his life. That had never happened before. She'd been studiously independent, needing no one, nothing but her own company, her career, to sustain her. But now she felt a deep, gnawing hunger for something more. For a man. For sharing, and quiet loving and children.

But last night she'd already come to the conclusion, as she slept in that lonely room, that Nicholas had only wanted her as a passing fancy. He'd said himself that he wasn't playing anymore. They were going to be friends again. Just friends. Because he'd never gotten over Misty and he had nothing more than desire to give a woman.

She followed him onto the front porch where a tall, buxom lady was giving him a hug, and an equally tall but thin old gentleman behind them smiled.

"Keena, this is Jesse Collins and his wife, Maude. They manage Manteau Gris for me," Nicholas said as she joined them, and there was a chorus of how-do-you-dos before they went inside.

The wooden floors were spotlessly clean and waxed, and that spiral staircase Nicholas had mentioned was truly dazzling. As the huge double doors were closed, her eyes were drawn to the fanlight above them, and the slight imperfection of the glass in it hinted at its age.

A Persian rug graced the center hall, its pattern a mixture of burgundy, cream and blue. There was a large front room just off to the left, its floors covered with other luxurious Oriental rugs, its furniture mostly mahogany that glistened with polished brass fittings.

"The furniture," Keena asked softly, her gaze moving from the gorgeous antiques to the paintings and then to the huge stone fireplace, "is it West Indian?"

"A discerning eye the young lady has." Mrs. Collins laughed, her whole broad face friendly and warm. "Yes, ma'am, it is. The first Mr. Coleman to own Gray Cloak—" she glanced apologetically at Nicholas for using the English version "—married the daughter of a West Indian planter, and these pieces were part of her dowry. And I could tell you some tales about that pair, I could."

"But not before you bring us some coffee," Nicholas said with a smile. "It's been a long morning."

"And you working yourself to death into the bargain, I'll say," Mrs. Collins said disapprovingly. "What you need is a few weeks here, so that I can look after you proper. I'll fix some sandwiches and cake for you, as well. You haven't had breakfast, either, I don't imagine," she muttered as she left the room, closing the door behind her.

"They never let you grow up," he said quietly, shaking his head. His eyes roamed the room, as hers had. "I've missed this."

She studied his broad back in the dark brown suit, seeing

the way the fabric strained across his powerful muscles. "I'm
sorry about what I said. I didn't think."

He half turned. "Will you stop apologizing?" he growled.
"My God, that's all you do lately. You know you don't have
to pull your punches with me. You never have."

She shifted her shoulders uncomfortably, helplessly. "But I
didn't want you to think…"

His eyes darkened. "The problem was with Misty," he
said shortly. "Not me. Even for my age I'm damned fertile.
Tests don't lie."

"You had tests?" she asked softly.

"I had to," he murmured, turning, a hand restlessly combing through his dark hair, "for my own peace of mind. I had
to know."

She didn't know what to say to him, how to find the words.
A child would have been such a comfort to him in his grief.
Of course, it had been six years, but did he still grieve? Did
he still love Misty to the exclusion of everything else? Was
that why he drove himself so relentlessly, even now?

He pulled a cigarette from his pocket and lit it. At least
he'd cut down on that, she thought idly. He hardly smoked
at all anymore.

She looked away. "I've sometimes wondered why you and
Misty never had children, that's all."

"Well, now you know," he said simply. "It wasn't because
I never wanted them. I did. I still do." He went to the window and stared out at the live oaks, bare of leaves, but still
covered with the long, curling strands of Spanish moss, dark
gray against the gray winter sky.

She looked down at the floor. She had somehow managed
to anger him again, to cause him to withdraw from her, and
she wished she'd never agreed to come here. It was more of
an ordeal than she could have imagined. Just the sight of him

hurt suddenly. Here they were, alone in the same room with only fifteen feet or so separating them. But she might as well have been in New York. Was this the pattern for their future? Had they lost even the friendship that they'd had?

She opened her mouth to tell him that she wanted to cut this visit short and go straight on to Ashton alone. But before she could get the words out, Mrs. Collins came bustling back in, all smiles, with a heavily laden tray of snacks and coffee.

"Here we are," she cooed, setting the tray gently down on the coffee table. "Now, you make the young lady eat something, too, Mr. Nick," she admonished as she went out the door. "She needs some feeding up."

Keena kept her eyes lowered, reaching out to pour coffee into the cups. They were fine-bone china, with a rose pattern, and very old.

"You should be properly flattered," Nicholas said, dropping into a huge armchair across from the sofa, holding the dainty cup and saucer easily in one hand. "Mrs. Collins rarely uses the rose china except for the most important visitors."

"I'm honored," she laughed bitterly. "I would think I hardly qualify."

"You do to some people—to Harris, surely?" he asked with a strange, cruel smile.

She shifted restlessly, sipping the blistering-hot coffee. "Surely," she replied sarcastically.

"When are you planning this party to end all parties?" he asked carelessly.

Her eyes ricocheted off his and back to her cup. "Mandy sent out the invitations the day I left," she informed him. "She's already contacted the caterer and arranged for a band by now."

"How organized," he replied. He sipped his own coffee, reminiscent of some regal baron as he filled that massive chair.

"I am, after all, a businesswoman," she reminded him coolly.

"All business," he returned politely. "Very little woman."

She finished her coffee, refusing to let him see how he was hurting her. "How much longer are we going to be here?"

He leaned forward and put down his cup. "I thought you might like to see the grounds before we rush away," he said bitterly.

"If you can spare the time to show them to me," she returned with dripping sweetness.

They barely spoke as he led her out the back door and onto the yellowed grass. They walked under the tremendous gnarled branches of the oaks, and far away was the sound of the river running, the whisper of pines touching high above against the gray sky.

"The…the flowers must be lovely in bloom," she said.

"They are," he replied. "Azaleas, camellias, dogwood, magnolias, roses—it's a symphony of color in the spring and early summer."

"Your wife," she murmured, watching the leaves fly as her feet lifted them, "did she plant any of them?"

"Misty was too delicate for gardening," he said shortly. His eyes darted sideways to catch hers. "Why are you trying so hard to dredge up ghosts? Are you that afraid of me? I'm through trying to seduce you!"

"Yes, the game is over. Isn't that the way you put it?" she broke out. To her horror, she felt the hot sting of tears filling her eyes.

His jaw clenched. "Oh, God, Keena," he ground out, moving toward her. He caught her arms and slammed her body against his, crushing her in a warm, hurting embrace. He rocked her against his warm, hard chest, and she could feel the heavy slam of his heart against her breasts, even through the layers of clothing that separated them. Her hands, flat against his shirtfront under the jacket, gloried in the warm strength of the concealed muscles.

"Can you imagine how I felt when I knew?" he whispered roughly, his voice muffled against her hair. "My God, I walked out of that apartment wanting to kill Harris." He drew in a deep, steadying breath, his arms contracting again. "Of course I didn't sleep. How could I? I'd wanted it to be perfect with us, absolutely perfect the first time we made love."

Tears flooded her face as she pressed her cheek to his broad chest. "I wanted you, you know," she managed tearfully.

"Yes," he said heavily.

She drew back and looked up at him with a watery smile. "It was delicious while it lasted," she choked.

"Was it?" he murmured, searching her eyes with a slight frown.

He traced her lips with one broad-tipped finger, watching it hungrily. "I don't dare imagine how much better it could have been," he whispered back. "You respond so wonderfully to me, my little love—so warm and giving and passionate. You very nearly drove me mad yesterday And then not being able to have you after all..."

The memory of it made her heart go wild. Her body trembled with it; her eyes told him how it had been for her.

"I want you," she whispered shakily.

"I want you, too," he replied quietly. "But for the time being, we're going to let it stand the way it is between us."

She hit his broad chest in silent frustration. "Nicholas!"

"Do you honestly think you're ready for that kind of commitment?" he asked harshly.

Her green eyes were wide and confused as they looked up into his.

His hands held her in front of him, firmly caressing her

upper arms through the soft oyster-white jacket of her suit.
"Keena, sex is a responsibility," he said gently. "Unless it's
understood as a business proposition, there's more to it than
the easing of an ache. Have you thought about precautions?"
he asked levelly.

She felt very young when he asked questions like that. "Not
really," she replied.

He smiled. "Well?"

She glanced at him and down again. "You take care of it."

He laughed softly. His eyes were patient, gleaming with
quiet amusement. "With you? Like hell I could. When I managed to tear myself away from you yesterday, I didn't know
my name. No, honey, don't expect me to take care of it. I
thought I could at the beginning, but I'm wiser now."

She traced the button on his shirt. "Aren't men supposed
to be more in control of themselves at your age, Mr. Coleman?" she teased gently.

His fingers trailed down her throat to trace the high, full
thrust of her breasts. "Not when they want a woman the way
I want you," he murmured. "Why do you bother with a bra?"

She could hardly breathe for the slam of her heart as those
slow, very wise fingers did impossible things to her self-con-
trol.

Her hands slid up to his broad, strong neck, and her nails
tangled in the thick hair at its nape, her eyes closed while he
touched and teased.

"Look at me," he whispered huskily.

She raised her misty eyes to his, watching the darkness
grow in them as he undid, one by one, the buttons on her
blouse. Her lips parted under a rush of breath, but she didn't
make an effort to stop him.

His hands started to reach around her for the clasp of her
bra, but she shook her head slowly, her eyes never leaving his.

"It fastens…in front," she whispered shakily.

"Do you want to be touched?" he asked as he found the catch and very slowly loosened it, his fingers brushing the wispy lace away from the high, perfect curves of her breasts.

"Only by you," she managed in a tight, muffled voice.

His hands swallowed her, took the soft weight of her, caressed and cherished and warmed her while she bit hard on her lower lip to keep from crying out, her eyes involuntarily closing.

"Sweet, sweet love," he whispered, lowering his dark head. "Kiss me."

She reached up and drew his mouth down onto hers, letting her lips part, inviting him, luring him, her body trembling as if with a fever as his mouth bit into hers with a hunger that was incredibly tender, loving, deeper than anything they'd ever shared. They rocked together, a tremor shaking his body as hers quaked with the kiss that locked them together for all of one long, breathless, aching minute.

He drew back a breath, his eyes dropping to the soft white treasure swallowed in his big hands, and he bent suddenly to put his mouth reverently to each hard pink tip, the moistness making the cold seem unusually fierce to Keena as it brushed her bareness.

"We must both be out of our minds," he whispered as he refastened the catch and buttoned the blouse back into place. "You'll have pneumonia."

"It's so beautiful when you touch me," she told him with a piercing tenderness in her soft eyes, "when you look at me. Nicholas, I'll never let another man touch me like that."

"I know," he said tightly. "Keena, you're the most beautiful thing I've ever seen. I could eat you from head to toe. Do you know that? Every soft, pearly inch of you, God!" He ground her body against his, holding her so close she could barely breathe. "I could take you here on the ground," he breathed harshly. "Oh, God, I hurt!"

"I'm sorry," she whispered, soothing him, her hands comforting, warm and tender as she smoothed his hair and crooned. "I know, I know. Nicholas, you can have me," she whispered into his ear. "Right now, right here, standing up, lying down, any way at all, don't you know that?"

"Yes, I know," he whispered tautly, but with some measure of control. His big arms tightened. "You've always been willing to give me anything I needed. Even sex, is that how it goes?"

"I'd do anything for you," she said simply, meeting his eyes as he lifted his leonine head. "Anything in the world."

"Why?" he asked quietly, and searched her eyes deeply while he waited for her to answer him.

She blinked, vaguely confused by the question. "Because… I care about you," she said finally. "Because we're friends."

"Would you really give yourself to me out of friendship alone?" he asked very gently.

"You're confusing me!"

"I think we're confusing each other," he replied drily. He bent and brushed his mouth gently across hers. He laughed softly. "Can you imagine what making love on the ground would have done to that suit you're wearing?" he teased.

She flushed, but she didn't look away. "Shades of Hemingway," she murmured.

"We don't have a sleeping bag," he pointed out.

"The earth moved, anyway," she laughed, lowering her hot face.

"It did for me, too, honey," he murmured against her forehead. He linked his hands behind her and drew back, his chest lifting with a deep sigh. "Have your damned party, if it means so much to you. But you can't have Harris. Not now."

Wanting to irritate him, just for mischief, she grinned up at him and asked, "Why not?"

But he wasn't playing. "Because you're mine," he said quietly.

She studied him curiously. "I don't understand."

"Remind me to explain it to you when you've got this crazy scheme out of your system." He jerked her playfully. "What the hell does it matter now what happened nine years ago, Keena?" he wanted to know. "It's in the past, where it's best left, including the man you thought you couldn't live without. What kind of life could you have with him?"

"Nick..." she protested weakly.

"We have to live in the present. But I can see I'm going to have to let you find that out for yourself." He let her go and moved away to light a cigarette.

She stared after him until he noticed that he was walking alone and turned to wait for her.

"I don't understand," she said blankly.

"What?" he asked.

"You...you want me, but you won't do anything about it, and we're friends, but we're not," she stammered. "Nick, what do you want with me? What do you want from me?"

His dark eyes ate her from her jet-black hair to her black-and-white pumps. "Honey, you'd be amazed."

"I already am," she murmured. "You could have any woman you wanted..."

"You're the only one who's never wanted me," he returned, "or my money."

"Is that why?" she persisted.

He turned away. "We'll have to talk about it someday. But not now, honey. I've got work to do. We'd better hit the road."

★ ★ ★

In no time at all, it seemed, they were back at the rambling old house in Ashton. Mandy smothered her with kisses and rattled off about the invitations, the decorator's bill, the caterers, the lack of phone calls, and half a dozen related subjects until Nicholas's rigid posture in the hall caught her eye and she vanished with a quick smile into the kitchen.

"Don't you want coffee?" Keena asked him.

He shook his head. His big hands were deep in his pockets and he looked strangely alone, standing by the door, his eyes quiet and faintly sad.

"You didn't bring your valises in," she added.

"I've already had them sent back to New York," he replied. A faint smile touched his hard mouth, "I'm not staying."

She should have been relieved. She should have shouted for joy and jumped up and down. But instead she felt a foreign urge to bawl and scream.

"Why not?" she asked.

"Business, love," he replied. "Things I can't handle from here. A labor dispute in the knitting mill, an equipment breakdown in Chattanooga…and on it goes."

"But you said—"

"I know what I said," he agreed. "Keena, you're a grown woman. I can't protect you from life, no matter how much I might want to. There's something called trust in any worthwhile relationship. It's time I let go of you, love. It's time I let you stand alone."

Her heart felt like heavy stone in her chest. "But, Nick, you'll miss the party," she said plaintively.

One corner of his mouth went up. "Send me an invitation."

She returned the smile a little shakily. "I'll do that. Nick, you aren't still angry at me?" she asked with a burst of apprehension. "You aren't saying goodbye…"

He went toward her, catching her waist with two big, warm hands to draw her unresistingly against his body, so that she could feel every inch of him touching her.

"Goodbye isn't a word we're ever going to use," he said gently. "I'm giving you some breathing room, that's all. We've come a long way in a little time, but you've got to be sure. I've said that before, now I'm saying it again. Have your party. Get Harris out of your system. Spend some time with him. But nothing further, Miss Liberty," he warned, something dangerous in his gaze. "Not unless you tell me first. I want your word on that."

She had to force herself to speak. "You sound very possessive," she whispered.

"You belong to me," he replied simply. "I'm not handing you over to any other man unless I'm damned sure it's right for you, and that's why I want a promise. Now."

"All right," she agreed without knowing why she did it.

He nodded. "And if you need me, you know where I am."

Her hands smoothed his shirtfront, already feeling the pain of separation. "Will you call me?"

"No."

"Why not?" she asked, incredulous.

"I'll be busy. Remember that invitation."

"Yes, Nicholas." It was going to be worse than ever. Even when he left the country, he called her. She felt desolation move over her like an icy wind.

"What a sad little voice," he murmured gently. "None of that. Smile for me."

She raised her sad eyes to his. "I don't feel like smiling. I'll miss you."

He searched her face. "I hope so," he murmured. "So long, my own."

She studied his mouth. "Are you going to kiss me?" she whispered.

"If you want me to."

She glowered at him and moved away. "Never mind, if it's such a trial to you."

He laughed softly, and she waited for his hard arms to come around her, her eyes closed, a dreaming smile on her mouth. A minute later she heard the door open.

She whirled, shock in her eyes, but he didn't look back. He closed the door behind him.

"Nick," she whispered in anguish.

She ran after him, but he was already down the steps, and by the time she got to the top step, he was cranking the Rolls's soft engine.

She folded her arms tight over her breasts, hurting. She didn't understand Nicholas or herself, but she understood the ache within. She felt alone, as she hadn't felt since her early teens. She felt completely, hopelessly alone and she didn't know how she was going to go on living without Nicholas somewhere in her life. Had he said goodbye forever, and all that talk about coming to the party and giving her some freedom was nothing but a placebo? Oh, Nicholas!

CHAPTER EIGHT

In six years it was the first time she'd gone more than two weeks without seeing or hearing from Nicholas. As the days passed, she felt herself withering, a flower without sunlight to sustain it.

James, whose company had entertained her once or twice a week, barely seemed to notice that she wasn't overly communicative. He enjoyed talking more than listening, anyway, and he didn't know Keena well enough to sense that there was anything wrong.

At her encouragement he'd contacted Nicholas, and the mill was in the process of being gobbled up by Coleman Textiles. But not one word about Keena had entered the negotiations. She had probed carefully in an effort to find out, and had been disappointed at the answer. After all those years of friendship, had Nicholas really forgotten about her? Didn't he care?

"You're seeing a lot of that Harris man," Mandy commented one night as Keena waited for James to pick her up.

Keena only shrugged, tugging the cowl neckline of the

pale green silk that washed down her slender body like a second skin. It was a simple design, but elegant enough even for Ashton's best restaurant.

"Nick doesn't care," she said bitterly. "He hasn't bothered to call, and it's been three weeks! The party is Friday night," she added, which was only two days away.

"He got an invitation," Mandy murmured. "I sent it by itself to make sure."

Keena's full mouth pouted. "He won't come."

"I wouldn't count on that." She admired the dress and smiled. "Very pretty. Does Mr. Harris appreciate the effort?"

She laughed softly. "He appreciates my encouraging him to ask Nicholas about buying the plant, that's all. He's a nice man, Mandy. A little devious, a little boyish, but very nice."

"Only that?" Mandy asked.

Keena sighed. "Yes. Isn't it sad? All these years I couldn't wait to come back and have my revenge on James for all that humiliation I thought I suffered from him and his friends. And do you know what? Nicholas was right. What attracted me the most about James was that I couldn't get him nine years ago. How sad."

"And Nicholas?" Mandy asked softly.

Keena's fingers pleated the soft silk nervously. "He doesn't care about me," she repeated.

"You can't cage a wild sparrow," Mandy said, in one of her enigmatic moods. "You have to free it and hope it will fly back to you."

Keena stared at her. "Have you been into the brandy?"

The doorbell sounded and Keena paused just long enough to grab up her red fox jacket and toss it over her shoulders. Nicholas would love the new addition to her wardrobe, she thought bitterly. It would only reinforce his pet name for her. She wrapped it close, and in her mind she felt again the hard crush of his bare arms, the feel of his body against hers, bare and hard and all masculine perfection. And she wanted him even more now than she had then. Wanted him in every way there was.

"You're very quiet," James said later as they finished the creamy dessert they'd been served with second cups of rich black coffee and cream.

Keena smiled apologetically. "I'm tired. Making preparations, you know."

"Oh, yes." He leaned back in his chair, the picture of elegance, smiling. "Everyone's talking about it. Imagine, a famous fashion designer in our midst, and all those sophisticated New Yorkers." He grinned. "I hear you've even invited some Broadway stars."

"You're right." She laughed. "Betty Sims and Jack Jackson," she added, naming two top performers from one of the newest hit shows, who were good customers as well as good friends. "Not to mention Demp Cashley."

"Cashley? The star pitcher for the—"

"Himself," she replied. "It's going to be quite a bash."

"And cost you quite a bundle," he added, and she could see the dollar signs adding up in his eyes.

She leaned back, shrugging lightly. "I can afford it," she murmured.

"So I hear. And see," he added, noting the emerald bracelet that she'd redeemed by paying off the loan. He grimaced. "What a skyrocketing success. From poverty to the top of the heap in nine short years."

"With a little work in between," she reminded him.

He shook his head. "And none of us thought you had it in you," he sighed. "Me, most of all. When I think about some of the callous things I used to say about you…"

"I remember," she said, and the cut was less sharp than

usual. "You said that I didn't belong in the same company with you and your friends, and that your mother would be horrified to find me there. I was standing around the corner from you when you said it."

He looked faintly shocked. "You didn't hear the rest?" he asked softly.

She stared at him. "What rest?"

"That I thought my mother was a horrible snob and if she opened her mouth to you, I'd give her hell," he replied quietly.

She couldn't believe her ears. "But you also said that awful thing about making love to me…"

"I was furious at Larry because of the way he was looking at you," he replied coolly. "I'd wanted to ask you to the party myself, but I wasn't sure you'd go because I was so much older." He smiled. "Earlier, you'd been so sweet to tease and take around places, until that night we were in Jack's apartment. Then I began to get serious.

"It would never have worked, you know. My mother would have destroyed you, and I hadn't reached the point of being independent financially. It was hopeless, and I saw it. So I broke it off. That party simply precipitated things. You left town before I was able to explain it to you." He looked sheepish. "I was frankly glad about that. I'd dreaded it."

"And I never dreamed the truth," she murmured, searching his blue eyes.

"It's just as well," he said quietly. "We're older now, more mature. This time we could make a go of it, and there's no one to interfere."

That's what you think, she told herself mentally, but she only smiled at him. She couldn't tell him that the man he was today could hardly take the place of the much younger man she'd loved as a teenager. Been infatuated with, she corrected herself. Love lasted, and this hadn't. Nicholas had been right all along. Nicholas…

"What would you say," he murmured, "to a nice, old-fashioned engagement ring?"

She mulled over her answer before she gave it. "I'm very fond of you," she began. "I've enjoyed going out with you again, and I'm grateful to you for telling me the truth. But we're different people now. I've changed too much, James, to be satisfied by what you have to offer. I'm not eighteen anymore, you see," she ended sadly. "I grew up."

He flexed his shoulders with a wistful little smile. "I wish I hadn't," he murmured. "You were such a lovely little girl. If only…"

"Sad words, my friend," she said, reaching impulsively across the table to touch his hand. She smiled into his blue eyes. "I do like you very much."

He smiled back. "You're not bad yourself. How about another cup of coffee?"

She nodded. He had made it so easy for her. She smiled with relief.

"You have a lovely smile," he said simply, smiling back. "You always did." He motioned to the waiter. "Here, I'll get us a refill."

The night of the party finally came. Keena had designed something unique for it—a royal blue dress in deep, iridescent satin with gold swirls at the strapless bodice, the nipped waist, and the hem of the full skirt. It had a stole of matching fabric, and the design was worth a small fortune. In it, Keena looked absolutely queenly.

But her mind wasn't on her looks or her dress. It was on whether or not Nicholas was going to be among her illustrious guests. Her heart pounded at just the thought of seeing

him again, of being held in his arms even in an insignificant
dance. She'd missed him as she'd never dreamed it was possible to miss another human being, and if he didn't come, she
didn't know how she was going to bear the evening.

She made her entrance after half the guests had already arrived. The rambling house was filled with sounds of laughter
and music. High society mingled with local culture; Broadway stars chatted with the president of the local utility company. And everyone seemed to be having a wonderful time.

James was standing at the foot of the staircase when she
came down, all eyes and approving smiles. But Keena's eyes
were already darting around, looking for a dark head towering over everyone, for an imposing-looking man in evening
clothes. But she didn't find it. Nicholas wasn't there.

"Don't look so somber," James teased. "You're gorgeous,
and just take a peek at the stares you're drawing."

She didn't tell him that she couldn't have cared less, even
though one pair of approving, kind eyes belonged to one of
her worst female enemies in high school. All of a sudden the
past didn't matter. Only one thing did—and that was Nicholas.

She liked the band Mandy had found. There were six of
them, and they played some of the prettiest music Keena had
heard short of New York. She found herself paying more attention to them than she did to her dancing partners, most
of whom wanted to rave about her success.

James rescued her from one particularly heavy-footed partner who managed to squash one of her toes before she got
away from him.

"Thanks," she murmured weakly. "My feet were in danger of being permanently damaged."

"My pleasure." He studied her wan little face. "Keena,
you're very depressed tonight. Can I help?"

Only by becoming considerably taller, brawnier, and developing brown hair and eyes, she thought, but she only smiled and shook her head.

"I'm just tired," she lied. "I've had a lot of coordinating to do between here and my office. But the mad rush is temporarily over, and things will get better."

Of course they would. After all, the party had been in full swing for more than two hours, and there was still no sign of Nicholas.

She grabbed a Scotch and water from a passing waiter's tray and finished it in three large gulps. It had been a long time since she'd had hard liquor, but she didn't think about that. In fact, she grabbed a whiskey sour to top it off with, and only moments later she felt suddenly brighter.

She melted into James's arms, to his delight, and didn't make a sound when he bent and brushed his mouth across her cheek and in her hair when his arms caught her scandalously close as they danced.

And as fate would have it, that was the moment Nicholas Coleman chose to enter the room, resplendent in black evening clothes with a stark-white shirt, bow tie and a scowl black enough to curdle milk.

CHAPTER NINE

She stared at him across James's thin chest, her eyes as wide and uncomprehending as if she'd seen three ghosts playing jump rope.

He looked back, and his eyes weren't throwing roses at her.

She pried herself away from James with a nervous laugh as the big man came straight toward them.

"Mr. Coleman," James said politely, offering his hand and a smile.

Nicholas ignored both. He had eyes only for Keena. "I'd like to talk to you," he said shortly.

"Yes…of course," she stammered. "James, if you'll excuse me…"

"Of course," James replied courteously, moving away to get himself a drink.

"Hello, Nicholas," she said. Her eyes had trouble focusing on him, but he looked as big and dark and imposing as ever, and she noticed traces of his fiery French ancestry not for the first time in that flinty expression.

"Did you invite everyone south of Charleston?" he asked, casting a quick eye around the room.

"Only the very *best* people," she said haughtily and with a mischievous smile. She held out her arms. "Dance with me," she pouted.

"I'd rather take poison," he said shortly.

Her face fell tragically. All the weeks of waiting, of standing by windows looking out, hoping to see that ridiculous white car—weeks of jumping every time the phone rang, hoping it would be him. For this.

She turned and went ahead of him out of the big front room that had been cleared for dancing, across the hall to the small study. She waited for him to join her before she closed the sliding doors and sat down in the nearest chair.

"Sorry I can't offer you a drink," she said tautly, "unless you'd care to brave the crowd again."

He was smoking, his fingers lifting the cigarette to his mouth with jerky precision.

"Enjoying yourself?" he asked with a sharp glare.

"Up until about five minutes ago, yes, thanks," she replied with equal venom.

He walked to the darkened window and stood staring blankly out it, smoking quietly while the strains of a familiar love song echoed through the house, through the tense silence that stretched between them.

"Realizing your dreams, little fox?" he asked with his back to her.

"Right now it feels more like a nightmare," she murmured, dropping her hands to her full, stiff skirt. It misted under her gaze. "I missed you," she whispered miserably.

"It looked like it," he agreed, his voice smooth with sarcasm.

She couldn't bear that hard, level gaze. "I had a Scotch

and water, followed by a whiskey sour, and I'm feeling it, all right?"

"Why were you drinking?"

She clammed up. Not for worlds would she admit to this cold stranger that she'd wanted him beyond bearing, and the liquor had been nothing more than a painkiller.

"I just came to tell you that I'm transferring some of my smaller cuts to Harris's plant," he said quietly, his back still to her so that she missed the expression on his face. "Yours is going to be one of them. You'll deal directly with him."

"But…he sold you the plant," she murmured.

"He still has the management of it," he replied coolly. "Didn't he mention it?"

She shook her head. Her world was falling apart. Was he telling her to get out of his life?

"Are…are we going to see each other anymore, Nicholas?" she asked hesitantly.

He took a long draw from the cigarette before he answered her. "It might be wiser if we didn't, Keena."

She'd never taken a killing blow, but this felt like one. She hurt in a way she'd never imagined, as if he'd torn out her heart. She could hardly bear the pain.

Her eyes memorized him, every line of that huge, wrestler's frame, his shaggy, dark hair, the leonine features of his face, the nose she'd traced, the chest her fingers had explored so thoroughly, the square jaw that—set as it was now—spoke volumes on immovability. He was telling her goodbye for good, and there wasn't a thing she could say or do to make him change his mind.

She'd been right from the first. He'd wanted her, but only for a brief affair, and now he was easing her out of his life. It was what she knew he was planning, but even then she'd hoped against hope that she was wrong.

She stood up, very regal in her royal blue satin, too proud to let him see the anguish in her eyes.

"If that's what you think best," she said gently. "Thank you for…for everything, Nicholas. We've had some good times together."

He nodded. "They outnumbered the bad."

She met his eyes and turned quickly away before he could see the tears. "You might remember to send me a Christmas card next year," she said, fighting to control her voice, to keep it light.

"I'll do that."

She stopped in the hallway, still with her back to him. "Have a safe trip home, won't you?" she managed.

"You might at least turn around and look at me when you're saying goodbye," he growled harshly.

"No, I don't think I can do that," she whispered as the first of the tears rolled down her cheeks. She all but ran to James, hiding her tearful face against his spotless black jacket. Above the sound of the band, she winced when she heard the door open and close firmly.

"So that's how it is," James murmured gently.

But she couldn't answer him. She felt raw and wounded inside.

She managed somehow to survive the rest of the evening, smiling at her guests, saying all the right things, taking compliments with finesse, handing them out sometimes with sheer grit. She carried it off perfectly, and it wasn't until every single guest had gone home that she collapsed in tears on the sofa.

Mandy smoothed her tousled hair, cooed comforting words, pried that last confrontation with Nicholas out of her and finally dried the tears.

"Did you tell him you weren't interested in James?" Mandy asked gently.

"No," came the sharp reply.

"Don't you realize what it must have looked like when he walked in and saw you dancing like that with him?"

She shifted restlessly. "I couldn't tell him, not after he'd literally moved me out of his life. I have to deal with James now." She wiped the tears from her cheeks. "At least it will give me a reason not to go back to New York for a while. I think I'll move my office down here, too, and Ann and Faye…"

"You like it here, dear, but they may not," Mandy reminded her.

"Then I'll commute." Her face clouded up again. "I don't want to see Nicholas again, ever," she wept, and her slender body collapsed again on the sofa. "I can't! I can't bear it, Mandy, I can't!"

"Do you hate him so much, sweetheart?" Mandy asked her.

"I love him," Keena corrected, lifting a tear-wet face to her housekeeper's kind eyes. "I didn't even discover it until we got to Charleston, and it was already too late. Mandy, I do love him so, and all I have in the world won't amount to one single day with him. Do you know that? All the money and fame in the world isn't worth anything without Nicholas."

"May I make a suggestion?" Mandy asked.

"Is it reasonable?"

"Why don't you go and tell him how you feel?"

"And have him pat me on the back and soothe me?" Keena asked on a sob. "Because that's what he'd do. I'm just another responsibility to him. One he's grown tired of."

"Has it ever occurred to you that Nicholas might be in love with you?" Mandy asked in a soft, gentle tone.

"You didn't hear him," came the wailing reply.

"Amazing," Mandy sighed, "how he came two thousand miles in the middle of the night to see someone he hates."

Keena blinked. "He...he only came to tell me about the changeover."

"He could have done that on the phone. And what, pray tell, was the first thing he saw when he walked in the door?"

She shrugged. "Me. And James."

"Nick's always been wildly jealous of you," Mandy reminded her. "You may not have noticed it as much as I did. I've seen him watching you, honey, and most women would give anything to be looked at like that by a man like Nick. You think about it."

Keena's lower lip trembled; her eyes watered. "But what can I do? It's too late."

"Oh, no, it's not. You just wait right there." Mandy got up and left the room, and a minute later Keena heard her dialing. Three phone calls later she was back.

"I've got a plane waiting at the airport to take you to Charleston, and a driver waiting there to take you to Nicholas's house. The rest is up to you," she said.

"I—I'll have to change," she murmured, looking down at the satin dress.

"Why bother?" Mandy asked. "You'll just be wasting time. Get a move on, honey. He's only there for the night!"

"Well, what about a cab?"

"There it comes," Mandy murmured with a grin. She kissed the younger woman. "Give Nick my love."

Without stopping to think, Keena wrapped the stole around her and ran out the door.

The manor house was quiet when she got out of the cab in front of it, but she girded up her courage and knocked on the door. The worst thing that could happen would be that Nicholas would throw her out. At any rate, she had to try. She loved him, and her pride wasn't going to sustain her through the long, empty years without him. She might as well risk everything.

Mrs. Collins ambled to the door in a long dressing gown, her face alternately astonished and delighted when she saw Keena standing at the door.

"Saints alive!" she exclaimed. "Now talk about coincidences, Miss Keena. Remind me to tell you one day about how the first Mr. Coleman found his wife-to-be on his doorstep late one night. Did you come to see Mr. Nick?" she added, her voice stealthy.

Keena only nodded. Her heart jumped. "He...he is here?"

"Oh, he's here," Mrs. Collins sighed. "Roaring around upstairs for the better part of two hours, he was, throwing things about. He came here in a devil of a mood." Her old eyes twinkled. "I'm hoping you'll improve it, ma'am."

"I'll do my best," Keena promised.

But all her bravado threatened to leave her when she was climbing the long, dark staircase up to Nicholas's room. It was now or never. But suppose Mandy had read the whole situation wrong? Suppose Nicholas meant every word he said? He wouldn't appreciate being chased. He wasn't the kind of man who would.

She paused just outside his door. There was a sliver of yellow light peeking out from under it. Obviously, he wasn't asleep, although no sound came from the other side of the heavy door.

Well, it was why she'd come, wasn't it, to talk to him? She couldn't do it from the hall. She took a deep, sharp breath and opened the door.

She walked in before she had time for second thoughts, and closed it behind her. It was just as well that she had something to lean against, because Nicholas was stretched out on the bed without a stitch of clothing on, his dark eyes incredulous as they met hers.

"This," he said with faint humor, "is getting to be a habit with you."

She swallowed down a surge of embarrassment, her eyes involuntarily touching every powerful line of him. "Is it my fault that you won't wear pajamas?" she asked, trying to be nonchalant about it.

He laughed shortly. "May I ask what brings you here in the middle of the night?" he asked. "Isn't Harris enough for you?"

She girded her pride around her, only to let it fall again when she met those dark, devastating eyes. "I don't want James," she said quietly.

He cocked a dark eyebrow at her. "No? That wasn't what it looked like earlier."

Her lower lip trembled. "What did you expect, damn you?" she burst out. "You stayed away for almost a month, without calling or coming to see me. I spent all that time looking out windows, listening for the phone. Then, the night of the party, I jumped every time the doorbell rang, waiting, hoping…and you didn't come!" Tears misted her eyes. "I wanted you so, and you…didn't come. So I—I had a few drinks—" she laughed tearfully "—and I danced with James. And I… hated you with all my heart."

He hadn't said a word, moved a muscle. But now he threw his powerful legs over the side of the bed and stood up.

"Are…aren't you going to put on a robe?" she asked, her voice wildly high-pitched as he approached her.

"Why bother?" he asked. "I'd just have to take it off again."

"B-but…" she stammered as he stopped just in front of her, his big, bare, muscular arms trapping her against the door, his hair-rough chest making a fleshy wall in front of her.

"Don't stop now, honey," he murmured, watching her ex-

pression. "It was just getting interesting. Why did you want
me at the party?"

She stared straight ahead at the hard muscles of his massive chest. "Does it matter?" she asked tightly. "You think
I'm sleeping with James, don't you?"

He moved closer so that she had to look up or have her
nose crushed against him. "You wouldn't have come this far,
this fast, if you were," he murmured, letting his eyes lower
to her soft mouth. "You'll go through that door if you try to
get any closer to it," he whispered sensuously. "Why don't
you stop fighting and do what you really want to do, Keena?"

She studied his broad, hard face. "What do I want to do?"
she whispered shakily.

For an answer he caught her cold, nervous hands and placed
them on his lean, warm hips, moving them up and across
until they followed the arrowing of dark hair up his body to
tangle them in the crisp, soft hair on his chest.

"This," he murmured as he bent to brush his mouth slowly,
gently, against hers. "You want to touch me all over. You
want to lie in my arms and feel my body over yours, taking
absolute possession of it. Or are you going to tell me that's
not why you came?"

Tears welled in her eyes. He was right. Of course he was.
But it was more than that, so much more. She relaxed in his
close embrace, letting his mouth have hers, letting his tongue
reach into the dark, sweet warmth of her mouth to taste it,
to probe and tease and kindle fires that flamed through her
slender body like an explosion of sensation.

She moaned achingly, feeling every muscle in her body
contract before she arched it uncontrollably against the massive warmth of his, feeling it fit exactly into the hard contours of his powerful body until even the air couldn't have
managed to pass between them.

His hands caught the backs of her thighs and pressed her hips roughly into his, pressing her against him in a slow, sweet rotation that made her murmur against his mouth.

"Tell me it won't…be just…sex," she pleaded against his devouring mouth.

"It wouldn't have been just sex if I'd taken you six years ago," he ground out, drawing back just enough to let his fierce gaze capture her startled eyes. "My God, you've tied me up like a sheaf of grain. Didn't you know? I meant it to be a game before I went to Paris. I needed to feel whole again when Maria and I broke up. But my God, honey, you haunted me the whole time I was gone. When I came back, when I kissed you for the first time, the whole thing blew up in my face." He slid his hands up to her hips, pressing them sharply against his. "I wanted you this much the day we met, but the time was never right. Maybe that was a good thing, because I want a hell of a lot more from you now than this sexy young body."

"What…what do you want, Nicholas?" she whispered at his lips, while her hands began, tentatively, to explore his bronzed torso.

He looked straight down into her eyes, his own beginning to flare up with dark lights. "I want you to give me a child."

She felt the words as if they'd touched her physically. "Why?" She mouthed it more than said it.

He laughed shortly. "Because I'm insanely in love with you, you crazy little witch," he growled softly, bending to lift her completely off the floor in his hard arms, crushing his mouth down against hers in a kiss that was as passionate as it was possessive. "Oh, God, I love you," he whispered into her mouth, "need you, want you. Keena, I wanted to kill Harris for just holding you, for touching you. I won't ask more than you can give me, but let me have you tonight. Stay with me."

Tears burned in her eyes as she returned the soft, clinging kisses, her eyes slitted, her breath coming in shuddering gasps.

"It…it may take more than one night," she managed shakily.

"What?" he murmured as he laid her down in the crisp brown sheets that still bore traces of the heat from his big body.

"For…to get…"

"For a child?" he whispered, his eyes more tender than she'd ever seen them, his hands gentle as he smoothed the folds of the dress from her body to leave her clad only in her brief panties beneath his slow, possessive gaze. "In that case, it might be a good idea if you married me," he murmured. "To keep the gossip down, of course."

Her hands reached up to his neck and drew him down to her. "As if you cared about gossip, you blackguard," she whispered, glorying in the feel of his hands sliding over her, the newness of his eyes eating every soft, pink inch of her. It was magic, like a fantasy coming true, and tears welled up in her eyes at the intensity of love she felt. "Oh, Nick, I'd do anything you wanted me to," she whispered fervently. "Anything. I'd be your mistress, if that was all I could have. I'd give you a child and disgrace myself forever and not even count the cost."

His dark eyes stared into hers for a long, sweet moment. "You said something similar out on the grounds, not so very long ago. I asked you why you'd do anything for me, and you said you didn't know. Don't you, really?"

Her fingers touched his hard, warm mouth. "It's because I love you, my darling," she whispered tearfully. "Because you're the beginning and end of my whole world."

His eyes closed briefly, and when they opened again, there was a look in them that shattered her. "God knows you're that and more to me, love. And one more thing. I loved my first wife. But not in the same way that I love you. I'm not living with ghosts, and there won't be any between us, not tonight or any other night."

"When did you know," she whispered, "that you loved me?"

He smiled tenderly. "I knew for sure when I drove up in your front yard and saw you flirting with Harris. I wanted to set fire to his trousers." His hands moved to take slow, sweet possession of her slender body. "But we'll talk about the whens and wherefores later. Right now, Miss Whitman," he whispered, easing down beside her, "I want your absolute and undivided attention."

Her breasts rose and fell quickly at the look in his eyes, at the sensations he was just beginning to arouse. "Nick, is loving you going to be enough?" she whispered. "I'm more than willing, but I know so little..."

"It doesn't matter," he murmured as his arms swallowed her, as his mouth burned down against hers in a kiss as slow and tender as it was passionate. "All you have to do," he added in a deep whisper, "is relax and do what I tell you to. I'm going to show you all the slow, tender ways that a man expresses love. I'm going to be very gentle, and you're not going to be afraid of me. All right?"

Her arms looped around his neck and she felt with a sense of wonder his warm, hair-covered flesh melting down over her soft, bare body until she felt the brush of every fascinating inch of it. Her eyes widened and she gasped, her eyes telling him all that she felt. "Nick, I want to give you everything," she whispered, gasping under his hands, the satin brush of his hard mouth touching her in ways, in places, that she'd never dreamed of even in her most erotic fantasies. "Love me," she whispered, arching her body toward his mouth.

He chuckled softly, delightedly, as his hand reached over to turn out the light.

★ ★ ★

It was morning when she woke to find herself looking up into patient, loving, dark eyes with all the memories of the night before in them. Nicholas had been patient and tender, intent on giving pleasure as well as getting it. His expertise had quickly ignited Keena with a passion that bordered on anguish. She remembered opening her eyes at that instant and looking straight into his, amazed to find him watching her, his face taut with desire, his gaze fiercely loving as his powerful body overwhelmed hers.

"You...you watched me," she whispered shakily, still half-awake.

He bent and kissed her mouth tenderly, reverently. "I had to," he whispered. "It was beautiful. The moonlight, brighter than day on your face, those tiny, amazed little cries purring out of you, your body trembling... I'll dream about it for the rest of our lives, Keena. You were exquisite."

Her fingers edged into his dark hair, where it was silver at the temples, tangling in its unruly thickness. "So were you," she whispered with a quiet smile. "Oh, Nick, I do love you so!"

He bent and kissed her open mouth roughly. "No less than I love you," he whispered. "How do you want to be married? In a church, with all the trimmings, or by a justice of the peace?"

"Any way at all," she murmured fervently.

"By a justice of the peace, then," he replied, "because I want my ring on your finger as soon as possible."

"I won't change my mind," she assured him gently.

One corner of his mouth went up wickedly. "That isn't why."

Both her eyebrows went up as she searched his eyes.

He chuckled softly, smoothing a big hand across her flat stomach. "We've jumped the gun, honey."

She flushed delicately. "Afraid of wagging tongues?" she teased.

"Terrified of the stork," he whispered against her mouth. "I'm a respectable businessman, a pillar of the community..."

"A seducer of innocents," she whispered back, drawing his dark head down so that she could kiss him slowly.

"But you love me," he whispered with a broad grin.

"More than my own life. Even more," she said, laughing, "than my fabulous career."

"And now you have a whole new career," he murmured against her seeking mouth as he lowered his powerful body completely against hers.

"Hmmm?" she murmured breathlessly.

"Loving me," he replied, and her soft laughter was drowned out by the pressure of his smiling lips.

★ ★ ★ ★ ★

A LOVING ARRANGEMENT

CHAPTER ONE

The rain had been fierce, and Abby Summer dripped puddles into the rich carpet at her desk as she eased out of her beige trench coat and removed the jaunty little brimmed hat from her braided coil of silvery hair. Even wet, she had a grace and elegance about her that caught and held the eye. She was twenty-six, but looked years younger with her slender build, her delicate features.

The fingers that slid her wet coat onto a hanger were long and the nails expertly manicured. There wasn't a hair out of place on her head, or a smudge on her high cheekbones that wasn't deliberate. Her dark green eyes were as cool, as calm, as the face she presented to the world. Abby was notorious around the law offices of McCallum, Doppler, Hedelwhite and Smith for her serenity in the face of impossible odds. In the year she'd been Greyson McCallum's executive secretary, she'd never fainted, shouted back, burst into tears, or resigned. That, in itself, was a mark of heroism. Greyson McCallum had his own reputation, and serenity was certainly not part of it.

McCallum and old Mr. Doppler were the senior partners in

the firm. Dick Hedelwhite was long dead, but his name was left out of respect, and Jerry Smith's just had been added. Abby and Jan Dickinson shared the secretarial duties, but Abby got the lion's share because of McCallum's larger clientele. He was nationally famous as a trial lawyer, attracting clients from as far away as New York, while Doppler and Smith specialized in divorce cases and civil suits. Besides, Jan had the advantage of working for two patient men. Nobody, ever, would have described McCallum as patient.

Abby uncovered her electric typewriter and reached in her middle drawer for the daily appointment book. When it didn't peer up at her, she blinked in amazement. It was always in the middle drawer.

She searched through the side drawer and found it tucked on top of a box of carbon paper where it had no business being. Odd, she didn't remember placing it there Friday at quitting time.

Her fingers opened the pages to Monday and she quickly scanned the familiar names and times until a heavy black scrawl stood out against the neatness of her crisp handwriting. McCallum had written in a name of his own for 4 p.m. and Abby felt the blood leave her face in a frantic rush.

Her hands trembled, dropping the black-bound appointment book on the glassy surface of her desk. Her eyes had widened at the name, and she felt a surge of panic that made her want to run out of the office. Robert C. Dalton, 4 p.m., Robert C. Dalton, 4 p.m.—the words ran around wildly in her mind.

Of course, it wasn't impossible that Atlanta could have produced a Robert C. Dalton. The phone book must have held at least a score of them. But Abby had a hunted sensation, and she'd have bet a week's salary that this particular Robert C. Dalton hailed from Charleston, that he was married to the heiress of a shipping empire, and that unless she found a way to be out of the office by 4 p.m. she was going to be drawing her unemployment by quitting time.

She'd been so interested in that name that she hadn't heard the intercom the first time it buzzed. The second sharp, impatient jab caught her attention, and she depressed the button with trembling fingers.

"Yes, sir?" she managed weakly.

"Bring your pad," a deep, curt voice replied.

She automatically reached for her steno pad and a pencil, dropping it once before she got to her feet. It was court week, and McCallum had a case set for 9.30 a.m. in superior court. It was just barely 9:00 a.m. now. It would take him ten minutes to get to the courthouse—five, the way he drove his sleek Porsche—and he'd just found something he wanted to add to a petition. By the time he dictated it, she'd have less than five minutes to type it, with copies, in the spotless manner he demanded. And she knew before she tapped at the door and went in that she'd never be able to manage it in her present, shaken state.

"Sit down," McCallum growled without lifting his dark, leonine face from the transcript his eyes were glued to.

Abby sat, poised gracefully on the edge of one of the brown leather chairs, her eyes lingering on his broad shoulders, the big, square-tipped fingers that were gripping the transcript. He looked more like a professional wrestler than a famous trial lawyer. And it wasn't only his tall, powerful physique that commanded attention. He could use words more effectively than any weapon. Abby had seen him reduce grown men to tears on the witness stand. He could literally strip the hide off a stubborn witness without ever raising his deep, velvety voice.

No doubt, he curbed those aggressive instincts when he was with women, because the office always seemed to be full of

them. Sophisticated, very mature women who looked vaguely
alike, merging into one specific type: tall, brunette, gener-
ously endowed and faintly bored. The zombies, Abby called
them when she needed a mental boost. And their conversation always seemed to center around their newest perfume
or McCallum's most recent gift. They all fawned on him.
And none of them had ever lasted longer than a few weeks.
At forty, he was still very much a bachelor, and in no evident
hurry to change his status.

"Studying me?" he asked curtly, and his strange pale gray
eyes suddenly caught hers in a hammerlock.

She fought back a snappy answer, barely maintaining her
cool, efficient image. Abby kept her vibrant personality under
tight wraps, disguising it in clothes like the plain gray suit she
was wearing, the glasses she didn't need. She'd landed the job
that way. Don't come on like a career woman, or a hothouse
flower, her friend Jan had warned her when she applied for
the job. Only McCallum's women were allowed to be colorful and vivacious. He only wanted an efficient wallflower
at his typewriter, someone restful. So Abby had toned down
her clothes and her personality, forgotten the outgoing charm
that had made her a successful reporter, and walked right into
the job. And she almost never missed the old life, the excite-
ment. Almost never.

"Was I staring, Mr. McCallum?" she asked with a polite
smile.

His eyes narrowed, and he watched her in that way he had,
a piercing stare that seemed to reach deep inside to all the secret places that were locked away from the light.

Without replying, he neatly removed a sheet of yellow legal
paper from the pad in front of him and slid it across the desk.

"Type that," he said curtly. "Then call Miss Nichols at

her apartment and tell her I'll pick her up at seven tomorrow night for the ballet."

Without me, Greyson McCallum, you'd never be able to keep a love affair going, she mused silently. It was up to Abby to send them flowers and candy, run interference, soothe them when he broke dates, put them off gently when he was busy…it was almost as exciting as writing a gossip column.

"Yes, sir," she said, jotting down the note in the margin of her steno pad.

"Call my brother and tell him to cancel his flight to Paris," he added darkly. "He is not, repeat *not*, following that French prostitute home. And call my mother and tell her I'm heading him off."

More dirty work, she sighed, making another note. Nick wasn't going to like that. He was genuinely infatuated with Collette, and whether or not she deserved McCallum's careless appellation was up for grabs. Mandy McCallum wasn't going to be thrilled by the news, either—she doted on her youngest son, but she wasn't up to her eldest's temper. She muttered a lot, carefully making her remarks when Grey was out of earshot.

"And you don't approve of that, do you?" he asked suddenly.

She jumped at the suddenness of the remark. "Why… I…"

"Don't give me that sweet, vague little smile," he growled. "I can read you like the cover of a glossy magazine, Miss Summer. But I don't require your approval, merely your co-operation."

And my blind obedience, yes, sir, she thought, hiding the mutinous twinkle in her green eyes.

"He is twenty-five," she reminded him.

"Twenty-five, eh? And since when has a man's age had anything at all to do with responsibility when a woman like that is concerned?" He leaned back in his massive chair, lifting his hands behind his shaggy mane of hair. The action stretched his tailored white shirt over his broad chest, its sheerness hinting sensuously at the heavy, thick mat of black hair over those powerful muscles. "Hell, Miss Summer, you can't know much about men if you consider that brother of mine responsible."

That aggressive masculinity disturbed Abby. She distrusted it. He'd never made a bona fide pass at her, although she sometimes felt that it had crossed his mind. She deliberately made herself as unnoticeable as possible. McCallum was the kind of man no sane woman would risk her heart on. He was too arrogant, too independent and too fond of variety. A brief affair was as much as he had to offer, and Abby had no faith at all in her ability to weather that type of arrangement. Despite a brief, unhappy marriage, she was still remarkably inhibited for a woman of her age, something of an anachronism in the modern world. She'd had her fingers burned badly, and she was wary of enticing flames.

"I said, do you think Nick is responsible?" he repeated, surging forward in the chair to rest his elbows on the desk, while his glittering eyes studied her from under his jutting brow. "What the hell is wrong with you this morning?"

She looked away from him and down at her pad. Well, she thought, it was tell him or make a run for it. "There's an appointment on your calendar for today that I didn't make," she said quietly, hoping against hope that it could be explained away, that it was a useless fear.

"Well, my God, do I need your permission to make an appointment on my own?" he demanded with a black glance.

"Oh, no, I didn't mean that," she said quickly. She hunched her shoulders helplessly. "I meant... Mr. McCallum, is Mr.

Dalton… I know it's none of my business, but is Robert Dalton from Charleston?"

A strange expression passed over his face. One eye narrowed ominously. "Yes, Bob Dalton is from Charleston. Why? Do you know him? From where?"

She should have known better. She could have pumped old Mr. Doppler later if she'd kept her head, and he was so fuzzy-minded, he wouldn't have asked for a reason. But McCallum was asking, and he meant to have an answer. She read it in his taut face as he watched her down his arrogant nose.

"It's nine-ten," she reminded him. "You have a client waiting…"

"He can damned well wait, or the judge can postpone the arraignment, or Jerry Smith can handle it for me, but you're not leaving this office until I get an answer." He took a cigarette out of his shirt pocket and lit it, dragging the big ashtray toward him. He leaned back again. "Well?"

"It's none of…"

"I hired you," he reminded her. "And not without reservations. If you think that disguise you wear has fooled me, you're crazy. You're shook up today, Miss Summer. As shaken as I've ever seen you, and unless I miss my guess, Bob Dalton is the reason. Care to tell me about it, Abby, or shall I call Dalton and ask him?"

"Is he a friend of yours?" she asked weakly.

"In a manner of speaking," he said, nodding. One silvery eye narrowed. "Come on, woman, talk."

She lifted her face proudly, hating the betraying tremor of her lower lip. "His wife found him on the bed with me," she said steadily, watching the surprise lift his heavy brows. "She had me fired from my job, and I left Charleston…because of the mess."

He stared at her levelly for several seconds before he spoke. "When?"

"Over a year ago," she said evenly. "I was the assistant news editor on an afternoon daily at the time."

There was a long pause before he suddenly picked up the receiver and punched a number out. A minute later he was telling his junior partner to take the case for him, and giving instructions.

"You can pick up the brief here, and get the lead out, boy, you've only got fifteen minutes!" He slammed the receiver down.

He stared at her silently for several seconds, taking a long draw from the cigarette before he spoke.

"Were you in love with him?" he asked.

She shrugged. "I thought I was, yes. I could have died when his wife opened that door. She went white in the face and began to scream obscenities…" Her eyes closed on the terrible memory.

"What did Dalton do?"

The question stung, because it brought back the humiliation full force. "He told her that I'd seduced him," she replied with a bitter little smile. "His wife had the moneyed background, you see. A divorce would have cost him everything, and I wasn't worth that. So I left Charleston and he kept his empire."

"You knew that he was married?" he asked, and she saw a glint in his eyes that she couldn't identify.

"Yes, I knew." She laughed mirthlessly. "Strangely enough, it didn't matter. I loved him too much to care. And we'd spoken often enough about his loveless marriage, his plans to get a divorce. I wanted to believe him. I hadn't learned that it's dangerous to want anything too much."

"How do you feel about him now?" he asked quietly.

She met his eyes with an effort. "I don't know. I haven't seen him since it happened. And I don't want to. I'm afraid," she admitted in a whisper. *Afraid that I'm not over him, that he'll smile at me and make excuses, and I'll believe them because I want to believe them,* her thoughts ran on. "I haven't even dated anyone since I left Charleston."

"I know," he replied, and something in the way he said it puzzled her. "You needn't look so puzzled, Miss Summer. I read people very well. You've worn a suit of armor since the day you walked into my office. It's very effective."

"I didn't want to get involved with anyone," she said, wanting him to understand. It was suddenly important to make him understand, not only that she was afraid of Dalton, but also why—because she'd never given herself to him completely. His wife had barged in just in the nick of time. But McCallum's eyes had gone past her to the door.

"Come in, Jerry," he said, motioning his tall, fair-haired partner into the office. "Here," he said, handing him the brief and tacking on a flurry of instructions.

"Don't worry, boss." Jerry grinned, winking at Abby. "I've been well taught. I'll murder 'em!"

"I don't have time to defend you, so don't go past contempt of court," McCallum said drily.

"You bet. See you!" And he was gone with a wave.

McCallum swept his piercing gaze back to Abby. "What do you want to do? I don't have time to break in a new secretary with my present calendar," he added menacingly, "so don't mention resigning. It'll take three weeks night and day to train a new girl, and I can't spare the time. I'm not that easy to please."

"If you weren't so impatient..." she began.

"Damn it, don't start trying to make me over," he shot back. "I'm too set in my ways. I don't want a teenager who'll get hysterical every time I lose my temper, and I can't take simpering spinsters. It took me long enough to get you over bouts of crying in the ladies' lounge."

She glared at him. "It was only once, and you threw a book at me!"

"The hell I did!" he growled, sitting up straight. "It sailed off the desk into your lap, but I didn't throw it. It slipped."

"You have a nasty temper, Mr. McCallum, and I'd hate to sacrifice some poor young girl to replace me, but I can't stay here if you and Bob Dalton are going to be working together for any length of time."

"I'm taking him on as a business partner," he said, confirming her worst fears. "And you're not quitting me. So just calm down and we'll work something out."

"What did you have in mind, Your Worship, hiding me in your closet when he comes to town?" she asked sarcastically.

One thick eyebrow went up, and there was faint amusement in his silver eyes. "Your mask slipped."

"Don't think it's been easy keeping it on around you… sir," she replied.

"Then why bother in the first place?" he asked impatiently.

"Because Jan said you wanted someone efficient, cool and unflappable," she replied coolly.

One corner of his chiseled, hard mouth turned up and his eyes were suddenly speculative. "Well, well. Now you're making me curious, Miss Summer."

"About what?" she muttered.

"About what you're like under that facade. I think I'm going to have to find out."

"You won't have time," she assured him, getting to her feet. "If Bob Dalton is coming here at four, I'm leaving permanently at three. I've had my life turned upside down once. I'll just pass on this round. There are other jobs."

"Like what—reporting?" he challenged.

She swallowed. "It left a bad taste in my mouth for a while, but yes, I think I could go back to it now."

"Running?" he taunted.

"Exercising the better part of valor," she corrected, firing up at his mocking smile.

"I thought you were interested in writing novels," he remarked.

She flushed. "So?" she challenged.

"So don't throw away your new life without a fight," he said, rising from his own chair to tower over her.

"I can't stay!" she cried, her eyes wild, her face flushed.

"Of course you can," he corrected, moving closer. He looked down at her with dancing eyes. "All you have to do is move in with me."

CHAPTER TWO

She stared at his solemn face blankly while she tried to decide whether or not she'd misunderstood him.

"You heard me," he said, reading the question in her eyes. "If you're obviously living with me, he won't dare make a pass at you. He wants this deal between us to work out too much to risk it, even for you."

That was true enough. McCallum's size alone was enough of a deterrent. And he was blatantly possessive about his acquisitions, especially his female ones.

"Do you think I have to actually move in?" She tried to sound her usual cool and reasonable self, but she could hear her voice faltering just a bit. "Couldn't we just appear to be having a very *obvious* affair?"

He sat back down in his chair, eyeing her in that totally unnerving way of his. "Certainly a possibility," he replied. "But tell me, Miss Summer, if Bob Dalton turned up on your doorstep late one lonely night, would you be able to keep him on the other side of that door?"

She stared back at him for a long moment, then down at

her hands clasped in her lap. She gave no reply to his question, and he seemed to acknowledge that none was necessary.

"But Mr. Doppler and Jerry…and your mother and brother, what would they think?" she countered to his silence. "Everyone would know!"

"It would hardly be effective if we kept it a secret," he reminded her with a dry smile. He stuck his hands in his pockets. "If you're worried about sex, you needn't be," he said bluntly. "You must have noticed by now that my tastes run to brunettes who don't interfere with my work. You won't have to lock me out of your bed."

The blush was unexpected, and it seemed to fascinate him. A faint smile touched his lips.

"Well?" he asked. "This is the twentieth century, honey," he reminded her gently. "People are living together all over the city. And you aren't still in pigtails."

That hurt, but she wasn't going to waste her breath trying to explain her feeling about such things to him. Twentieth century or not. It didn't seem to matter to him, anyway. He was so matter-of-fact about it, as nonchalant as if he asked women to live with him every day. She studied him quietly. Perhaps he did. And he was offering her his protection, without any risk of involvement. It would keep Bob away from her, of that she was sure. Robert Dalton's cowardice had surfaced once during their brief relationship and she did not flatter herself into thinking for one instant that he would risk losing this deal with McCallum for her sake.

Besides, she told herself, her parents wouldn't have to know and Grey's family would understand, she hoped. She couldn't bear to have them think less of her for it. Their opinion mattered. Grey's opinion mattered, and she'd only just realized it. She stared at him helplessly, wanting to put it into words that she couldn't seem to find.

"How long would I have to live with you?" she asked practically, after a minute.

"Two weeks," he replied. "Dalton will be in town that long while we discuss business—and he's going to visit friends in Dunwoody. After that it won't matter anymore and you can move back into your own apartment."

"When do I have to pack?" she asked.

"This morning, obviously," he replied with a curt laugh. "He's having dinner with me tonight. Mrs. McDougal is cooking seafood for us."

"Oh." She couldn't imagine how she was going to get everything packed by late afternoon. And she couldn't imagine, either, how she'd let herself be talked into this. No wonder McCallum had such a reputation for charming judges and juries. She didn't know what had hit her, and she'd seen it coming!

He turned and hit the intercom switch. "George," he told Mr. Doppler, "Abby and I are going to be out for the rest of the morning. If I have any calls, have Jan take them, will you? Thanks."

He flicked off the switch and the next thing Abby knew, she was being put into her raincoat and hat and herded out the door.

It felt strange, having Greyson McCallum in her apartment. He'd been there before, to give her a lift to work once when her car was in the shop, or to deliver a sheaf of scribbling that he needed typed on Saturday. But having him sit on her dark brown sofa sipping a cup of coffee, with his pale eyes watching her narrowly while she darted around getting books and essentials packed, was disturbing. He made the small efficiency apartment seem even smaller.

"I'm still not sure I'm doing the right thing," she said a few minutes later, with her suitcase packed and sitting on the rug by her floral upholstered easy chair while she shared a last cup of coffee with him.

"Afraid of what people will say?" he chided.

She flushed, the rosy color complementing her creamy complexion and lighting her wan face. "Yes, a little. I've always been pretty conventional. I don't know if I'm going to like having people stare at me like a kept woman."

"Haven't you learned by now that people can only hurt you if you let them?" he asked with a cocked eyebrow. "Who the hell cares what people think?"

She stared down into her fragrant coffee. "You forget I've been there before," she reminded him. "And I've got the scars to prove it."

He crossed his long legs and stared at her over the rim of the cup. "How old are you?"

"Twenty-six," she said without thinking.

"You look like a twenty-year-old, trying to impersonate my maiden aunt in that outfit," he laughed softly. "I hope you aren't planning to wear it tonight?"

She bristled. It was an expensive suit. "What's wrong with it?"

"It isn't the kind of outfit a sophisticated woman wears," he said matter-of-factly. "You'll have Dalton questioning my eyesight. And I presume you didn't dress like that for him?"

Damn his bluntness! Her small chin lifted proudly. "I won't disgrace you," she said sharply.

"Don't bristle," he admonished. "Do you need those glasses?"

With a self-conscious grimace, she took them off and folded them, placing them on the table beside her.

"Or to screw up your hair in that ridiculous bun you always wear?"

With an exaggerated sigh, she took out the hairpins and let her long, silver hair flow around her shoulders. The effect was stunning. He watched her with a steady, narrow gaze that made her want to lock a door between them. He'd never looked at her in quite that way before, and she wasn't sure how to take it.

"Tell me about Dalton. How did it begin?" he asked.

She drew in a deep breath. "There isn't a lot to tell. He was running for office, for city commission, and I interviewed him. He was easy to talk to, very charming. He invited me to tour his shipyards, I went, and we started seeing each other. It was just an occasional cup of coffee at first, and then one day…" She shifted restlessly, remembering the feel of the tall, blond man's arms around her, the stunned expression on his face that first time he'd kissed her, the feel of his hard, expert mouth on hers…

"Stop daydreaming and finish it!" McCallum said curtly.

She dragged her mind back to the present. "He said he loved me," she replied, skipping over the rest. "I believed him, perhaps because I wanted to so much." Her eyes dropped as she remembered Dalton's silky voice pleading with his fiery wife, denying his own part in it, assuring his wife that Abby had tempted him one time too many…

"Was it worth it?" he asked with a bite in his voice, and her temper ruffled. Not for worlds would she have told him the truth then, that it had never gone the last mile between Dalton and herself.

She glared at him.

"How long did you stay around after his wife caught you?" he asked.

"Two days. It was either run or be run out of town. Dalton's wife comes from a family with plenty of pull. So, I ran. Atlanta was home," she explained. "I grew up with Jan," she added. "She said I might be able to work for you, since your secretary was leaving to get married. But she said I'd have to blend in with the woodwork."

"So you became a chair," he mused. "I see. And didn't you miss chasing ambulances, Miss Summer?"

"Not after the first month," she confessed, glancing at him with a shy smile. "You have some of the most incredible people around you. There's always something going on where you are."

"The next best thing to the police beat?" he asked.

"Or the social page," she murmured, grinning. "Your love life is one big, ongoing adventure…"

"Don't bring love into it, honey," he corrected with a half smile. "That's a word I'm not used to."

She shrugged. "Whatever. Working for you is never dull."

He scowled at her. "You look different without your disguise."

Her hands made a helpless little gesture. "I don't suppose you were fooled from the first, were you?"

"No, but I was curious." He lit a cigarette and blew out a cloud of smoke. "I wondered why a girl with your intelligence would be working as a secretary. And why you went to such lengths to hide your beauty and avoided every pass my brother made at you." He chuckled at her blush. "At first I thought you might have undergone some trauma in adolescence. You wore an invisible 'don't touch' sign. But you were efficient, and dependable, and I kept you on despite my initial doubts. You were very restful," he added with a grin.

He got to his feet, staring down at her intently. "No turning back," he warned softly. "If you commit yourself this far, you're going the whole way. Walk one step toward Dalton and you'll rue the day you met me."

She believed him. That raw power in him was more obvious now that she'd seen it in a personal way. She knew how ruthless he could be, and she didn't want to have that wall fall on her.

"I won't back out," she promised. Her eyes searched his narrow ones. "Why are you doing this for me?"

He smiled mockingly. "I don't want to lose the best secretary I've ever had."

"Oh."

"I hope you packed an evening dress," he added.

She smiled, thinking of the sexy little black dress in her suitcase. "Oh, I think you'll approve, even though you don't like blondes."

"You'd better thank your stars that I don't," he replied in his deep, gravelly voice as he went to open the door with her suitcase in his big hand. "Otherwise, you might be jumping out of the frying pan and into the fire."

"What is Mrs. McDougal going to think?" she asked, frowning.

"Will you stop?" he growled. "For all I care, she and the whole bunch can think we're madly in love and too inflamed by passion to stay off each other."

"They'll know better," she stammered.

He lifted an arrogant eyebrow at her. "Then we'll just have to let them find us making love on the couch, won't we?"

She'd never thought of him that way. But the pictures that flashed suddenly into her mind were graphic and embarrassing. To lie in those big, powerful arms and let his mouth crush down against hers. To feel the hunger in it and taste it, to feel his skin under her hands…

She followed him out the door in a stunned silence. She hadn't counted on being curious about him, physically. That changed things, and she wasn't sure in what way.

★ ★ ★

His apartment was like the man himself—big, sophisti-cated, elegant and imposing with flagrant contrasts at every turn. The furniture was antique—genuine; she was sure. The rugs were Oriental, the statuary was modern, marble pieces mostly. There was a plush gray sofa around a fireplace, down in the sunken living room.

"Where shall I put my things?" she asked hesitantly.

He led her down the hallway and opened a door into what was obviously the guest bedroom, with a deep blue decor that was pleasant and restful. He set her suitcase and overnight bag inside the door.

"This is yours for the duration," he said with a hint of humor in his tone. "But for the sake of appearances, when Dalton's here and you need to freshen up, use the master bed-room, not this one."

"All right. But…where is it?" she faltered.

He led her to the room across the hall and opened the door on a dark curved oak bedroom suite with a huge king-size bed overlaid by a silky chocolate quilted coverlet, flanked by heavy tables with broad-based lamps.

"No comment?" he asked, studying her averted face. "Not even on the size of the bed?"

She gave him a sneaking glance. "There's a lot of you," she agreed.

He laughed softly. "And I'd look strange in a canopied French Provincial bed," he added.

She couldn't stifle a laugh at just the thought of it. And then she remembered something and the laughter vanished. "Will Mrs. McDougal be in today?" she wondered aloud.

"Probably," he said. "Don't worry so. She's not a busybody. She never interferes."

But all the same, it wasn't going to be pleasant, having that very kind woman giving her curious looks. She'd known Mrs. McDougal for several months. She respected her, and she didn't want the plump housekeeper to think less of her. It was a crazy idea, anyway, and God only knew what effect it would have on McCallum's private life. Speaking of which…

. The phone interrupted her thoughts. McCallum answered it, and Abby went into the living room to give him some privacy. But it was a brief conversation, because barely two minutes later he joined her.

"That was Jan," he murmured. "Dalton won't be here until Wednesday." He glanced at her and smiled. "It's just as well. I wondered how we were going to break the news to the staff and make it believable."

She felt the relief all the way down to her toes. Two more days. In that length of time, a lot could happen. The world could end…

Her green eyes darted up to his. "What about Vinnie Nichols?" she asked. "Will you tell her the truth?"

"I might as well take out an ad in the Sunday magazine section of the newspaper," he replied gruffly. "My God, you know what a gossip Vinnie is."

"But…" she faltered.

"We tell nobody the truth, Abby," he said curtly, his eyes level and silver. "Unless you'd rather back out?"

The alternatives were all unpleasant. There'd been enough change in her life in the past few years. She was weary of flight, of trying to outrun problems. She liked her job; she liked her life the way it was now. She shook her head slowly. "No, Mr. McCallum, I don't want to back out."

He lifted an eyebrow at her. "How many people are going to believe that you can still call me Mr. McCallum when you're supposed to be sleeping with me?" he asked.

She shifted uncomfortably. "I'm sorry, but old habits die

hard. I've never called you by name, even behind your back."
She studied him. "Although," she admitted drily, "I've called
you a lot of other names behind your back."

"No doubt." He smiled faintly. "Mother calls me Greyson.
Nick calls me Grey. Vinnie calls me Cal. Take your pick. But
no more 'Mr.' Fair enough?"

"I'll do my best," she promised.

He took her to a quiet little café around the corner and she
had a club sandwich and a cup of coffee while he acquainted
her with the routine of his apartment. She knew that breakfast
was at six sharp, that he liked peace and quiet, and he didn't
care for hose hanging in the shower.

"Oh, aye, aye, sir, I'll be sure to leave my collection of ab-
original fertility rite recordings at my old apartment," she
assured him.

"Twenty-six, did you say?" he asked mockingly.

Now she was finishing the first half of her sandwich and
watching him over her coffee cup. He was bigger close up
than he seemed to be in the office, broader and darker and
much more imposing.

"You're staring again," he remarked without looking at her
as he poured cream into his coffee.

She shifted. "Would you rather I stared at the man behind you?"

He chuckled softly. His silver eyes pinned her. "How have
you managed to be so sedate while you were taking dictation
all these months, Miss Summer?" he asked. "Surely you had
to bite through your tongue a few times."

"More than a few." She sipped her coffee, feeling awkward
without her coiffure and glasses. Her whole outlook was different now, with the facade taken away, as if age had fallen
away with the bobby pins. "But I liked my work, and I didn't

want to be fired." She glanced at him impishly. "I needed to blend in with the woodwork, you see."

"Jan exaggerates at times," he reminded her. "I did want an efficient secretary, but the role of an aging spinster hardly suits you." His eyes narrowed, studying her. "Didn't you tell me once that you were divorced?"

She didn't like even the memory of her marriage, but she nodded.

"How long ago?"

"Three years."

"Children?"

She shook her head stiffly.

Her fingers tightened on the cup. "Are there any more personal questions you'd like to ask me before we go back to the office?"

"Only one," he replied, not even ruffled by her rudeness. "Was Dalton involved emotionally?"

"He never told me. I think he was…" She studied the floor. "I was lonely and he was kind. Perhaps I was blinded by my own feelings."

"How long did the affair last before his wife caught you?" he asked casually.

"Ah, that's the irony of it all," she said with a bitter smile. "We'd only just realized that we were going to have an affair. Fortunately, she walked in while I still had some of my clothes on."

He set his cup down with deliberate slowness and stared at her across the table with narrowed, studious eyes. "In other words, he hasn't had you."

"Shades of the Spanish Inquisition!" she burst out.

"Is that how I sounded?" He finished his coffee. "I suppose I'm so used to the interrogation room and the courtroom that I tend to forget how to carry on normal conversations."

"What *are* you going to tell Miss Nichols?"

"Have you called her about the ballet?" he asked.

"But we rushed out of the office, and I didn't get time…"

"I'll talk to her this afternoon." He leaned back in the chair. "I'm going to tell her that we're having an affair."

"But she'll be so upset…" she protested, remembering how fragile-looking the small woman was. Abby liked her, despite the fact that she dyed her hair red and tended to put on airs.

"I'll console her with a diamond bracelet," he said carelessly. "She won't miss me."

She glanced down at the shiny surface of the table. "Is it always that easy for you to let go of people?"

"I love my freedom, Abby. I like a woman I can take or leave. Hadn't you noticed?" he added with a raised eyebrow.

"It's very hard to miss a parade," she agreed. "They don't last very long."

"I wear them out," he remarked with a slow, sensuous smile.

Sex was little more than an unpleasant memory for Abby, whose husband had expected everything and given nothing. It had been a part of her marriage that she tolerated, but never really enjoyed. Even with Robert Dalton, her caresses had been a way to please him, to repay him for his kindness. More enjoyable perhaps, but never thrilling. She'd never felt touched to her very soul, never out of control. She had the feeling that she was a little cold, a little frigid. She'd never wanted a man with the kind of raging passion she read about in her endless romance novels. It had often surprised her that she found those same love scenes so easy to write.

"Deep in thought, Abby?" he asked. "Don't you think I'd be a good lover?"

Her surprised gaze met his head-on. "I'd never thought about it."

"Ouch." He lit a cigarette with a wry smile on his face.

"No offense," she said quickly.

"None taken." He studied her face with a scrutiny that was just a little short of embarrassing. "Will you think about it now?" he asked with the bluntness that was characteristic.

She averted her face. "Shouldn't we get back?"

He stood up and paused to leave a tip under his saucer. He didn't say another word, but she had an odd feeling that she'd given him the answer he wanted just the same.

Two clients came and went before McCallum called Abby in for dictation.

After he got through the pile of letters that required answers, he watched her for a long time, his eyes going from the loosened, waving platinum hair, down the soft lines of her body to the sleek legs encased in smooth hose peeking out of her skirt.

"Now *you're* staring," she observed.

"You've got nice legs, Miss Summer," he murmured, and his narrowed eyes slid over them like caressing hands.

She laughed, her whole face lighting up at the unexpected compliment. "Thank you."

He grinned back at her. "My pleasure. Well, Abby, is it going to be today?" he asked, leaning back in his huge, padded chair to study her. The action pulled his shirt taut across the broad, hard muscles of his chest, and her eyes involuntarily went to it, curious about the sight of it, the feel of it. Her own thoughts were faintly shocking and she looked away.

"Today?" she echoed, only half hearing him.

"You do realize that if we're going to make Dalton believe we're having an affair, the office staff is going to have to believe it, as well?" he asked quietly.

"Yes, of course." She stared at him, waiting.

"Do you think telling them would be enough?" he taunted.

He pressed the intercom button to get Jan. "See if George has that Burlough file, honey. I'd like to look through it."

"Yes, sir," came the pleasant reply.

McCallum's silver eyes caught Abby's and held them, while something prodded her heart, causing it to beat wildly. Her breath caught.

"Open the door a little, Abby," he said in a deep, slow tone that was as rich as velvet.

Like an automaton, she laid down her pad and went to open the door a couple of feet.

"Now, come here," he added softly.

She went around the desk, but hesitated at his side, looking down at all that vibrant masculinity, the darkness of his hair, the uncompromising lines of his face. She was surprised to find herself a little afraid of him, a little shy.

He reached out and caught her around the waist, pulling her down onto his lap with a short laugh at her involuntary gasp.

Her eyes stared into his from a distance of inches. Her cheek pressed against the fine fabric of his suit jacket. She could hear the regular, strong beat of his heart under her ear. He smelled of expensive cologne, and his face was immaculately clean-shaven, his mouth chiseled and firm and wide.

"That's right, look at me," he murmured deeply. "You never have."

Her lips parted on a shaky sigh. Her fingers laid nervously on his white shirt, and under it she could feel warm flesh and the springiness of chest hair, and it made her pulse tremble with new sensations.

One big finger traced a sensuous line around her full lips, teasing them, tantalizing them. "I've wondered if that pretty mouth was as soft as it looked," he murmured before he bent his head to find out. She looked up into darkening eyes with an expression she couldn't fathom as his mouth brushed softly against hers in a slow, lazy rhythm. Her eyes closed involuntarily, her body still rigid from the newness of intimacy with him, her lips faintly stiff as he traced them with his own.

His hands moved to her back, soothing, softly caressing while his hard mouth gently parted her lips and moved between them with a firm, but controlled pressure.

"Relax, Abby," he whispered, his voice deeply amused, "I'm only kissing you."

It didn't feel like only a kiss, though. There was a world of experience in that expert, taunting mouth, in the hands that knew so well where to touch, how to touch. She was aware of his hard-muscled, powerful thighs under her, his massive chest against her. She felt as nervous as a schoolgirl with him, and it was unexpected to find that she liked the way he was kissing her.

"Stop holding yourself away from me," he whispered against her mouth. "It's like making love to a virgin. Give in, Abby. Stop fighting me."

"I'm trying," she whispered. "Grey, it's been a long time…"

"This isn't going to convince anyone," he growled. "But maybe reason is less effective than this…"

He took her mouth roughly, and she felt his tongue darting into it, taking possession, while his massive arms swallowed her against him. She couldn't even fight, it was too devastating. This was a lover's kiss, and even Dalton's hadn't been so sensuous.

Desire welled up in her slender body as his tongue thrust slowly, deeply, into her mouth with a demanding pressure that made her body curl into his. He lifted her even closer, one hand in her hair, the other sliding down to her spine to urge her flat stomach against his in a new, urgent intimacy.

She gasped under his ardent mouth, her hands flat against his chest. She could feel the warmth of it, the steely muscles under the spring of curling hair. She wanted to open the buttons. She wanted to touch him, to press her face against his warm skin, to hold him against every trembling inch of her body.

There was a sound outside the office door that barely penetrated her whirling mind, followed by a faint gasp and the sound of footsteps retreating quickly. Abby was only aware of it on some subconscious level until McCallum lifted his head, glanced toward the doorway and smiled mockingly.

"Discovery," he murmured, glancing down at Abby. He was as calm as if he'd been fishing. His pulse was regular and slow, his breathing normal, not a hair mussed. Abby's heart was punishing her, and she could barely breathe. She couldn't believe he'd weathered that stormy interlude without any effect, but perhaps it was only an appetizer to him.

"Jan, unless I miss my guess," he said, gazing at her flushed face, parted lips and wildly disordered hair. "A little cooperation on your part would have been welcomed, but I think she got the picture just the same."

"I... I did cooperate," she murmured, puzzled.

"Did you?" He studied her quietly.

Abby brushed a strand of hair away from her misty eyes and sat up on his hard thighs. "Well, I learned one thing," she said with a little of her irrepressible humor returning as she glanced at him. "I learned why there's a parade through here."

He chuckled softly. His narrow eyes studied her for a minute. "Just for the record," he asked as she struggled to her feet and moved demurely away from him, "how long has it been since a man kissed you?"

She gave him her haughtiest smile while he drew up an ashtray and lit a cigarette. "Nick did, as a matter of fact, at the Christmas party. Very nicely, too. Which reminds me, are you really determined to make him stop seeing Collette?"

He glared at her. "My private life, and my family's, is none of your concern, Miss Summer. Don't you have some letters to type?"

The sudden change from lover to autocratic employer hit her like jet lag. She hesitated just an instant before she retrieved her pad from his desk and walked back into the outer office, closing the door without looking back at him. In the months that she'd been his secretary, he'd never spoken so coldly to her before.

Jan cornered her in the ladies' room during break, her eyes wide and openly curious.

"Busy?" she asked.

"He's got a full calendar." Abby could just barely meet her friend's dark eyes. She hated the deception already. "The White case comes up next week, you know, in criminal court."

"Do I remember," Jan groaned. "I had to help you make phone calls and set up appointments and type petitions…at least we got paid for all that overtime. Can you imagine the DA's face," she added with a mischievous grin, "when he sees all those exhibits McCallum's taking into court? Not to mention the surprise witness."

"It will be war," Abby agreed, grimacing. "And, as usual, he'll call up here and want to grind Mr. McCallum into grits, and guess who'll get to soothe him?"

"I'll take you out to the new lobster place that day," Jan promised.

"You're a nice person," Abby told the short brunette.

Jan glanced at her and away. "Uh, Abby, I…well, there was a file Mr. McCallum asked me to bring in a few minutes ago."

Abby was busy trying to repair the damage McCallum had done to her mouth and hair. "And?" she asked, forcing herself not to blurt out the whole painful story.

"He was kissing you," came the soft reply. "Whew! Was he kissing you!" the smaller woman added with rolling eyes.

And hadn't felt it at all, Abby could have told her, but why that should be disturbing puzzled her. "He…he asked me to move in with him," she blurted out, waiting tautly for the reaction.

"With McCallum? You're going to live with McCallum?" Her friend sat down in one of the two chairs and sighed. "I should be so lucky. What about that bottled redhead?"

"I don't know," she replied quietly. "He said he'd tell her goodbye with a diamond bracelet."

"I'd rather have McCallum," Jan giggled. "Wouldn't you?"

"What a question!" She ran a small brush through her glorious tangle of platinum hair.

"It's just like that novel of yours you let me read the first few chapters of," came the wistful reply. "You know, where the business executive falls in love with his secretary and has to take her away from his best friend?"

Abby put her brush back into her purse with a sigh. "But there's no married and living happily-ever-after in it," she said. "Or with McCallum, either."

"Once he gets to know you, who knows?" Jan asked softly. "Far as I know he's never lived with anyone before."

If only she could tell Jan the truth. She hated the lies, but when she thought about Robert Dalton, she knew there was no other way.

In her mind, she could still see him. Tall, blond, slightly graying—a sophisticated man with a kind of tenderness she'd never experienced. It had been the tenderness more than anything else that had attracted her. Life hadn't been gentle with

Abby. The very newness of being treated like porcelain had undermined all her nervous defenses.

McCallum hadn't been tender, she recalled suddenly. She could remember vividly the hard crush of his mouth, the leashed strength in his big body as he'd held her so intimately. She'd never realized just how experienced he was. How could she, when he'd never touched her. Even at the Christmas party, she'd been afraid to let McCallum catch her under the mistletoe. Although, honestly, he hadn't even bothered and that had stung. So had his remark about her lack of "coop-eration" in his office a few minutes ago. She hadn't fought him. She flushed. She hadn't kissed him back, either. A small part of her was afraid to wake the sleeping lion in that vibrant body, for fear of what it might cause. And she didn't take time to explore that nagging curiosity, either.

"How about some coffee?" Jan asked as they went back out into the carpeted reception area where their desks were spaced widely apart. "I just made a fresh pot."

"I'd love it. Maybe I'll have time to finish the scene I was working on last night while we have our break."

"Abby, honestly, do you ever do anything except write?" came the exasperated reply, followed by a gasp and a giggle. "What a silly question. Sorry!"

Still smiling, Abby sat down at her desk and pulled out the long yellow legal pad that contained her scribbled notes. Mc-Callum and Jerry and even old Mr. Doppler teased her about her writing ambitions. Everyone knew that it was her dream to become a novelist. She ate, slept and breathed it, a habit that even went back to the old days in journalism. Writing was what kept her going, the one thing that gave her lone-liness dignity, that made life bearable. It was more than an ambition. It was husband and child.

She scanned the page, a torrid love scene that led her two

main characters into a fiery argument—the old ploy of getting them together while keeping them skillfully apart until
the end of the book.

"Abby, what do you want in your coffee?" Jan called.

"Oh, I'll fix it." Abby jumped up, leaving the legal pad on
her desk to join her friend in the office's compact conference
room. The coffee smelled delicious, its rich aroma meeting
her at the door.

"Aren't we lucky?" she sighed, taking her cup gratefully
from the small brunette. "Our very own coffeepot."

"Not to mention our own doughnuts." Jan grinned, lifting the lid of the small toaster oven to let the sweet fragrance
of doughnuts escape. "Have one."

"Jan, you angel! I came without breakfast this morning, and
all I got for lunch was half a club sandwich, and no dessert…"

Jan watched her munch happily on the doughnut. "Which
you didn't have time for, I gather. Doesn't he feed you?"

She laughed. "I was too busy talking to eat, that's all."

"Miss Summer!"

Abby jumped. That deep roar was as familiar as her face
in the mirror. She put down the coffee cup and ran for the
door. It must be something terrible to make him bellow like
that on a full stomach.

She opened the door to McCallum's office without stopping long enough to knock. "Yes, sir?" she asked breathlessly,
her face flushed, her hair disheveled.

He glared at her, and his silver eyes had the cold brilliance
of ice in the sun. "What the hell is this?" he demanded, glancing down at the pad in his big hand. "'His cruel mouth fastened on her soft…'"

"No!" she screamed, making a dive for the legal pad. She
jerked it out of his light grasp and clutched it possessively to

her breast, staring horrified at him over the top of it. "It's mine!"

"Then where is mine?" he asked sharply. "All my notes on that burglary involved in the White murder case were on it, and it's gone!"

"But it was on your desk Friday when I locked up," she protested. "Maybe Jerry picked it up by accident when he took that brief to court this morning."

He was still scowling at her. His big body was poised on the edge of the swivel chair that was just barely adequate for his massive size.

"Are you sure that isn't mine?" he persisted gruffly.

She thumbed through the pages and found each one covered with her own high scrawl. "No, I'm positive, it's definitely not yours," she replied. The thought of his eyes on that torrid love scene made her want to go down under the carpet. Nothing could have been more embarrassing.

"Damn it, I need those notes." He drew in a deep, short breath. "Well, why isn't Jerry back? Where is he?"

"I don't know…"

"Don't just stand there, damn it, find him!" he grumbled. "Call the courthouse, talk to the clerk, see if he left word where he was going. Ask Jan, maybe she knows, but find him!"

She closed the door softly behind her and leaned against it to get her breath. It was like closing the door between herself and a hungry lion, and the relief was equally great. This fierce, angry man was reminiscent of the old McCallum she'd met head-on during her first week in the office. He'd mellowed just a little since then, but something had sprung the lock on his impatient temper, and she sincerely hoped that he wouldn't carry it home with him. If he did, it was going to be an impossible two weeks.

She went back to the conference room where Jan was waiting, wide-eyed, and picked up her coffee and her doughnut.
He could just wait while she finished her coffee, temper or
no temper. Heaven knew, he worked her hard enough to deserve a break now and then.

"What's going on?" Jan asked, glancing at the legal pad
Abby had placed on the shiny conference table.

"McCallum got my legal pad by mistake," Abby grimaced,
remembering. "Do you know where Jerry is? I've got to find
him or I'm going to be cut to ribbons."

"He had to see a client this afternoon," Jan said, watching her friend gulp coffee and cram half a doughnut into her
mouth. "He should be yelling at me, not you. You're going
to live with him."

"Oh, I just can't wait!" Abby said in her best theatrical
voice. "It will be like living among mistreated tigers."

Jan looked at her out of the corner of her eye. "I'll draw
you up a will, if you like."

"Do you know where Jerry's client lives?"

"At the county jail." Jan grinned. "You can call that dashing Lieutenant James, you know him. He'll find Jerry and
have him phone in."

"Lieutenant James is sixty," Abby observed. "His dashing
days are past." She gulped down her coffee. "However, a retired dasher is better than nothing. Thanks for the coffee."

"Next time, I'll dissolve some vitamin pills in it," Jan called
after her.

Even with Lieutenant James's help, it took ten minutes for
Abby to get in touch with Jerry. Her nerves weren't soothed
by the fact that McCallum stood over her the whole time,
wearing ruts in the carpet under his elegant shoes.

"You sound frantic, Abby," Jerry laughed when he answered. "What's wrong?"

"Have you got Mr. McCallum's legal pad?" she asked. Her voice sounded breathless, but she couldn't help it. McCallum was standing less than two feet away with blazing gray eyes.

"His legal pad? Just a minute. Let me go and check my briefcase. Hold on…"

"He's checking," Abby told McCallum.

He didn't even speak. His face was like steel, and about as readable. His eyes slid idly down her body, and back up again. She tried not to notice, but her pulse went wild at the scrutiny.

"Yes, Abby, I've got it," Jerry said a minute later. "Does he need it right away? I'll be through here in about ten minutes and I can come straight back."

She looked up at McCallum. "He's got it. Can you wait ten minutes while he finishes with his client?"

He rammed his big hands into his pockets. "He can have twenty—to get here."

"Mr. McCallum will expect you in his office in twenty minutes, Jerry," she said sweetly.

"Giving you hell, is he?" came the knowing reply. "I'll be there. Bye."

She put down the receiver. "Is there anything else, sir?" she asked with her professional voice.

"Only one," he replied, shouldering away from the door facing. "When a man's mouth fastens on that portion of a woman's anatomy, it's better for both of them if it isn't 'cruel,'" he murmured, tossing her a glance that contained equal parts of impatience and humor.

He went into his office and closed the door.

Abby quickly slid the legal pad into her desk drawer and started working on the letters McCallum had dictated after lunch.

CHAPTER THREE

It was almost quitting time when she remembered that she hadn't called Nick, McCallum's first order of the day. She was wary of antagonizing him any further, so she jerked up the phone and dialed his mother's number.

Four rings later a sleepy voice mumbled, "Hello?"

Relief flooded through Abby's body. At least he hadn't caught the plane yet. "Nicky?"

"Abby?" He seemed to wake up all at once. "What's wrong?"

"Oh, nothing, just an order from the top," she murmured drily. "The boss says to cancel your flight to Paris or else. He didn't mention what the *or else* might be."

"He doesn't have to. I already know," Nicky sighed. "He won't have to start wielding his sword. I've already canceled it."

"Oh, Nicky, why do you let him tell you what to do?" she groaned.

She could hear the grin in his voice. "Because, my friend,

Collette is still in town. She doesn't go home until next week. *Then* I'll follow her home."

"Good boy!" She laughed.

"When are you going to come see us?" he asked. "I'll take you riding. I'll even let you ride Grey's horse, if you promise not to tell."

That brought to mind the lie that was very shortly going to make the rounds of the office. She hesitated, wondering how to break the news to Nicky, and how she was going to face Mandy McCallum after it was out in the open.

"What's gotten into you?" Nicky prodded. "You sound strange."

She chewed on her lower lip. "Nicky, what would you say if I told you I was moving in with your brother?"

"That you must be desperate for a roommate," he replied immediately. "Are you really? For the obvious reason?"

She swallowed. "Yes."

He hesitated. "Scared?" he teased.

"Terrified!"

He laughed delightedly. "I wondered if he was going to stay blind forever. Now that it's come to a head, remind me to tell you what he said to me after our Christmas party," he added mysteriously. "Don't be nervous, Abby. He doesn't yell nearly as much at home as he does at work. Mother will be beside herself," he added as if the thought tickled him madly.

"She won't be shocked…?"

"At Grey?" he burst out. "She'll be convinced that he's finally ready to settle down. You know how possessive Grey is about his privacy. The mere fact that he's willing to let you share it says a lot."

She felt her spine tingle and looked around to find McCallum watching her. He moved so silently for such a big man. It was unnerving.

"Time to go home," he told her, eyeing the phone. "Who are you talking to?"

"Nicky," she said involuntarily.

He moved forward, holding out his hand for the receiver. She gave it to him without an argument. "Nick?" he asked curtly. "If you get on that plane...you aren't? Fine, we'll talk about it later. Tell Mother I'm bringing Abby down for supper tomorrow night. Did you? Yes, you're right, she is. See you." He hung up, leaving Abby to wonder what he was talking about.

"Well, are you coming or not?" he asked curtly. "It's been a damned long day and I'm tired."

Without another word, she got up and put on her light coat, covered the typewriter and picked up her purse. She called goodbye to Jan and Jerry, and waved at George Doppler as they passed his office. When the door closed behind them, she heard scurrying footsteps, and she knew Jan was on her way to tell the others the news. She sighed. Well, at least everybody knew now. That was the hump, and she was over it.

Mrs. McDougal had dinner on the table minutes after they walked into McCallum's apartment. She smiled and nodded at Abby, a strange, appraising look in her blue eyes as she moved around the table to place their meal on it.

"Everything's fixed, and your dessert is on the stove," she said after a minute. She went to get her coat, whipping it easily around her ample girth. "Now, just leave those dishes, Miss Abby. I'll get them in the morning." She nodded her silver head, winked at Abby, smiled mischievously at McCallum and slid out the door like an oversize fairy.

They were alone. And Abby's uneasiness seemed to make McCallum's short temper even shorter.

"For God's sake, will you stop pacing and sit down?" he

demanded curtly, taking his place at the head of the table with unconscious grace.

"Yes, sir," she said, deciding that it might be best to humor him.

"Don't call me sir."

"No, sir."

"Abby!"

She reached for her coffee cup, lifting it in unsteady hands. It had already been a traumatic day, but this was getting rough. She took a deep breath and sipped her hot black coffee.

"She knows?" she asked softly.

"McDougal?" he grumbled. "Yes, she knows. My God, couldn't you tell? All those twinkling glances and sickening winks and smiles…she's positive that I'm head over heels in love."

"Poor, demented soul," she said in her most serious tone, meeting his eyes levelly.

He glared at her over a mound of mashed potatoes. "Pass the potatoes," he growled.

"You're already dishing them up," she pointed out.

"Then pass me the rolls!"

She did, smothering the uproarious laughter that was clamoring for escape. She ate the rest of the meal in silence, her mind quickly losing its sense of humor at the taciturn, smoldering look on his broad face. It wasn't going to work; that was already evident. He hated having her around. She was going to cost him his privacy, his love life, and subject him to the kind of teasing that would assault his dignity. She'd never dreamed the subterfuge would have such sweeping repercussions. She wondered if he hadn't considered the consequences when he made his gallant offer. It wasn't like McCallum to do anything on impulse, without thinking the action through. It was that attention to detail that made him such a fine attorney.

"We can still call it off," she said after she'd served up the delicious cherry flan Mrs. McDougal had provided for dessert.

He put down his fork with cold deliberation, and she knew with a shiver that she'd finally given him the opening he was waiting for. His eyes glittered like shards of metal.

"Isn't it a little late for that?" he asked curtly. "The word's out, in case you've forgotten. Vinnie wailing all over me on the phone, Nick making cute remarks, Mrs. McDougal sighing like cupid on Valentine's Day… My God, if I'd had any idea what I was letting myself in for…"

"I'll go right now," Abby said soothingly. "I'll call Miss Nichols and Nick myself. Everything will work out fine." She put down her napkin and left the table. It was almost a relief. The way he was acting, even having to face Robert Dalton wouldn't be a fraction of the strain.

She'd just opened the top drawer of her bureau to start taking out neatly folded tops and blouses when he paused in the doorway.

"Abby…" he began hesitantly.

"It's all right, really," she assured him. "It's probably for the best. I can get a job with the wire services and ask for an assignment to Central America…"

"You're breaking my heart," he growled.

She glared at him. "A lot you'd care if I got shot down in the streets," she muttered.

"It would depend on how much of my correspondence you'd answered," he replied matter-of-factly.

She wanted to throw something at him. The only problem was that she wasn't quite sure how he'd retaliate.

"Calm down, Abby." He chuckled.

She tossed back her long hair impatiently. "Calm down! How can I? You make me feel as welcome as a typhoid carrier. I realize that I'm in your way, and I'm sorry, but this was your idea, not mine."

"I know." He moved into the room, taking the blouse out of her hands. He tossed it lightly on top of the chest of drawers and caught her by the shoulders to study her.

"I've lived alone most of my life since I came out of the service," he said quietly. "Adjusting to another person is never easy. You might remember that from your marriage."

"I didn't have to adjust to Gene," she said bitterly. "He was never at home."

He paused. "Other women?"

"Yes. Other women."

His fingers tightened before he let her go and moved away. "Come and drink some coffee with me. Then you'll have to amuse yourself. I've got some phone calls to make."

"I don't expect to be entertained," she murmured as they walked back to the living room. "I'm used to being alone, too. I have a manuscript I work on in the evenings."

"The one about the man with the cruel mouth and the 'wise, patient hands'?" he asked, tongue in cheek.

She hated the ruby blush that highlighted her high cheekbones. "Fie on you, counselor," she grumbled. "One of these days, I'm going to sell that book, and you'll be laughing through your teeth."

He chuckled deeply. "I hope you can write to music. I rarely watch anything on television except the evening news."

"Neither do I," she admitted. She glanced at him nervously. "There's one show on this week that I've just got to watch, though," she said hesitantly. "I'll turn it down very low…"

He looked irritated. "Well, which one? A soap opera, no doubt."

She glared at him. "No, it isn't. It's a special on public television about a dig in Egypt…"

"*In the Valley of the Kings?*" he asked sharply. "The one about the site that had to be moved because of the Aswan Dam?"

She felt shocked. "Why, yes."

"I've seen it once, but I'll gladly sit through it again with you." He moved to the record player, his eyes puzzled. "Is that a fluke, or do you like archaeology?"

"I'm nuts about it," she admitted. "I read every book I can find on the subject. I subscribe to magazines about it. I watch all the specials."

"So do I," he admitted with a slow smile. "When you're not writing the Great American Novel, dig into my bookshelves." He nodded toward the bookcase that lined the walls. "I've got some excellent volumes with pages of color photos, all on Egypt, Greece, Mexico, Peru…"

"I'll never get any writing done," she wailed, her eyes greedy on the titles as she walked down the row of subjects. "Oh, how wonderful!"

"Do you like Rachmaninoff?" he murmured as he started the record player and the rich strains filled the room.

"The second piano concerto? I love it," she murmured, her nose already buried in a thick text on the Inca civilization.

He laughed softly as he went toward his study in what would have been a third bedroom before its bed was replaced by a desk. "I think we'll get along all right," he murmured.

The next evening they had supper with McCallum's mother and brother, and if she'd expected them to be shocked, she was in for a surprise.

"I've seen it coming for months," Mandy said with a quiet smile, her dark hair and gray eyes leaving no doubt about which of his parents McCallum favored the most. She was a tall woman, but slender, and the blue dress she was wearing flattered her. "I wasn't even surprised when Nicky told me."

"Neither was I." Nicky grinned, glancing from McCallum's taciturn face to Abby's smiling one. Nicky was as different from his brother as midnight from dawn. He had light brown hair and blue eyes, and he was half Greyson McCallum's size.

"A likely story," Mandy teased. "Who was it who went around the house for ten minutes laughing about the irony of it? Didn't you also mention something about beauty and the..."

"How about some more coffee?" Nicky asked quickly. He jumped to his feet. "I'll get the pot."

"Anyway," Mandy continued, "Greyson, I do hope that this arrangement is only temporary. Marriage may be old-fashioned, but you just can't bring children into the world..."

"Children!" McCallum burst out.

Mandy glanced at him warily. "I did remember to tell you what caused them?"

It was the first time Abby could ever remember seeing him flustered. He was holding his coffee cup as if he expected it to try to escape. His face was stiff with indignation.

"Abby will want children, won't you, dear?" Mandy asked her gently.

Abby felt the question to her toes. Yes, she wanted them; she always had. But she'd never thought about them in connection with Greyson McCallum. Now she did. And it shocked her to discover that she wouldn't mind having his child. She stared at him with the shock of discovery in her eyes.

"Don't you recognize stark terror when you see it, Mother?" McCallum asked wryly, indicating Abby's face. "Not everyone thinks children are the ultimate pleasure in a relationship."

Mandy glanced up as Nicky came into the room with the percolator in his hand. "What took you so long?" she teased. "Was there a woman hiding in the closet?"

Abby burst out laughing. It would have been so in character for Nicky to have a girlfriend hiding there. She couldn't help her reaction.

"You see?" Mandy laughed. "Abby wouldn't be surprised, either. Honestly, Nicky, why don't you think about starting a family, as well? At this rate I may not be around to spoil my first grandchild."

"Oh, I very much doubt that," McCallum said drily.

Mandy made a face at him. "Have some more pudding, Abby. Pass it here, Nicky."

"You sweet little tyrant, you," Nicky teased as he handed over the dish.

The older woman smiled complacently. "I had to be to raise Greyson," she reminded him.

"Was he really that bad?" Abby had to ask.

Mandy studied her eldest with pure love in her eyes. "He was my anchor, my dear," she said in a sincere tone. "I don't think the family would have survived without him. We certainly wouldn't have had so much," she added, referring to the spacious home and its multiacred surroundings on the outskirts of the city.

"You'd have managed," Grey chuckled.

Nicky checked his watch. "Oops," he muttered, rising. "I've got to get going. I'm taking my best girl to the ballet."

"Best girl?" McCallum murmured suspiciously.

"Yes," Nicky said over his shoulder. "Collette's still in town. Didn't Abby mention it?"

McCallum glared across the table at Abby. He didn't say a word, but she knew when they got back to the apartment that she was going to be on the receiving end of some unpleasant words.

And she was. They were no sooner inside the door when McCallum let loose with both barrels.

"Was there some special reason for not telling me about that French disaster?" he demanded.

She drew herself up and glared back at him. "Why should I? It's Nicky's business."

"Nicky's a boy."

"He's twenty-five and part owner of a public relations firm. When are you going to realize that he's a grown man?"

"When he begins to act like one," he shot back. "I've worked like hell to support my family, to keep it together. I'm not going to have it all go down the tube because Nicky's infatuated with some call girl!"

"She isn't a call girl!"

"How would you know?" he asked gruffly. His big hand shot out to jerk her roughly against his massive body. "You cold little piece of porcelain," he accused. "What would you know about women who exchange their bodies for favors?"

She stared up at him helplessly, her temper gone, her senses staggered by his sudden nearness.

He tangled one hand in her hair and pulled her head back slowly. "No wonder your husband went astray, Abby," he ground out as he bent his head. "You don't give an inch!"

His mouth crushed down on hers and hurt, the anger in it merciless as he twisted her soft lips under his to force them to part. His tongue shot into the sweet darkness of her mouth while his hands slid down her back to grip the backs of her thighs and grind her hips against his.

She gasped under his hard mouth at the intimate contact that she hadn't known in such a long time. She could feel every hard muscle of his thighs and stomach in that forced embrace as his hands relentlessly lifted her even closer into it. His mouth demanded, possessed, while she drew up inside at the unbridled fury she could taste in the overpowering ardor.

He was hell-bent on his own pleasure, not knowing or caring if she was receiving anything from it.

"No," she begged against his hard mouth. "Grey, no, not in anger. Please…"

The pleading of her shaky voice seemed to bring him to his senses. He drew back, his eyes on her mouth while he slowed his breath. His big hands relaxed their rough hold on her thighs, sliding sensuously up over her hips to catch her by the waist.

She looked back at him with all the old feelings of inadequacy gripping her. His careless words had hurt. She'd always felt guilty that Gene had gone from her bed to other women's, but she hadn't been able to give him anything in a physical sense. She'd expected that side of marriage to fall automatically into place with the ring on her finger, but it hadn't. She'd only been infatuated, and Gene's rough treatment of her on their wedding night had been the first in a series of embarrassingly brief and unsatisfying encounters. Even though she'd tried naively to please her new husband, she'd never been able to give him passion. He'd accused her of being cold, and she'd accepted the criticism without protest, believing it to be true. When he'd asked for a divorce, she'd given it willingly. But the scars had remained with her, and now McCallum had reopened and rubbed salt in them.

"Let me go, please," she said in a choked voice.

He removed his hands absently as if he hadn't even realized that they were still holding her.

She drew back from him, her eyes mirroring all the pain and fear that lingered.

"You were right, Mr. McCallum," she said in a tiny voice. "Your private life is none of my business. I… I won't forget again." She turned and walked briskly to the room he'd given her. Once inside, she locked the door behind her and the scalding tears ran freely down her cheeks.

She didn't sleep. Memories came back to taunt her, of Gene's late nights, his endless criticism of her as a woman. Why had McCallum chosen that particular way of getting even? He had the killer instinct to a frightening degree. It was what made him such a good criminal lawyer, because he wasn't afraid to hit where it hurt the most.

She dragged out of bed at five-thirty, took her shower and dressed in a white pleated skirt and silky blouse, complemented by a navy blazer and matching navy pumps. She brushed her hair and put on the maximum of eye makeup. But the hollows under her eyes stood out despite her best efforts. She gathered her purse and went down the hall to the dining room.

McCallum, faultless in a pale brown business suit, was sitting quietly at the table while Mrs. McDougal spooned a panful of scrambled eggs into the serving dish and placed it on the table. There was already a plate of fresh biscuits and a platter of bacon on the polished surface of the hardwood table.

"Good morning," Abby told Mrs. McDougal with a wan smile.

"Good morning, love. Sit down and have breakfast. I'll pour the coffee as soon as I've put this pan in to soak." She vanished through the swinging door that led into the kitchen.

McCallum was buttering a biscuit, but his gray eyes didn't miss much as they scanned Abby's face. "That was a nasty remark I made to you last night," he said quietly. "I apologize for it."

She forked a piece of bacon onto her own plate. "I had no right to comment on your personal affairs," she said quietly.

"That doesn't excuse me."

Her shoulders lifted and fell. "It doesn't matter. By the way, Jerry wants to know if I can go to the clerk's office with him this morning. He's got to get some information on a land transfer and he needs me to take it down as he dictates it."

There was a long pause. "All right. For an hour or two, no more. Dalton's coming this afternoon."

She felt her body stiffen. In all the emotional turmoil of the night before, she'd forgotten. Incredibly, she'd forgotten. "Yes," she murmured.

They ate breakfast in a tense silence, broken only by Mrs. McDougal's soft humming in the kitchen while she cleaned up the pots and pans. They had a last cup of coffee before they left for work. When they rose, and McCallum started to take her arm, she flinched.

His expression was indescribable. He held her all the same, staring down at her with a face that rivaled a diamond for hardness.

"That won't do, Abby," he said tautly. "We're not going to fool Dalton if you flinch every time I come near you."

"Sorry," she said with an attempt at lightness. "I'll work on it night and day."

"I hurt you last night, didn't I?" he asked in a strange, deep tone.

She moved away from him to go in the living room and get her purse. "We'll be late," she said, but she wouldn't look at him.

He hesitated for an instant before he went to open the door for her.

She stayed out of his way until lunch, and then there was no avoiding him. He came out of his office with a determined look on his face and stood over her until she gave up on the letter she was trying to type and looked at him.

"It's noon. Let's get some lunch," he told her.

She fished for an excuse. "Uh, Jan was going with me…"

"I'm going with you," he corrected. "Now."

She knew the tone. It meant he was going to get his way if he had to pick her up and carry her out of the building. With a resigned sigh, she got her purse out of the drawer and went peaceably.

There was a small Italian restaurant a block from the office, tucked between a furniture store and a smart little boutique. In the middle of busy Atlanta, it was like finding a misplaced piece of Italy. There were red-checkered tablecloths with candles in wine bottles and flowers on the tables, and a smiling proprietor who greeted guests while friendly waiters took orders.

The spaghetti was just right, and the garlic bread was a temptation Abby couldn't resist. She hadn't wanted to come with McCallum, but she was enjoying it despite her intentions.

"At least you don't starve yourself," he murmured as he sipped a second cup of coffee over an empty plate.

She glanced at him before she finished the last of her spaghetti. "I don't have to. I never gain."

"A few pounds wouldn't hurt you," he replied. His eyes studied what was visible of her slender body above the table, narrow and appraising.

She ignored the look. "Thank you for lunch," she said and leaned back with her coffee cupped in her hands. "It was delicious."

"I'm glad you enjoyed it." He lit a cigarette and studied her through the smoke. "I want to explain something to you. I want you to understand why I'm so concerned about Nicky."

She flushed uncomfortably. "You don't owe me any explanations, Mr. McCallum," she said tautly.

"My father committed suicide when I was sixteen."

She tried to speak and couldn't. Her eyes looked into his helplessly.

"My father was a sharecropper," he said quietly. "A farmer who gets a share of the profits he makes on rented land. He'd saved all his life to buy a tract of land all his own and get out of debt. He'd just managed that when Mother got pregnant with Nicky. There were complications, and he only had life insurance, no health insurance. He had to sell the land to meet the debts, but that was only the beginning. By the time Nicky was born, the bills amounted to more than Dad could make sharecropping in twenty years, even if he'd been blessed with perfect weather." He took a long draw from the cigarette. "He took a stab at it. He tried. But eventually the hopelessness of the situation depressed him to the extent that he began to drink. Nicky was a year old the night Dad took his old army revolver out onto the front porch and blew his brains out."

She'd wondered many times why McCallum was as strong as he was—and now that iron in his makeup began to make sense.

"How did you manage?" she asked.

His face grew hard. "On the charity of one of Mother's uncles. For the last year I was in school. After that I went into the army and had an allotment made out for Mother and Nicky. I stayed in four years during Vietnam, got a job on a construction gang when I got my discharge and went through law school at night. A few years later I began to make a living," he chuckled, and Abby knew what he meant. It was hard finding a good law firm to join with a law degree that didn't come from full-time status as a student. Although McCallum had managed it very well. "A stint in the DA's office as a prosecuting attorney got me where I am," he added. "But what it adds up to is this. I backed Nicky in that public relations firm he owns half of. He's getting his head above water for the first time and I want him to keep it there. A woman, especially one who likes expensive trinkets, could bankrupt him overnight. Now do you understand? Mother will always be my responsibility, and I don't mind it a bit. But Nicky needs to stand on his own. It's past time."

She felt vaguely ashamed of herself. "I see," she said quietly. "And I'm sorry I spoke out of turn. I thought you came from a moneyed background. I didn't realize…" She shifted restlessly.

"Silver spoons and a white-coated butler?" he mused. "I could afford them now. But I don't have the inclination for status symbols, or much patience with people who deal in them."

"I wish you wouldn't judge people so harshly on first impressions, that's all," she continued softly. "Collette is such a sweet girl." She glanced at him and away. "I… I may be porcelain," she said with a bitter laugh, "but I'm not all that bad at summing up people. Reporters learn that trick along with lead sentences. She struck me as a very sheltered young lady on her own for the first time."

He studied her averted face for a long time. "Are you ever going to forgive me for calling you that?" he asked in a deep, gentle tone.

"Why should I have to?" Her laugh was bitter. "It was true."

He caught her hand in his and ignored her feeble attempt to drag it away. "You've never talked about your marriage," he said, watching her. "It left scars, didn't it? Did he accuse you of being cold, Abby? Is that the excuse he used to have other women?"

"No fair, counselor," she said coldly, jerking her hand away. Her lower lip thrust forward accusingly. "That's badgering." She stood up. "Please, can we go?"

He stood up with a hard sigh, crushing his cigarette in the ashtray. "What's the matter, honey, did I hit too close to the truth?" he asked with a hard laugh as he went to pay the check.

She didn't even answer him. Her voice would have wobbled if she'd tried, with mingled anger and indignation. McCallum, she decided, would try the patience of a saint.

She found excuses to help Jerry or Jan for the rest of the day. Anything to keep out of McCallum's way. It was puzzling that she'd managed to get along with him so well until these past two days. It was like being in a combat zone, now that she was living with him. She was grateful that Dalton was coming. It would be like having the cavalry come over the hill! At least Robert had never thought she was cold...

It was almost four o'clock on the nose when he walked into the waiting room and came face-to-face with Abby.

He seemed to contract all over, standing statue-still in the doorway, his pale eyes wide with shock.

"Abby!" he exclaimed.

CHAPTER FOUR

He hadn't changed a lot in one year. He was much the same as she remembered him, tall and very dignified. Utterly charming. But her reaction to him was different. It confused her. She'd expected to be wildly flustered and attracted. And she wasn't.

"Abby," he repeated softly, shock in the handsome face she remembered so well. "My God, what are you doing here?"

"Working," she said drily. She got up and extended her hand. Amazing how easy it was to be friendly and nothing more. "It's nice to see you again, Mr. Dalton."

"Robert," he corrected. He clasped her hand between both of his. His eyes made a meal of her face. "Abby, I've wondered all this time where you went, how you were. I felt like ten kinds of a heel after what I put you through… Abby, you'll never know how I hated myself for that cowardly display."

He'd never know how she'd hated him, or how she'd wanted revenge for it. He'd never know how he'd hurt her. But somewhere in the months since it had happened, she'd become wrapped up in McCallum's world. Charleston had retreated into the past, like a dimly remembered nightmare.

"It was a long time ago, Robert," she said gently. Her green eyes studied him. She'd forgotten that he was almost twenty years her senior. His blond hair had a liberal sprinkling of silver and there were deep lines beside his eyes and mouth. But the charm was still there, and the tenderness. He wasn't sensual like McCallum, but he had appeal.

"Yes, a long time ago," he agreed. His pale blue eyes searched her face. "Liz and I are separated now," he said slowly. "You brought all the problems to a head. We worked out a settlement just two weeks later." He sighed heavily. "I tried to find you, but you'd vanished. Abby, perhaps now..."

Before he could suggest what he was thinking, McCallum's office door opened and he came through it, his narrow silver eyes darting from Abby to Dalton.

"Hello, Robert," he said formally, extending his hand. "Good to see you."

"Same here, Grey," he replied cordially, glancing warmly at Abby. "I've just been renewing my acquaintance with your charming secretary. We knew each other in Charleston."

"Did you?" McCallum asked.

Dalton's eyes caught Abby's. "I was just telling her about my separation from Liz. I thought I might be able to persuade her to join me for dinner this evening."

The expression that darkened McCallum's face was an open threat. He moved closer to Abby almost imperceptibly, one big arm sliding around her shoulders in a gesture that was possessive as well as supportive.

"I don't think so," he said. His voice was deep and mea-sured—his courtroom voice.

Dalton seemed to shrink. "Oh?"

McCallum's glittering silver eyes dropped to Abby's face

with something resembling hunger. "However, we'd both enjoy having you join us for dinner this evening at our apartment," he said frankly. "Wouldn't we, Abby?"

"Of course," she agreed, mainly because she couldn't bear the thought of another evening alone with McCallum. Since their confrontation the night before, she was wary of him.

She felt the arm around her contract as if in bridled anger, but she didn't try to pull away.

"I'd like that," Dalton said. "What time?"

"About seven." McCallum gave Abby a long look and turned toward his office. "Come on in. I'll give you directions to the apartment before we discuss this deal." He closed the door behind them, and Dalton still hadn't regained his composure. It gave Abby a tiny nudge of pleasure. She went back to her desk smiling.

The silence in McCallum's apartment would have been deafening without Mrs. McDougal's pleasant chatter while she prepared a delicious steak dinner, complete with home-made rolls and a superb spinach salad, and apple pie and cream for dessert.

McCallum's narrow eyes were tracing Abby like an artist's brush on a canvas. She was wearing a slinky taffeta dress, long skirted with a nipped waist, black spaghetti straps and a fitted, low-cut bodice with corselet ties that left a strip of skin acutely bare down to her waist. She'd worn it in defiance, to show him that she did know how to dress to catch a man's eye. But she hadn't counted on catching his to this extent. Her fingers went nervously to her high-piled coiffure, to the dangling gold shimmer of her earrings.

He himself was striking in dark evening clothes. It was the first time they'd dressed for dinner, and it would serve Dalton right if he showed up in a sports coat, she thought amusedly.

"Martini, Abby?" he asked after a minute, rising from his seat on the sofa to go to the bar.

She shook her head. "But I'd love a glass of wine if you have it." She sat down in the chair beside the sofa, careful not to wrinkle the elegant skirt of her dress.

"Sweet, no doubt," he teased lightly, glancing at her. "The only thing I have is a very dry sherry. How about brandy?"

"That would be nice, thank you."

"Nervous?" he asked. He poured the amber liquid into a snifter and turned to pour himself a whiskey before he brought it to her.

"Just a little," she admitted with a shy smile. *But because of you, not Robert*, she added to herself.

He sat down across from her, crossing one long, powerful leg over the other. "Afraid to sit by me?" he taunted.

"I… I'm just being careful of my dress," she lied, straightening the skirt. "Taffeta wrinkles easily."

He sipped the whiskey. "Was it as bad as you expected, seeing him again?"

She shook her head. "Not nearly." She sipped the brandy slowly. "He hasn't changed."

"He's a great deal older than you," he observed.

"Twenty years."

He leaned back on the sofa, his head slightly to one side as he studied her. "Was his age the main attraction?" he asked gruffly.

Her eyes jerked up. "I beg your pardon?"

"Did you think he wouldn't be too demanding in bed?"

She felt the blood rush to her face as the question penetrated to her mind. Slamming the snifter down on the table as she got to her feet. "You abominable…!"

"What's the matter, honey, did I hit a nerve?" he broke in, rising to tower over her, his eyes narrow and calculating.

"Come on, Abby, talk. Were you looking for a man who wouldn't pose a threat to you sexually? Are you afraid of sex?"

She started blindly past him, with some wild idea of staying in her room until Dalton got there. Thank goodness Mrs. McDougal was out of earshot...

But McCallum, for so large a man, was incredibly light on his feet. Before she could get away, he was in front of her, barring the way.

"No, you don't," he said calmly. "No more running. I want to know, and you're going to tell me."

"Oh, no, I'm not," she shot back at him, her stance pure bravado. "I don't owe you that kind of answer, counselor."

"But I'm going to get it," he said in his courtroom voice. He moved forward like an uncoiling spring to catch her by the waist, holding her helplessly before him. "What was the attraction, Abby?" he kept on relentlessly. His glittering eyes filled the room, filled the world; his fingers around her waist hurt. "A man old enough to be your father."

"You almost are!" she hit back, wanting to wound in return.

"Nice try, honey," he laughed shortly, "but not good enough. Are you frigid, Abby?"

"All right!" she cried, shaking with mingled fury and pain. Tears rushed into her dark green eyes. "All right, yes, I'm frigid, is that what you want? I cringed every time my husband touched me, until one day he left and didn't come back!"

His eyes studied her pale, tear-washed face quietly. The fingers on her waist became tender, caressing. "Didn't you want him?" he asked quietly.

Her eyes closed, squeezing out the rest of the gathered tears. She sniffed and took a steadying breath. Just to talk about it was a relief beyond words, she'd held it in for so long.

"No," she whispered, admitting it at last. "No, I didn't

want him in any physical way. I thought I loved him." She laughed. "I thought he loved me. I didn't realize that all he wanted was a more important position with my father's bank. He thought marrying me would accomplish it."

"Did it?"

She shook her head. "Bank presidents don't get that far up the ladder without being able to size up employees. Gene didn't have managerial ability, and Dad knew it. He never really cared for Gene. Mother didn't, either. They tolerated him, for my sake."

"You never talk about your parents, either."

She smiled wetly, taking the handkerchief he offered and wiping her face with it. "They live in Panama City, and I dote on them. I miss them too much to talk about them. I get homesick."

He laughed softly. "I'll fly you down one day soon."

She crumpled the handkerchief in a small fist against his evening jacket, staring up at him curiously. "I don't understand you."

"Why? Because I force things out of you that you don't want to admit—not even to yourself?" He drew her closer, until her thighs felt the hard warmth of his, even through the layers of fabric. "I'm insatiably curious, Abby," he murmured. "Digging out secrets is my profession."

"I have a right to privacy," she reminded him.

"Not with me, you don't," he told her, something dark and soft in his tone. He had an actor's voice; he could shade it in a dozen different ways to reflect anger, command, indignation. But this shade was like velvet, rich and smooth, and it affected her in strange ways.

"You…there are things you don't need to know," she protested. The warmth of his big body, the elusive fragrance of his cologne, were making deep impressions, weakening her.

"I need to know everything," he replied. One big hand moved up between them, a darkly beautiful hand with flat, immaculate nails and a sprinkling of hairs on its back. It toyed with the string of the first bow that held her bodice together and slowly, lazily, tugged until it came loose.

Abby's breath caught at the back of her throat. She looked up at him in disbelief, not moving, not speaking. Her eyes looked into his, searchingly, as he repeated the action with the second bow. There was only one left, but already she felt the coolness of the room against her bare skin.

"The advantage of small breasts," he said very softly, easing a long finger into the opening to touch, lightly, the hard, pink peak of one breast, "is that you don't need to bother with a bra."

She felt the color burn into her face and wondered at the effect he was having on her. Her slender body began to tremble delicately, and a tiny part of her mind wondered why she was permitting this kind of intimacy.

The other hand speared into the hair at the nape of her neck, where it was swept up into the sophisticated topknot. He unfastened it with deliberate movements, watching it tumble down around her shoulders.

"Don't put it up again," he said. "I like it like this, long and sexy." His eyes dropped to her bodice, where that maddening finger was tracing a fiery path against her breast.

"Grey..." she whispered, her lips parting, her eyes half-closed as the touch aroused sensations long forgotten.

His mouth brushed against hers softly, teasingly. His finger touched and lifted inside the bodice, and she realized belatedly that her body was twisting, lifting toward it, trying to capture it against the swelling softness of her breast.

One big hand ran down her spine to her buttocks, pressing her lips into intimate contact with the hardening muscles of his own. "What do you want, Abby?" he whispered against her trembling mouth.

"Want…?" she echoed in an unsteady whisper.

He chuckled softly, dangerously, against her parting lips, his mouth easing sensuously between them as his warm fingers suddenly burrowed lazily under the bodice to take the weight of her breast, his palm pressing deeply against the taut, aching nipple.

A strange, high-pitched whimper broke out of her throat and whispered into his mouth.

He drew back a breath to look down at her, his silver eyes taking in the wildness of her dilating green eyes, the drawn look in her cheeks. "Now, that's sexy," he murmured. He bent to brush his mouth over hers tantalizingly.

"What…is?" she managed, not even bothering to protest the possessive hand cupping her breast.

"That wild little sound you just made," he replied, "not to mention the way your body is melting against mine."

She hadn't realized that it was, but all at once she felt the hardness of his thighs where hers were lifting and falling, and she tensed.

"Self-conscious?" He lifted his head and looked down at the bodice of her gown, where the black fabric showed up the skin of his wrist. His fingers moved, sliding half of the bodice completely away from her high, firm breast to bare it to his narrowed eyes. "My God, your skin is fair," he murmured, noticing the contrast of his dark fingers against the whiteness of her soft flesh.

Her cheek was resting on his shoulder, her eyes watching him helplessly while her heart threatened to beat itself to death. It had never been like this before; she'd never been vulnerable like this with any man.

"No protests?" he whispered gently. His eyes searched hers

while his fingers stroked her, feeling the trembling softness lift toward them. "Suppose I do this, Abby…" With a smooth, deft movement, he drew the other strap down her arm until the bodice fell to her waist. Both big, warm hands swallowed her then, his thumbs flicking the taut nipples, his eyes strangely watchful on her face.

"Oh, Grey," she whispered, her aching voice a stranger's, her hands trembling as she reached up to lock them behind his broad neck and pressed herself against him. "Don't— don't stop."

"Like this?" His big hands contracted gently, caressing, probing. His mouth opened over hers, nudging it softly, his tongue teasing, tracing, the long line of her lips before it shot into her mouth, no longer teasing. "Unbutton my shirt," he ground out. "I want to feel your bare skin against mine."

"Mrs… McDougal…" she whispered brokenly.

He muttered something, lifting his head. His breath was coming as erratically as hers; she could feel the roughness of his heartbeat against her.

Without a word, he caught her by the hand and pulled her into the room he used for a study, closing the door firmly behind him. His eyes lanced over her bare breasts while his fingers tore at the tie, tossing it into a chair before they flicked open the buttons over his hair-roughened chest.

"Now," he muttered, lifting her body against his, watching her taut nipples vanish in the thick nest of hair over his muscular chest. "Oh, God, now…!" His head bent to her smooth shoulders, his mouth insistent as it slid roughly against the silky skin, burning where it touched.

Abby could barely breathe at all. Her arms were locked around him, her head thrown back, her eyes closed as she let her body drown in sensation. The pleasure was so intense it made her ache. She moved restlessly, dragging her breasts against his hard chest, the thick hair tickling, deliciously abrasive against the tender flesh.

"Cold?" he ground out, his voice husky, faintly unsteady. "My God…!" His mouth slid down to cover one taut nipple, his tongue hard against it, his lips swallowing it, savoring it.

She held his head against her rigid body, her fingers digging into the nape of his strong neck. "Grey," she whispered achingly, "Grey, I ache so…!"

His mouth slid up her body, all the way up to cover her lips. His hands slid down, lifting her by the thighs until her hips were crushed against his blatant masculinity, letting her feel the arousal she could taste on his demanding mouth.

She trembled wildly against him. Her fingers tangled in the thick hair on his chest, tugging at it sensuously while his mouth drained hers in a silence that pulsed with hunger. Her breath rasped, mingling with the unnatural tenor of his.

"Do you know how much I want you, Abby?" he asked in a deep, harsh tone.

"I…thought you didn't want me," she whispered against his mouth, "…before."

His fingers bit into her soft thighs, pressing her sensuously to him. "You can feel how much I want you now," he murmured huskily. "I want you naked in my arms, Abby," he whispered achingly. "I want to warm every inch of you. I want to hear you crying out with the pleasure I'm going to give you…"

Her eyes looked straight into his, misty with the hungers he'd aroused. "Take me to bed, Grey," she whispered softly. "Make love to me."

His big body shuddered with the words, his eyes blazing into hers, his hands contracting, hurting her. "Now?" he whispered roughly.

"Now," she whispered back. She leaned forward and traced his firm, chiseled mouth with just the tip of her tongue.

The sudden blast of the doorbell's loud chime was like a spray of ice water. Abby jerked in his embrace, stunned at the interruption.

McCallum bit off a harsh curse. He let Abby slide down his body until her feet touched the floor, but he still held her to him. His arms drew her close, comforting now, soothing. His hands on her bare back were faintly trembling.

"Dalton, no doubt," he murmured in her hair.

She stiffened. "Mrs. McDougal won't...come in here, will she?" she asked nervously.

He chuckled softly and caught her shoulders, moving her away from him just enough to give his glittering eyes access to her high, swollen breasts.

"Poor Dalton," he murmured, staring boldly at the soft curves.

Passion had sliced away her inhibitions, but with the return of sanity came self-consciousness. She drew back, her nervous fingers drawing the bodice back in place.

He laughed softly, watching her fumble with the ties while he fastened his shirt and replaced his tie.

"Embarrassed, Abby?" he chided.

She couldn't find the courage to meet his eyes. She was embarrassed, all right, but more than that she was shocked. That uninhibited woman Grey had released had been a complete stranger to her.

She tied the last bow and drew in a long, steadying breath.

"Oh, Mr. McCallum, your company's here!" Mrs. McDougal's voice burst down the long hall toward the bedrooms.

McCallum chuckled softly as Abby worked at her tangled hair with her fingers.

"Leave it, honey," he said softly, coming up behind her to

catch her by the shoulders. "You look like you've been making love, which is exactly the impression I wanted Dalton to get."

Something went cold inside her. "Was…was that why?" she asked, steadying her voice.

"What do you think?" he asked carelessly.

She turned around, her green eyes dark and sensuous, her lips rosy from the long, sweet contact with his, her hair disheveled but flattering. "I think you're dangerous," she said.

One corner of his chiseled mouth went up; his amused eyes searched hers. "You might keep it in mind the next time you wear a dress like that," he told her, studying the bows with a devastating boldness. "Those damned bows are a temptation no man can resist."

The words brought back the feel of his slightly rough hands on her velvety skin, and her breathing accelerated just enough to be visible.

"I thought self-restraint was something you learned in law school," she muttered.

"It only applies to law, honey, not to women. Except in one respect," he added with a slow, sensuous smile. "Would you like me to explain that?"

She could feel the heat in her cheeks. "No, thanks." She turned toward the door. "Robert will wonder where we are."

"Not when he gets a look at you, Miss Summer," he said with a soft laugh.

She glared at him over one bare shoulder. "I think you're despicable," she grumbled.

Both dark eyebrows lifted toward the ceiling. "Can this be the same passionate woman who, less than five minutes ago, was begging me to take her to bed?"

She could have strangled him. Words boiled up into her mouth, but couldn't manage to get out.

"Think of it this way," he murmured as he moved to her

side to open the door. "A good writer draws upon experience. And now you'll have something to draw upon, won't you?" And he opened the door and went through it before she could get past her involuntary gasp.

The look in Robert Dalton's eyes when he saw Abby was something she couldn't describe. The tall, dignified man seemed to age all at once when he saw the telltale marks of McCallum's violent lovemaking on her face.

"Abby, how lovely you look," he said with genuine appreciation, moving forward to take both her hands in his and study her, smiling. "You make me feel my age."

"Oh, I make Mr. McCallum feel his, too," Abby murmured with a glance in her boss's direction that earned her a black scowl.

"Mr. McCallum?" Dalton teased lightly.

"She's called me worse," McCallum muttered.

"Greyson," she warned, glaring at him.

He only grinned. "Would you like a martini, Bob, or something stronger?"

"A brandy would do me," the older man replied with a smile. He was still watching Abby with a steady, intense gaze. "I can't get over the change," he said quietly.

"I'm older," she agreed.

"That wasn't what I meant." His eyes grew sad. "How long have you and Grey been…together?"

"Over a year," McCallum said, pausing to retrieve Abby's snifter and hand it to her as he brought Dalton's drink.

"We, uh, we haven't been living together that long, though," Abby murmured, accepting the glass with a smile.

"Oh?" Dalton brightened.

McCallum's eyes narrowed. "We would have been, if I'd

managed to turn the heat up far enough," he murmured quietly, staring at her.

"How is the shipping business?" Abby asked Dalton quickly.

"Oh, I've ditched my interests," he said pleasantly. "I sold out to Liz. Now I'm more interested in real estate. I own a chain of realty companies, and Grey, as I'm sure you know, has a well-run construction operation. We're trying to work out a deal, and let Grey's brother build us an image."

No, Abby hadn't known because McCallum was as tight-lipped as a clam about his private business. Abby was privy only to what concerned the legal practice.

"Bob's secretary has been handling the paperwork," McCallum said. He moved to Abby's side and drew her up against him with a casual motion that wasn't really casual at all. He was claiming possession, daring Dalton to challenge that claim.

"Didn't trust me, huh, counselor?" Abby teased.

He looked down at her with a slight frown. "I'd trust you with anything I have, Abby," he said softly.

She looked away from that disturbing glance with a nervous smile.

"Dinner is served!" Mrs. McDougal called from the dining room.

All through the delicious meal, Dalton's eyes never left Abby. By the time Mrs. McDougal brought in the homemade apple pie with cream, McCallum was smoldering quietly at the head of the table. His gray eyes met Abby's once, and there was blatant accusation in them, as if Dalton's interest was her fault. In a way, she thought, it probably was. She hadn't actually rejected his subtle overtures. She couldn't. There was something barely begun and still unfinished between them. And even though she'd told herself it was over, even though she'd responded unconditionally to McCallum's passion, a small part of her still responded to Robert Dalton. How much was something she had to find out alone.

When Mrs. McDougal called Grey aside to check with him about menus, Dalton saw his chance and took it.

"Abby, I've got to talk to you," he said urgently. "Have dinner with me tomorrow. Just that, just dinner. Surely you can spare me that much of your time?"

She felt the discomfort like a touch. Her eyes flicked to McCallum, to find him talking to Mrs. McDougal but looking straight at her with a challenging glint to them. The glint decided her. She wasn't his possession, despite his possessive attitude.

"I'll have dinner with you," she said. "We can go straight from the office tomorrow afternoon. I get off at five."

His face lit up. He smiled. "I've missed you."

She'd missed him, too. It had been an ache that had almost driven her mad soon after she left Charleston. But like all aches it had faded with time. Now, seeing him, watching him, she wasn't sure that it had completely gone. That was why she needed time. She needed to be sure.

"Abby's agreed to have dinner with me tomorrow night," Dalton said without preamble after McCallum had let Mrs. McDougal out of the apartment. "I hope you don't mind."

He did. It showed in every rigid line of his face, in the flash of silver eyes that pierced Abby's. "Just bring her home early," McCallum said with a smile she didn't like. "Let's get down to business, shall we? Abby's working on a manuscript. She can amuse herself."

"I'll say good-night, if you don't mind," she told Dalton, giving him her hand. "I like to work in my room, that way I don't disturb Grey."

"Our room, darling," McCallum retorted with a mocking

smile. "You shouldn't have any trouble finishing that scene you were working on this afternoon," he added, "now that you've researched it."

She just escaped a livid blush. "Good night," she murmured, flashing a glare at him.

"Surely you can do better than that?" he purred.

She was going to have to kiss him, and in front of Dalton. It was the last straw. Well, two could play his game. She'd give him something to color his dreams.

With a sensuous smile, she moved toward him, standing on tiptoe to reach his disciplined mouth.

"See you later, darling," she whispered sweetly, and her fingers tangled in his dark hair to bring his mouth down over hers. Out of the corner of her eye, she noticed Dalton turning his head discreetly to study the books in the bookcase. Feeling utterly wicked, she pressed her hips hard against Grey's and her tongue teased his mouth before it shot into the warm darkness, tempting him, seducing him. She felt his breath quicken, felt his fingers digging violently into her waist as he suddenly took over. His mouth crushed hers, his tongue taught her sensations she hadn't felt even in the privacy of the study earlier that night. His hands caught her hips and moved them sensuously against his. She'd been bluffing, but he wasn't. He knew all the moves, and to her horror, an anguished little moan tore out of her throat as the ache rose like a river in flood inside her body.

Grey put her away from him suddenly, smiling like a rake. "Sleep well," he murmured.

As if she'd sleep a wink after that, she thought as she wobbled down the hall. Damned arrogant man.

CHAPTER FIVE

How she slept at all after their dinner with Dalton and Mc-Callum's good-night kiss was a minor miracle. But she woke up with a nagging headache and a strange new sense of emptiness. Greyson McCallum had kindled fires in her body that she hadn't dreamed of. It had faintly shocked her to find out how passionately she could respond to a man. She'd never felt that way with Gene. In all honesty, she'd never felt that way with Robert Dalton.

She glanced at the clock beside the bed and suddenly jumped to her feet. Breakfast would be in ten minutes and McCallum wouldn't wait. Her face colored slightly as she thought about how it was going to be when she looked into those hard gray eyes again. Despite his relentless chiding, he'd been every bit as involved as she was last night. She could still feel the rough sigh of his breath against her mouth, the hardness of his demanding body against every soft, aching inch of hers. In all the long months she'd worked with him, she'd never dreamed there was such an ardent lover under that monumental reserve of his.

She dressed in a two-piece tweed suit with a long-sleeved blouse, all in different shades of brown and beige. The effect, with her long, loosened blond hair, was memorable. She slid her feet into a pair of beige pumps and hurriedly dabbed on some lipstick and powder before she grabbed her purse and went down the hall toward the kitchen.

McCallum was already working his way through an egg and mushroom omelet. The smile Abby had felt surging up to her lips died somewhere in her throat when he looked up. The expression was familiar. It was the one he wore when the district attorney's name was mentioned, or when he, rarely, lost a case. It was accompanied by a black scowl and glittering eyes, and right now Abby was being treated to both.

"You're late," he said shortly. "Go and tell Mrs. McDougal what you want, and be quick. I'm leaving here in exactly ten minutes."

She wanted to tell him where he could go in those ten minutes, but it didn't seem like the best time.

"Yes, Your Worship," she murmured under her breath as she went through the door to the kitchen, not waiting to catch his response.

"Ill-tempered as a wet hornet this morning, he is," Mrs. McDougal murmured, muffling a smile when Abby joined her. "He always has three eggs in his omelet—this morning he wanted one. I buttered the toast, and he wanted it plain. The coffee was too strong. Too strong! He's always wanted it twice-boiled, and this morning I made it just a bit weaker than usual!" She shook her head. "If he takes his mean disposition to the office, you will have all the sympathy I can muster."

"Thanks, I'll need it. Just toast for me, Mrs. McDougal," she said with a twinkling smile. "It's hard to enjoy a meal when you're eating in a tiger's cage."

"I'll not argue with that." Mrs. McDougal grinned. "The

things love does to a man." She sighed, turning away just in time to miss Abby's flush.

When Abby took her toast back in, McCallum was creaming his second cup of coffee and looking even more impatient than usual. He was wearing a gray pin-striped suit with a charcoal-gray vest and a stark white shirt. His tie was a striped one in various shades of silvery gray and blue, and the combination emphasized his dark hair, his tanned complexion. He looked...extraordinarily handsome, she thought.

"Is that what you're wearing tonight?" he growled, glancing at her. "Or is Dalton bringing you here to change?"

She gave him a surprised look over the toast she was nibbling. "I'm wearing this," she said. "I don't need to change just for dinner."

"No? You're sure you wouldn't rather wear that little number you had on last night for him?" he chided.

Just the memory of his hands on her warm, soft body made the blood careen drunkenly through her veins.

She put the rest of her toast down and sipped her coffee. "I'm only having dinner with him, Mr. McCallum," she said tightly.

"That wasn't all you were having with him a year ago," he shot back. His eyes narrowed. "I told you at the beginning that I don't like being made to look like a fool. Dinner, okay. But just be sure you don't end up being dessert. You make one false move with him, and I'll make your life hell. That's a promise."

He didn't have to add that last sentence, she thought miserably. She knew McCallum well enough to have tacked it on all by herself. He didn't make idle threats.

"You're just furious because I wouldn't fall in line and do exactly what you said," she grumbled. "Is that what you expect from your women, McCallum? Blind obedience?"

"Among other things," he replied, and his darkening eyes said more than the words. They traced the soft curves of her breasts until she wanted to scream. "You've got a lot to learn, Miss Summer," he murmured deeply. "But you've got promise."

She let her eyes rest on the half-full cup of black coffee under her cool fingers. "We…we agreed that this was going to be just a business arrangement."

That hardened his face. "Did we? Then, by all means, Miss Summer, we'll stick to it." He drained his cup and got up from the chair, leaving her to follow.

He opened the apartment door for her, blocking it for just an instant as he looked down into her troubled eyes. "Are you ashamed of last night, Abby? Is that it?" he asked in a low, deep tone.

Her face flushed and she stared down at the carpet. "I'd rather forget last night," she choked.

"Did he make you feel like that?" he asked gently. "Did he make you beg?"

The flush got worse, and her hunted eyes met his. "No fair, counselor," she managed. "I… I had a lot to drink .."

"You had a sip of brandy," he corrected. "The only thing you were drunk on was passion."

"Damn you!" she cried. She ducked under his arm and almost ran ahead of him down the hall.

Fortunately, the preliminary preparation for the White murder trial kept McCallum busy when they got to the office. Abby lost track of the people who came and went, leaving behind bits and pieces that McCallum would wind into a case once he got into the courtroom. One of the visitors was his surprise witness, a nervous young brunette who was an eyewitness to the brutal slaying. McCallum had kept that fact close to home so that Clever Hardway, the hard-nosed district attorney, wouldn't get wind of the surprise witness and use her to his own advantage.

While she was still in conference with McCallum, Abby answered the phone and found Hardway breathing down her ear.

"What is he holding back?" he demanded without the courtesy of a greeting—unusual for the very gentlemanly manner he usually presented. "I'm hearing rumors I don't like, Abby. If he throws me any curves in this case, I'll barbecue him in front of God and the jury, I swear it!"

"Now, Mr. Hardway," she began in her best soothing tone, the one that worked ten percent of the time on McCallum, "I'm sure Mr. McCallum has told you everything…"

"He's told me everything but the truth," came the heated reply. "I'm sick to my argyle socks of having him introduce surprise witnesses just minutes before the closing arguments!"

Abby chewed delicately on one long, pink nail to keep from giggling. "But surely you'd know…" she protested gently.

"How could I know?" he burst out. "He bribes people to keep their mouths shut! He must, there's such a conspiracy of silence around here! You tell him…never mind, I'll tell him. Put him on the phone."

"I can't do that, Mr. Hardway. He's in conference…"

"He's always in conference," came the harried reply. "Or out on a personal emergency. Or eating lunch! It's impossible for any man to run a law practice and be out of the office as much as he is! And he won't return my calls. Not once has he ever returned one of my calls!" There was a slow, deliberate sigh on the other end of the line, and when it was over, Hardway's voice sounded calmer. "Tell Mr. McCallum, if you will, that I do *not* intend to be shown up in court on this one. I have done my homework. But if I hear one more rumor about a surprise witness, I will come over there and shake your employer by his ears until he levels with me. And you may quote me when you give him the message. Goodbye, Abby."

She stared at the receiver. A giggle tickled her throat and burst out despite her efforts to control it.

"What's so funny?" Jan asked as she passed the desk.

"Mr. Hardway," she replied, indicating the receiver. "He said that if McCallum brought in a surprise witness this time, he was going to come over and shake him by the ears."

Jan went away laughing. Clever Hardway, while a brilliant prosecuting attorney, was not up to McCallum's size by any stretch of imagination. The DA was only five foot six.

When the little brunette left McCallum's office, casting a nervous smile in Abby's direction, it was time for lunch. Abby was in the middle of an especially long petition with descriptions of the exhibits McCallum planned to have entered into evidence in the White trial, so she'd asked Jan to bring her back a sandwich and a soft drink.

McCallum glanced at her as he came through his open door. "Not taking lunch today?" he asked shortly.

She shook her head. "No time."

"So efficient, Miss Summer," he said with biting sarcasm.

"Don't sink your sharp teeth into me, please," she muttered. "I've just been nibbled on by the district attorney and I'm sore all over."

"Hardway called?" His eyebrows shot up. "What did he want?"

"He's hearing rumbles about your surprise witness," she told him.

He stuck his hands into his pockets and a half smile touched his firm mouth. "What kind of rumbles?"

"Rumors." She glanced up at him, still typing while she

talked. "He said that if you pull another surprise witness on him, he'll come over here and shake you by the ears."

That broke the black mood he'd been in all morning. He threw back his head and roared. "My God, is he going to use a stepladder?"

She bit back a smile. "He didn't say." She ran out of space on the page and drew the original and carbons out, replacing the carbons neatly on other legal-size sheets. "That reminds me. That luncheon your civic club is giving for Mr. Hardway is next Thursday at noon. It's an appreciation day lunch."

"I don't appreciate him," he shot back, his eyes glittering.

"I don't get the idea that he appreciates you very much, either." She laughed.

"Do I have to take a present? Find me a picture of a horse's—"

"Mr. McCallum!"

He studied her faintly flushed face with amusement. "Point taken." His eyes watched her, sketched her face. "Don't you think you're taking a hell of a risk by going out alone with Dalton?"

"It's only dinner," she protested.

"Is it?"

She looked up into his eyes and found them held, captured. Something intensely personal locked their gazes until her heart went wild inside her. She couldn't move, couldn't speak; she felt as if she were drowning in those deep gray eyes.

"Can he give you what we had last night, Abby?" he asked very quietly. And then, without another word, he turned and walked out the door.

She stared after him with conflicting emotions. No, Dalton couldn't give her the kind of pleasure McCallum had; it was ridiculous to assume that he could. Because Dalton no longer held her heart, and she was only just beginning to realize it.

★ ★ ★

It was one minute to five when Robert Dalton walked into the office, his fairness complemented by his expensive blue suit.

"Made it, just," he said with a smile. "Is Grey in?" he added.

"Uh, no, he didn't come back to the office after lunch," she said, and stopped short of admitting how unusual that was. "I'll just be a minute."

Dalton took her to an exclusive restaurant in an even more exclusive shopping center outside the city. It was faintly reminiscent of Charleston, especially when the delicious chilled prawns and spicy cocktail sauce were served. The lobster thermidor was excellent, like the aged white wine Dalton ordered to go with it, along with baked potatoes stuffed with bacon and chives and butter, and flaky homemade croissants. For dessert there was a lemon tart, served with luscious whipped cream, that Abby couldn't refuse.

"I don't know when I've enjoyed anything more," Abby sighed over her coffee, smiling at Dalton over the flower arrangement.

"My pleasure, Abby," he replied. He set his own cup down and stared at her. "How did you manage?" he asked gently, and there was genuine concern in his voice.

She smiled wistfully. "I went to work for McCallum," she explained. "I had very little time for self-pity or regret. He's... an unusual man."

He shifted uncomfortably. "I could have shot myself for my own cowardice," he said softly. "It took weeks to get over the look on your face when Liz walked in and I...put the blame on you." He grimaced. "It just burst out. Liz held the purse strings. I had money of my own, but all of it was tied up in investments. She could have and still can bankrupt me in a divorce suit. But what I did to you was unforgivable."

"No," she said gently. She reached out and touched his hand lightly. "Not unforgivable. We're all human, Robert."

"When Liz agreed to the separation, I looked for you," he admitted. "But you'd disappeared into thin air."

She laughed. "It was still a one-way street, you know," she told him, her voice soft. "There was no future for us."

He started to speak, but apparently thought better of it, and laughed shortly. "If by that, you mean I'd never have been able to offer you marriage, I suppose that's the truth. But, Abby, neither has McCallum. What kind of future can you expect with him?"

She'd never given that much thought, but like a lot of other new ideas, it rushed in to confound her. A future with McCallum. To live with him and be loved by him, to sit and watch him while he worked into the night, to take care of him when he was sick and have him to hold close to her late in the night...

"I've known Grey for years," he continued quietly. "Any woman who could last more than a few months with him would be unique indeed. Marriage isn't in his vocabulary."

"Yes, I know," she replied quietly. How often had she heard McCallum say that same thing? And it had made her laugh months ago. Now it made her want to cry.

Dalton saw that look and launched into memories of when they were getting to know each other in Charleston. She found to her amazement that she could look back at them without remorse. It was a closed chapter in her life, and surprisingly it didn't hurt too badly to look at it. It was a little like taking out an old photograph, one of a cherished memory, and revisiting it. There was no pain, only a feeling of mild pleasure.

It was just barely eleven o'clock when Dalton escorted her to the door of McCallum's apartment.

He looked down at her with a sad, wistful expression in his pale blue eyes, and smiled. "It's too late for us, isn't it, Abby?" he asked.

She managed a smile. "I'm afraid so."

He nodded toward the apartment. "Is he good to you?"

"Oh, yes," she lied, remembering how he'd spent the morning growling like a hungry lion.

Dalton nodded. "I hope he realizes what a treasure he has." His pale blue eyes were wistful as they scanned her face. "I'm sorry that I didn't. We could have had something very special, Abby."

She reached up and touched his cheek lightly. "There were good times, you know," she said gently. "I enjoyed being with you. You were kind to me at a time when I desperately needed kindness. I'll never forget that."

He smiled sadly. "Would you mind very much if I kissed you?"

She shook her head, moving closer. He bent and she felt the hard, firm crush of his mouth for the first time in over a year. He brought her closer, deepening the kiss as if trying to recapture what they'd once had. But now Abby had McCallum's rough ardor for comparison. Against it, Robert Dalton was almost an amateur. Abby felt a very gentle kind of pleasure in his embrace, but it was nothing like the fires McCallum had kindled. The difference was like that between a soothing breeze and a hurricane.

At last, Dalton drew back, frowning slightly at Abby's composed features. He let her go with a world-weary sigh. "You know something, Abby?" he said softly. "I used to think that I could be utterly content if I had enough wealth to satisfy every need and whim. Now I can do that. And it isn't enough. It will never be enough."

She felt a faint maternal stirring as she saw beneath the calm face, all the way to a deep, lingering emptiness. He wasn't a happy man; she wondered if he'd ever been happy. Some people, and he seemed to be one of them, had an outlook on life that precluded happiness in any form. They expected heartache, and of course it came running.

"Thank you for the evening," she said. She opened the door. "We'll see each other again before you go, I'm sure."

"So we will. But it won't be the same, Abby," he added wistfully. He smiled halfheartedly before he walked away.

The apartment was empty. McCallum wasn't home, and that was odd indeed. Nicky had said that he loved his privacy and didn't like sharing it, but Abby had assumed that he meant his older brother spent a lot of time at home. Now she began to wonder if the reverse wasn't true. Perhaps he was tired of Abby, of having a second person in his home. Perhaps, too, he was out with that bottled redhead. Something uncurled and yawned inside her, something unreasonable that suddenly wanted to start pulling out dyed red hair. Abby shook herself mentally. This was none of her business. McCallum had always had women, and that fact had never bothered her before. She thought of Vinnie Nichols and saw red; a red that had nothing to do with hair. McCallum, with that woman, when he was supposed to be living with Abby!

She tried to work on her novel, but she couldn't concentrate. She paced, she stared at the clock, she watched television programs without seeing them. In desperation, she took a bath. It was midnight, but still no McCallum.

At one o'clock she went to bed. She had to, or she knew she'd never be able to get up in the morning. But a part of her mind stayed alert, listening for the sound of a key in the door, a telephone call. What if he'd had an accident? She sat straight up in bed. After all, she reasoned, he'd been away from the office since lunch. What if he'd been hit by a car or something and the people at the hospital didn't know who he was? Or worse, what if Clever Hardway had sent the police out to arrest him for withholding evidence? What if the Martians had captured him? What if he'd turned into a puddle of mushroom gravy? With a groan she lay back down again. Lack of sleep was making her hysterical. Of course he was all right. He was just shacked up with that redhead. She rolled over and thumped the pillows violently, burying her hot face in them.

Just before she finally fell asleep, she had a deliciously satisfying fantasy in which McCallum broke his arm and Abby nursed him back to health, after which he confessed his passionate love for her. The thought caused a vivid dream from which she woke in a flushed daze.

The alarm clock was buzzing noisily when she opened her eyes and flung out a drowsy hand to shut it off. She felt as if she'd hardly slept at all, and the first thought she had was that McCallum might not have come home at all.

She felt a kindling rage like nothing she'd experienced before as she jumped out of bed, not even pausing long enough to sling on a robe as she padded over the carpet to the door and opened it angrily. Down the hall in the kitchen there were rattling sounds and soft humming, which meant that Mrs. McDougal was already getting breakfast. Was McCallum home or not?

Abby went across the hall to the master bedroom and opened the door with a savage jerk. *Philandering, miserable...* She froze in the doorway. McCallum was home, all right. Her wide eyes locked on to his big, masculine body sprawled completely naked and sound asleep on the cover of the bed.

CHAPTER SIX

It certainly wasn't the first time Abby had seen a man without clothes. But her memory of Gene's lean, pale body was no match for what she saw on the silky chocolate bedspread in front of her stunned eyes.

McCallum was solid muscle, from the tips of his toes all the way up, broad hair-roughened thighs, lean hips, massive hairy chest, powerful arms…he was tan all over, too, as if he spent his vacations sunbathing in the nude on those French beaches he favored. If a man could be called beautiful, he was; a candidate for a centerfold if ever there was one.

After a minute she managed to drag her eyes away from his blatant masculinity and turned to leave the room. On her way out, his hastily discarded shirt caught her eye. It was lying on top of his trousers in a chair, its spotless white front smeared from the second button to the collar with pale orange lipstick. That shade was instantly recognizable to Abby. She'd noticed distastefully how caked Vinnie Nichols's wide mouth always was with it.

So that was where he'd been, she thought venomously.

She gave his sleeping body one last, furious glance before she closed the door on the sight of him.

She was more composed when she went to have breakfast, wearing a becoming blue-green dress that was high-collared and beautifully pleated from shoulder to waist. It flattered her small waist and her firm, high breasts. She set it off with black sling-back shoes and a matching leather purse. And her green eyes were greener than burning emeralds under the frown she couldn't help.

"I'll have to go and wake Mr. McCallum," Mrs. McDougal sighed, noticing the time. "Or he'll never get to work on time."

"Uh, you needn't bother," Abby said quickly, remembering the sight of him. "He had a late night last night, and the sleep will do him good." She grinned at the thought of her punctual employer arriving late; it would shock old George, and Jan would giggle… She flushed, remembering what they were sure to think, and it wouldn't be only McCallum they'd be giggling at. But she couldn't wake him up—he'd still been out when she dropped off around one-thirty, which meant he'd surely only had a few hours of sleep. She grimaced. There was nothing to do but let him sleep. She wondered why he hadn't just spent the night with Vinnie. Perhaps he'd been hoping that Abby would be sitting in the apartment, getting more jealous by the minute. And of course, she had. But McCallum wasn't going to have the satisfaction of knowing that. No, sir.

"Are you sure he won't awaken roaring around and mad enough to fire me?" Mrs. McDougal laughed. "Oh, he's got a temper on him, that one."

"Just speak in a soft voice, don't show fear and don't make any sudden moves," Abby instructed. "It works every time."

Mrs. McDougal watched the younger woman finish half a piece of toast and wash it down with black coffee. "Now, that's a masterly bit of advice. May I ask where you learned it?"

Abby grinned at her. "I read an article once about what to do if you were ever confronted with an attack dog."

Mrs. McDougal went back into the kitchen, laughing so hard that tears streamed down her cheeks.

Abby's bus was five minutes late, and when she walked into the office, Jan was sitting on the edge of Abby's desk chewing a fingernail into shreds.

"Oh, thank goodness you're here!" the petite brunette sighed. "Abby, where's Mr. McCallum?" she added, staring around her friend as if she might be concealing the attorney behind her.

"At home asleep," Abby said shortly. "Why?"

Jan started to say something, but closed her mouth quickly at the expression on the taller woman's face. "It's that divorce case Jerry was handling," she explained. "He's got one, and Mr. McCallum has one he's handling as a favor to one of his friends, remember?"

"How could I forget?" Abby groaned. "That wailing woman has caused me grief in the middle of preparations for that murder trial. I've had to wipe away tears and listen to her on the phone, and track down McCallum at all hours of the day...anyway, what's wrong?"

Jan looked toward the ceiling. "Jerry called and left word for McCallum's client to be at the courthouse in the city at 9:30 a.m. and told his client to be in Addison at the same time today."

"So? You did know that the case had to be tried in the woman's county of residence?" Abby murmured absently as she uncovered her typewriter calmly.

"That's just the point." She sighed miserably. "Oh, Abby, Jerry called the wrong number. *Jerry's* client lives in this county. *She's* not supposed to be in Addison at 9:30 a.m. today, McCallum's client is. McCallum will chew his ears off—but right now what do I do? McCallum's supposed to handle that case, and Jerry's on his way to court in the city, and…"

"Sit down," Abby said gently, helping Jan into the chair behind the uncovered typewriter. "Take two deep breaths. Then type these letters for me—one is about a deposition McCallum wants taken in the White case, the other is to the legal organ to explain a notice of incorporation for a merger he's entering into with Robert Dalton. You take care of that. And I will save Jerry's life."

Jan smiled. "Now I know what true friendship is."

Abby smiled back. She opened the door to McCallum's office. "Now, let's see, what am I going to ask Jerry for in return? The keys to his car, his stereo, his credit card…"

It took all of thirty minutes, but Abby caught Jerry in time to have him send the woman McCallum was representing to Addison. At the same time she called the clerk of the court's office in Addison and had Jerry's client notified of the mix-up. Then she reached an attorney in Addison who was an old partner in the firm Jerry Smith had previously been associated with and sweet-talked him into substituting for McCallum. She hoped she'd be forgiven for telling the unsuspecting substitute that her absent boss was nursing a sudden illness. It sounded better than telling people he'd collapsed after a drunken orgy.

McCallum didn't come into the office until after eleven o'clock. He looked drawn under his scowl, and there were lines of fatigue carved into his rigid face. He glared at Abby, standing over her desk like a phantom in his black suit. She couldn't help thinking how the shade matched his expression.

"Well?" he asked silkily. "You told McDougal to let me sleep, didn't you? Don't you know I had a damned court case in Addison at nine-thirty?"

"All taken care of," she said distantly. "James Davis is handling it for you. I cleared the calendar for this morning and I've caught up the paperwork and the correspondence."

"Why the hell didn't you wake me up?" he asked shortly.

She lifted her eyebrows haughtily. "After your wild, mad night with your even wilder artist friend? God forbid."

He stared at her unblinkingly. "What makes you think I was with Vinnie?"

"The lipstick smeared all over your..." She stopped short, knowing already that the admission had told him everything.

He lifted an eyebrow and began to chuckle softly at the expression on her face. "Got an anatomy lesson, did you?"

She really flushed then, and he chuckled wickedly. "Oh, hush," she snapped. "You might have had the decency to put on a pair of pajamas."

"I don't wear pajamas, Abby," he remarked drily. "They only get in the way."

She avoided his pointed gaze. For a man who'd walked in looking ready to do murder, his mood had improved with incredible speed.

"You're supposed to meet Bill Sellers for lunch today at twelve at the Marble Room," she said, biting back a comment.

"Did you sit up and wait for me?" he chided.

"Did you expect me to?" she countered, eyes blazing. "It's none of my business if you want to spend your evenings getting drunk and getting..."

He started laughing and couldn't seem to stop. Abby sat and seethed, picturing a noose around his thick neck.

"I think you and I had better have a nice long talk after work today," he said finally. "We need to clear up a few things."

"Are you sure your poor throbbing head will stand it?" she taunted.

He cocked an eyebrow. "I don't have a hangover," he replied with a faint smile. "Were you hoping to spend the rest of the day slamming doors and making noise? Sorry to spoil your fun."

"You didn't," she said shortly. "Robert and I had a lovely evening."

"Did you?" He lifted his head and stared down his arrogant nose at her.

"A lovely evening," she repeated with a stage sigh and a dreamy smile.

"By that," he said with a cool smile, "I assume that you didn't have too much trouble helping the poor old doddering fellow in and out of cars?"

She picked up a paperweight and stared at him with furious eyes.

"It would only break," he informed her as he went sauntering into his office and closed the door.

Abby's temper didn't improve, but McCallum's certainly did. He was like a lamb around the office for the rest of the day. Not once did he yell or rake Abby over the coals for not getting a letter typed fast enough. He didn't complain about Jan's coffee or even give Jerry hell about the mix-up that morning. He seemed like a man with happy secrets—which made Abby all the madder. She just knew that he was remembering the night with Vinnie!

Abby was almost relieved when five o'clock came. Once

they got back to the apartment, she could lock herself in her room and write and just ignore the infuriating man.

But when she was comfortably seated in McCallum's sleek black Porsche, she suddenly realized that he wasn't driving in the direction of his apartment. He seemed to be heading out of town.

"Where are we going?" she asked, sitting up straight.

He took a long draw from his cigarette and his eyes slid toward her for just a minute. "To spend the night with Mother and Nick," he said. "Collette's going to be there."

"Wait a minute," she said quickly. "What do you mean *spend the night*? And what has Collette got to do with it?"

"You seem to think I've got the wrong impression of her, don't you?" he chided. "Well, this is my chance to see what she's really like."

"I suppose so. But there aren't that many bedrooms even though it's a big house..." She frowned.

"We'll worry about that later," he said. He grinned at her. "Come on, Abby, wouldn't you like a brisk morning ride in the woods? Peace and quiet, leaves rustling, mist on the river..."

"Well..." She felt herself weakening.

"Mother's making peach cobbler for dessert," he added.

"Oh, I'll go without another argument," she burst out, already tasting the delicacy that was her favorite; and nobody made it like Mandy McCallum. The sandwich she'd had at lunch had already left, and her stomach was feeling dreadfully empty.

"Hungry?" he teased.

"Terribly," she admitted. Her eyes flirted with him. "My boss is a slave driver. He's terrible to me."

"I am? My God, let me make amends right now!" He pulled the car off onto the side of the little-traveled county road and left it idling with the brake on. Before Abby knew what was happening, he'd undone her seat belt and jerked her out of her bucket seat and into his lap.

"But, Grey…!" she burst out.

"Hush, baby," he whispered against her mouth. "Just… hush."

His hard mouth bit at hers in brief, searing kisses that very quickly kindled the fires he'd lit once before. Her lips softened and parted; her fingers lifted to tangle in his thick, dark hair and pull his head even closer.

She felt his fingers lift under one high, firm breast and take its delicate weight while his thumb nudged the taut nipple in a slow, maddening motion.

She moaned involuntarily against his mouth and felt him smile.

"More?" he whispered sensuously. He opened the buttons at the front of her dress, his hand sliding up to the front catch of the lacy bra, flicking it open with the ease of long practice. She gasped as his fingers touched and teased the soft bareness of her body and made it writhe with the force of the pleasure. She buried her hot face in his throat, her nails digging into the soft fabric of his suit.

His hard lips brushed over her forehead, her closed eyes. "Look at me, honey," he whispered.

Her eyes slid open lazily, wide and dark green and misty with emotion, framed by disheveled blond hair that was more becoming than any hard-done coiffure.

"You're very good at this," she managed in a voice that shook.

"And you're very lovely," he said gently. His fingers moved, fastening the catch on her bra, then buttoning the front of her dress. "Didn't your husband even get around to teaching you the basics?" he asked quietly.

She shook her head. "He assumed that I already knew them." She smiled wistfully. "I didn't know anything except what I'd read and the little my parents taught me. I went to strict schools and I had an even stricter upbringing. The first time was a nightmare. The rest of my marriage was a little more bearable, I guess. Gene wasn't anybody's idea of the world's greatest lover. Perhaps he just didn't want me enough." She looked up at him briefly, her face flushing just a little. "I could never talk to him the way I can talk to you. I always thought I would never really enjoy making love."

She expected him to smile at that, but he didn't. He looked deeply somber. "But we know differently now, don't we?"

She dropped her eyes to his collar, stained with her lipstick. "You're smudged," she murmured. "And neither of us has a change of clothes to go riding in."

"I keep some clothes at the house." He grinned. "You can't wear mine, I don't imagine, but I'll bet you could wear a pair of Nick's jeans and one of his sweaters."

She couldn't argue with that; she was about Nick's build except for a few additional bulges. "I'd like to go riding with you," she admitted.

He drew a deep, slow breath, and something flared up in his silver eyes. "Honey, there are one hell of a lot of things I'd like to do with you. More than I ever realized…" He put her back into her own seat. "We'd better get down the road. I'm too old to let myself get arrested for public indecency— added to which," he murmured with a wicked smile, "Jerry would enjoy defending me too much."

She laughed with him. The idea kept her smiling all the way to the house.

Mandy McCallum met them at the door, all her misgivings showing in her face. "Oh, Grey, you aren't going to cause

trouble, are you?" she asked softly. "It's Nicky's birthday in
two days, and if you have a fight with him…"

"I'm not going to have a fight with him," McCallum said
with a smile. He bent and kissed the older woman's cheek.
"Say hello to Abby and stop worrying."

"Hello, Abby," she said obediently. "I made you a peach
cobbler. Did Grey tell you?"

"Yes," Abby agreed. Impulsively, she kissed Mandy, too.
"You're an angel."

"There you are!" Nick called from the doorway. He came
through it in a rush, dragging a shy little creature with short
dark hair and huge, shining eyes behind him. "Grey, Abby,
this is Collette."

McCallum stared down at the little Dresden-china doll, and
all the hard lines seemed to go out of his face. "Hello, Collette," he said in his kindest voice. "You're as lovely as Nick
told me you were," he added.

The French girl smiled shyly and her huge brown eyes sparkled as they briefly averted to Nick. "Thank you, Monsieur
Grey," she said. "I also have heard much of you. I am glad
that we meet at last." She edged closer to Nick and clung to
his arm like a lifeline.

Mandy breathed a visible sigh of relief. "There's nothing
better for my nerves than having my family all together at
once," she muttered as she led the way inside.

Mandy had outdone herself. There was chicken-fried steak
and gravy, homemade yeast rolls, a tossed salad, mashed potatoes, asparagus with a cheese sauce—and that delicious cobbler for dessert. Abby felt like a stuffed bird as she finished
the last morsel of the cobbler in her saucer.

"I'll put the rest of it in the refrigerator, Abby," Mandy told
her. "And if you get up before Nicky does, you can have it."

"Peach cobbler for breakfast?" McCallum burst out, gaping at Abby.

She sat up straighter. "There's nothing wrong with peach cobbler for breakfast. I've seen you eat steak," she reminded him.

"At least steak is civilized," he retorted.

"Not the way you eat it, it isn't." She giggled. "Your steaks try to run for it when they see you coming."

"Just like the witnesses the DA brings in," Nicky chuckled. "Grey's a lawyer," he reminded Collette.

"As you told me." The French girl smiled. "You must be very smart, Monsieur, to carry so much knowledge of the law around in your head."

"You flatter me," McCallum replied gently. "What do you do, Collette?"

"Do?" She glanced at Nicky. "Oh, a job, you mean? I have helped my father with the winery, so that someday I will earn the care of the vineyard when my father has retired. I am the only child, you see. They will be my responsibility, all the vines."

"Your father has a vineyard?" McCallum asked casually—too casually, as he leaned back in his chair and lit a cigarette.

Nicky chuckled. "Have you ever heard of d'Anece wines?"

McCallum's eyebrows shot up. "Who hasn't? They're internationally known for excellence."

"Collette's father is Raoul d'Anece."

It only took the older man an instant to recover. "You might have told me that at the beginning, little brother," he said with a smile that covered a vein of suppressed temper.

"We all need a few surprises to keep our mundane lives percolating, Grey," he replied, grinning merrily.

McCallum blew out a thin cloud of smoke and couldn't

hold back a chuckle. "That's one up for you," he admitted. "Now, how about a brandy and let's talk over some business."

"You've got an account for me?" Nick asked eagerly.

"That depends on how good you are at your job."

"Oh, Nicky is the best," Collette assured McCallum, and she gazed up at Nick with worshipful eyes. "Truly."

Abby saw the way Nick looked back at the girl, and she was glad things were working out. It looked as if McCallum's younger brother had finally found something he was willing to fight for.

McCallum and Nick talked business for most of the night, discussing campaigns, publicity and finance in terms that boggled Abby's mind. She sat on the sidelines with Mandy and Collette, sharing a new *Harper's Bazaar* while they discussed the latest fashions. Collette was knowledgeable about the trends, pointing out the latest styles that had caught on in Europe. Collette and Mandy seemed to get along well, too, which was a good thing if that look between Nick and the younger woman was anything to go by.

Abby's eyes, meanwhile, wandered restlessly over McCallum. He had shed his suit coat and vest and had rolled up his sleeves. Several of the buttons on his shirt were unfastened down the front, and every time he moved, the thin fabric strained sensuously over the broad muscles of his chest. She remembered achingly the feel and touch and taste of him, the way he'd looked stretched out so blatantly masculine on his bed. Her pulse hopscotched wildly when he looked up and caught that intense appraisal. He didn't smile, and the tension between them was suddenly tangible.

It was after eleven when the discussion broke up. Nicky had to drive Collette back to her hotel in town, and Abby admitted reluctantly that she was tired, too. McCallum grinned wickedly at the admission, and Abby instantly regretted the slip. Now he'd know for certain that she'd waited up half the night for him.

Mandy walked upstairs with Abby while Grey locked up and turned out most of the lights, leaving the porch light on for Nick.

"I've put you both in the guest bedroom," Mandy said. "If Nicky wasn't here, you could have his room, but…"

"No problem," McCallum said, coming upstairs behind them. "Abby and I are used to sharing. Aren't we, honey?"

Abby flushed. "Uh, supper was delicious," she told Mandy. "Thank you for having me."

"You're very welcome, love." Mandy smiled. She hugged Abby in the hall. "You'll probably leave before I get up in the morning, so come back soon. You're always welcome, even without Greyson."

"Thank you. I'll remember that," Abby promised.

McCallum opened the bedroom door and stood aside to let Abby go in first. The focal point was the huge double bed in the center of the room, decorated in blue and white patterns with a canopy and wispy curtains. It was all French Provincial, and Abby couldn't help but grin at the idea of as masculine a man as McCallum in that bed.

She peeked up at him. "A little…feminine, isn't it?"

He cocked an eyebrow. "A little. No loud protest, Abby?"

She shook her head. "It's a big bed."

"And neither of us has pajamas."

"I intend to do the decent thing and keep my slip on, thanks," she said with theatrical hauteur. "And if you were any kind of a gentleman, you'd wear your shorts."

"Now, what makes you think I'm any kind of a gentleman?" he asked amusedly.

She blinked. Now, there was a question. She put her purse

on the dresser. "Uh, if you don't mind, I'd like to go ahead and take my bath."

"Through there." He indicated a door. "It's a sunken tub with a heated whirlpool," he added. "Just the thing to relax tension."

"Thank you." She went into the bathroom, closing the door behind her, and found a plush washcloth and towel that matched the burgundy decor. The sunken tub was enormous, almost filling the room, almost big enough to swim in. Abby stripped down quickly after she'd filled it with water and activated the whirlpool unit. As an afterthought, she filled it with bubble bath, as well, sending up a cloud of delicious fragrance into the air.

She sank down into the swirling warmth of the water with a huge sigh, her hair loosely pinned atop her head to keep it dry. She closed her eyes and let her tired muscles relax. The whirlpool was just the thing to chase away tension. And wondering how she was going to manage a night in bed with McCallum without screaming from pure frustration was anybody's guess. She was viewing the situation with a jumble of emotions. A part of her wanted more than sleep. Another part was uneasy about that kind of commitment. What she felt for McCallum had grown from an uneasy friendship to a steaming inferno of desire, but not an altogether physical one. While she did want him desperately, she admitted to herself for the first time that she wanted more than a night in his arms. She wanted much more than that.

While she was trying to work out her emotions, she heard the door open. With shocked green eyes she appraised McCallum as he walked in, stark naked, and found himself a washcloth and towel.

She couldn't even get out a question. Her eyes were helplessly riveted to that muscular, tanned body as he got his electric razor from the cabinet and began to shave.

"I'm taking a bath," she said in a squeaky voice.

He glanced at her with an amused smile, noticing the line of soap bubbles that barely covered her creamy breasts. "So I see. Do you like the whirlpool?" he asked over the combined hums of the razor and the whirlpool unit.

"Oh, yes, I… I like it very much, thanks." Well, if he could be nonchalant about it, she could, too. They were both adults. She'd been married; she wasn't naive.

Her fascinated eyes ran up his muscular legs, over his slim hips and broad, heavy shoulders. He was so deliciously masculine, it was all she could do not to climb out of the tub and run her hands over him. She'd never wanted to touch Gene like that, but she'd have given a week's salary just to caress McCallum's smooth, bronzed skin.

"You were right about Collette," he admitted wryly. "But for future reference, I'm not usually wrong about people. She threw me a curve."

"Naturally. You aren't used to naive little things," she teased.

He lifted an eyebrow at her. "No? I've had you around long enough that I should be."

"I'm not naive."

"About sex, you most certainly are. Delightfully naive," he added sensuously, before she could take offense.

She dabbed at her face with the soapy cloth for something to do. She felt completely out of her element.

"No comment?" he teased. He finished with the razor and put it back in the cabinet, pausing to splash aftershave on his smooth cheeks. "Don't tell me you're shy?" he chided as he turned around.

She couldn't help the blush. It was simply unavoidable. She

dropped her eyes to the washcloth. "I'm not shy at all," she said bravely.

He laughed deeply. "Then why won't you look at me?"

"I'm bathing," she ground out.

"Which does sound like a good idea." And while she was still trying to figure that one out, he picked up his washcloth and towel, threw the latter onto a vanity chair beside the tub, and climbed down into the soap bubbles beside Abby.

CHAPTER SEVEN

Abby's face managed to capture shock, outrage and fascination in one expression as McCallum slid down into the water right beside her, the soap bubbles catching in the thick mat of hair across his broad chest.

He sighed deeply. "God, that feels good. I've thought about having one of these installed in the apartment, but somehow I never got around to it. Just the thing after a rough day, isn't it, Abby?"

"It's very nice," she agreed. His shoulder was touching hers, and she felt shock waves all the way to her toes, ripples of sweet sensation.

"Soap?"

She handed it to him. "Do you think Nicky is serious about Collette?" she asked with a valiant effort at nonchalance.

"I think it's a definite possibility," he admitted. He lathered his arms and his chest, and Abby watched him with a dull ache inside her tense body.

He glanced at her and lifted an eyebrow. "Ever fancied yourself as a geisha?" he teased. "How about doing my back?"

He handed her the soapy cloth and turned so that she could reach the muscles, silky with water and dotted with soap bubbles.

She took it and began to smooth it over his darkly tanned skin. She ached to be closer, to touch him without the cloth between her fingers and his hard-muscled body.

While she was trying to stifle the growing hunger, he turned around and saw that look in her eyes before she could erase it.

His chest rose and fell heavily while they looked at each other for a long moment. Then, wordlessly, he took the cloth out of her hand and tossed it into the water. His hands caught hers and lifted them to his soapy chest, moving them slowly, sensuously, against it until she got the idea and began to explore his warm torso without any further coaxing.

He smelled of soap and aftershave, and Abby thought there'd never been such a sensuous man in the whole of her life. Her hands moved down his rib cage, to his flat stomach, hesitating, fluttering, when they reached it.

Gently, he guided her hands down even farther, and she looked up at him as she touched him, read the pleasure in his darkening eyes that slowly closed, even as she felt the tiny tremor run through his massive body.

She inched toward him, sliding her hands delicately over his broad shoulders until the tips of her breasts were touching his chest. Her lips were parted, her breath coming unsteadily and fast, like his. She leaned forward and brushed her lips softly across his, drawing them back and forth in a whisper of a kiss as she moved again, letting her soft breasts crush down against his slick, hair-covered chest.

He was letting her take the initiative, letting her have all the time she needed, and he seemed to be enjoying it—more than enjoying it if the expression on his broad face was anything to go by. Leaning back, with his glittering eyes like slits under his heavy brows, he watched patiently every move she made. The only indication of emotion under that calm exterior was the thunderous pounding of his heart against her breasts.

"Enjoying yourself, little one?" he asked deeply, his voice as sensuous as a caress.

"I… I'd enjoy it more if you'd help me," she whispered against his mouth.

"Help you how?" he whispered. His hands moved then, to slide the length of her spine and back up again. "Like this? Or…like this…" They moved around her, and he eased her gently back so that his hands could swallow her taut breasts. His fingers caressed them gently, probing, stroking, until she moaned softly.

He eased her across him and one big hand arched her back. He bent to the taut nipples exposed by the motion and took first one, then the other, into his mouth to tease and caress them with his lips, his tongue, his teeth.

Abby's nails bit into his shoulder. She sighed with the pleasure. As his lips slid over her breasts and down to her flat stomach, she bit back a cry.

"For God's sake…" he gasped.

He stood up, taking her with him, and riveted her trembling body to the full, hard length of his. His mouth ground down into hers, his tongue thrusting hungrily into her soft mouth, his arms grinding her into him, telling her without words that he had to have more than this.

He broke off the kiss after a moment and reached for his towel. Without another word, he dried every aching inch of her, slowly, the movements of his hands a caress that enveloped her in a blind kind of pleasure. When he was through, he handed the towel to her and stood watching patiently while she did the same for him, her eyes openly adoring him as she dried him from head to toe.

He took the towel away from her, tossed it onto the floor. He lifted her gently in his arms and carried her through the bathroom into the bedroom, laying her down on the blue patterned coverlet of the bed. She watched as he eased down beside her, so hungry for him that she trembled from head to toe. All she wanted out of life at that moment was to please him, to give him a kind of pleasure he'd never find with anyone else. She wanted him more than life itself.

"I'll take care of you," he whispered as his head bent to her breasts.

She couldn't even answer him. She lay drowning in pleasure as his lips traveled lazily over every soft, sweet inch of her. She alternately moaned and sighed, biting on her lips to keep from crying out loud as he brought her to a crest of sensation that had her writhing like a wild thing.

She felt his broad, hard thighs parting hers, easing between them, and her arms reached up to draw the full weight of his warm, bare chest down over hers, the sensation of skin against skin unbearably sweet. She looked straight up into his eyes, watching him helplessly, as his body merged gently, completely, with hers.

She gasped, clinging, a wild little cry escaping her throat even as she stifled it.

"Mother and Nick sleep on the other side of the house," he said in a tight, rough whisper. "There's no one to hear you except me, sweetheart. And, God, Abby, I love the sound of you…!"

He took her mouth then, and she arched upward to meet the hungry, hard thrust of his body, her last sane thought that the lights were still on, and she hadn't even cared. Then she began to feel the first stirrings of a wild, savage sweetness that took her complete concentration as she reached, and reached and reached to try to catch it...

She nestled close into McCallum's big arms, damp with perspiration, trembling softly with fulfillment, her moist cheek pressed to the hair-roughened, padded muscles of his chest.

His big hand smoothed her hair tenderly while he smoked, as contented as a jungle cat.

She vaguely remembered murmuring close to his ear that she loved him, as the pleasure washed over her like a thunderous breaking wave. She couldn't remember if he'd acknowledged her words, sounds that may have been unintelligible to him. But she knew now that it was the truth, not part of the incredible passion they'd shared. She loved him.

"I meant to take longer than that," he murmured drowsily.

She smiled shyly. "I don't think I'd have survived if you had," she whispered.

He shifted to look down at her. She'd never seen that particular expression in the silver eyes that traced, deliberately, every exposed inch of her body before they came back to her eyes. "Sweet delight," he said in an uncommonly soft tone, "did I please you?"

"I hope I pleased you," she countered. She nuzzled close and let her eyelids fall.

"Couldn't you tell, honey?" he teased gently.

She smiled. "I hoped."

"Want to go riding with me in the morning?" he murmured.

"Mmm-hmm," she murmured drowsily.

"I'll set the clock. Good night, sweet."

"Good night, Grey," she whispered through a smile.

The last thing she remembered was Grey pulling the cov-

ers over them and fitting his body around the shape of hers
as she curled on her side and sank into a sweet, dark oblivion.

She woke up all at once, blinking against the daylight fil-
tering in the gauzy curtains. She sat up, and as the covers fell
to her waist, she realized that she wasn't wearing a gown—or
anything else. Then memory flooded back and she flushed
to her collarbone. She'd never meant to let that happen, but
the discovery that she loved him had been too much. She'd
never known that two people could give and get so much,
could please each other in ways that bordered on euphoria.
She was faintly embarrassed at the things she'd whispered so
feverishly, at the things Grey had whispered back...

She got out of bed and noticed the note on the other pillow. "If you're up by six, I'll be at the breakfast table," it read,
and he was hers, Grey. She smiled, reading it a second time,
and a third. Perhaps he did care, just a little. He wanted her
at least, and that was something. If only Robert Dalton's
words hadn't come back to haunt her. McCallum's women
only lasted a few months, he'd said. That was so, but Abby
wanted far more than a few months. Or even a few years. She
wanted the rest of her life with him.

She took a quick bath, trying not to remember what had
happened in the tub last night, and dressed in the jeans and
sweater that Nick had lent her early last night before she came
to bed. They were a little tight, but they felt good, and the
shamrock-green sweater brought out the vividness of her eyes.
She tossed back her hair with the brush, ignored makeup and
rushed down the stairs to the breakfast nook.

McCallum was just setting a platter of eggs and bacon on
the table. He looked up as she walked into the room. She
stood still in the doorway uncertainly. His face gave nothing
away, and she wondered if giving in to him had been the big-

gest mistake of her life. What if he thought she was cheap, that she was easy? Or even worse, what if that one encounter had wiped out his hunger for her, and he'd never touch her again?

CHAPTER EIGHT

His narrow eyes slid up and down her and suddenly he smiled. It was like daylight breaking on the horizon. All Abby's worries went up in smoke.

"I hope you like eggs and bacon and mushrooms in a messy omelet," he murmured with dry humor. "Because this is the only way I can fix them. The coffee's much better," he promised.

"I don't think I'd notice if it was mud," she admitted with a shy smile.

He put the platter down and moved quickly toward her, to jerk her body against his and kiss her with a warm, slow passion that the night hadn't apparently made a dent in. She felt the hunger in his mouth even as he drew her hips hard against his and told her without words how much he wanted her.

Her arms around his waist, she answered the kiss with a ready response that was new. As new as the look on McCallum's broad face when he lifted his head, and her lips clung unashamedly.

"I thought I'd dreamed it until I woke up and found you

sound asleep in my arms," he murmured quietly. "It took every ounce of willpower I had to leave you like that. I wanted to kiss you awake and start all over again."

She stood on tiptoe to kiss him, her lips soft and loving. "It was the loveliest dream I've ever had."

"Yes," he said. His voice was deep, his face solemn. He held her close for just an instant before he turned her loose and guided her to the seat beside his.

"Do you often cook breakfast when you're home?" she asked when he'd seated her and himself.

He handed her the platter while he poured the coffee into his mother's thin rose-patterned china cups. "Only when I'm entertaining a lady."

Her eyes jerked up, wounded.

"Abby," he breathed. "I've never brought a woman here before."

She felt embarrassed at letting him see how much it had mattered. She tried to laugh it off. "Oh, I see."

He reached over and covered her hand with his. "Would you like to hear a confession?" he asked gently. "I wasn't with Vinnie—well, I was, but not in the way you thought. She had a few drinks too many and called me to take her home from a party. I put her to bed, but I didn't climb in with her."

"You don't owe me any explanations," she murmured.

"Does that mean you aren't going to admit that you were jealous, Abby?" he murmured with a grin.

She smiled at him over her coffee cup. "That's exactly what it means, counselor."

Later, riding contentedly alongside him in the deep woods that bordered the McCallum property, Abby thought that she'd never seen him quite as relaxed or carefree as he seemed now. The familiar scowl was gone. The lines in his broad face had relaxed. And she felt a new intimacy with him that was devastating.

He caught her looking at him and smiled. "Having fun?" he asked.

"I love this," she admitted. She patted the roan's mane as it paced McCallum's big black gelding. "I used to ride when I was a little girl. One of Dad's friends owned some stables near our house. I got to ride whenever I felt like it."

"What are your parents like?" he asked.

She laughed. "Sunshine," she said without thinking. "I grew up with love and laughter, and I can only remember one honest argument that ended with Dad carrying Mother off to bed." She shook back her long hair delightedly. "They love each other terribly."

"Is your father retired now?"

She nodded. "Yes. As I told you, Mom and Dad are living in Panama City. He keeps busy. He's much too active a man to sit back and grow flowers."

He glanced at her. "I noticed quite a few pots of them at your apartment."

"I like flowers," she said defensively

He smiled. "I'll admit to an occasional urge to help Mother hoe the garden."

"Grey, what about Nicky and Collette?" she asked after a minute.

He drew in a deep breath and reined in long enough to light a cigarette. "I've done some thinking about that," he told her. "Perhaps I have infringed on Nick's territory a little. It's hard to admit to myself that he's a man now. I spent a lot of years helping Mother raise him. It's not easy, letting go."

She studied his hard face. "I know. It wasn't easy for me when my parents moved away. I still see them, of course, but it's not like having them a few miles away."

"I promised to fly you down there. I'll do it, the minute I get through with this case."

She smiled. "A few days in the sun wouldn't hurt you," she said. "You work too hard."

"It's been a habit with me," he admitted. His eyes clouded. "I'll never forget the way it used to be, Abby. Poverty leaves its mark. That, and my father's death, were bitter pills to swallow. Sometimes I work myself into a stupor just so that I won't have to think, to remember."

Abby had a feeling that he'd never told that to another living soul, not even his mother, and she felt warm and close to him.

"Come on," he said suddenly, irritation in his deep voice, "I'll show you the mist rising from the river. It's a sight you won't forget in a hurry."

He led the way and after a few minutes Abby could hear the gurgling sound of the river running lazily between its banks. McCallum reined in and dismounted at the side of a towering oak tree, the roots of which extended down into the river and were partially exposed on one side. He reached up for Abby, and deliberately let her body slide down his as he levered her to the ground.

"Mmm." He chuckled. "I like the way you feel. God, you're soft."

"You're not," she teased. She looked up at him for a long moment; just long enough for the hunger between them to kindle again.

His fingers tugged at the buttons of his brown shirt, not stopping until it was open all the way down the front over his broad chest. With a sensuous smile he drew Abby to him.

"What are you wearing under this?" he asked as his fingers tugged at the garment's hem idly.

"Not a thing, Grey," she whispered. Without stopping to

think, she reached down and pulled it up over her firm, high breasts just before she flattened them against the warmth of his bare chest by moving forward. She drew them lazily back and forth against him and drew in her breath sharply at the remembered sensations it triggered.

McCallum's hands went down to her hips and lifted her gently, sensuously, against the sudden hardness of his thighs, watching her face as the contact stiffened her body.

His eyes slid sideways to a couple of pine trees several yards away where pine straw covered the ground. "I don't know how comfortable this is going to be," he whispered, lifting her suddenly in his arms, "but at least we won't have to worry about interruptions this far from the house."

She drew his mouth onto hers and kissed him slowly, sweetly. He spread out his brown shirt and her sweater and then laid her down on the pine straw, her arms coaxing him down with her.

He moved, covering her trembling body with his so that every inch of them touched. His mouth opened; his tongue darted sharply into her mouth, again and again in a rhythm that matched the aching movements of his hard, heavy body on hers. Her nails dug into his hips and she gasped as the pressure increased the ache inside her until it was almost unbearable.

"I need you," she whispered, her voice shaking. "Please, Grey, oh, please, please...!"

"I need you just as much," he ground out, breathing harshly. His hand went between them to the zipper on her jeans. He was already easing it down when a new sound made its way to their feverish minds. It wasn't the soft creak of the trees, or the murmur of the river. It was the sound of horses' hooves and laughing conversation.

McCallum's head jerked up while he listened, and a harsh,

explicit word broke from his tight lips as he lifted his body away from Abby's and got to his feet.

"Nick! Of all the damned times to go riding," he muttered, yanking on his shirt. "By God, I'll kill him…!"

Abby got up, shaking, hastily picked up the sweater and quickly pulled it over her head. She pressed herself into McCallum's arms and moved close. "Hold me," she whispered shakily. "Grey, I ache so!"

His arms obliged her, crushing with mingled frustration and irritation. His head bent over her and he rocked her against his big body until they both calmed, until their stormy pulses began to throb normally. The voices were close now.

All of a sudden, his chest began to shake against her as laughter rumbled up from it. "I can't believe what I meant to do," he burst out, chuckling. "My God, right in the middle of a bridle path that half the riders in the neighborhood use, in broad daylight… You see what you do to me? I touch you and my common sense goes on vacation."

She laughed, too, glorying in the tight clasp of his arms. It was nice to know she affected him that way, even if it was only desire that caused it.

"Nicky and Collette would have gotten an eyeful, all right, and we'd never have been able to face your mother again."

He drew away and looked down at her with calm, watchful eyes. "I seem to pick the worst possible times and places to make love to you. In the apartment with Dalton due, in the car, here." He shook his head wistfully. His eyes narrowed, clouded. "Abby, after last night…how do you feel about Dalton?"

She started to speak, to tell him that Robert Dalton meant nothing to her now, that she loved Greyson McCallum, that last night had been heaven for her. But she hesitated, trying to find the right words, and his face closed up to her. He let her go abruptly as Nick and Collette rode into view a few yards away.

"Isn't it a great morning for a ride?" Nicky laughed, his dry gaze going from Abby's flushed face to McCallum's hard one. "Did we interrupt something?"

"Nothing that didn't need interrupting," McCallum said coolly.

Abby felt a sudden emptiness at the curtness in his tone, but she disguised it with a smile. "Hi, Collette," she said. "I wish I looked that good in jodhpurs and a hacking jacket." The young Frenchwoman smiled shyly at that.

"You don't look all that bad in my jeans and sweater," Nick teased with a broad wink. "Talk about a good fit…"

"When you get your ideas together on that campaign," McCallum told his brother, "give me a call and I'll arrange a meeting with Dalton. Abby and I have to get to the office."

"Sure, Grey. See you, Abby," he added.

McCallum, taciturn and unapproachable, helped Abby mount before he threw his leg over his own horse's back and led the way to the house.

McCallum lit a cigarette, ignoring Abby, once they were on the way to the city again.

"What have I done?" she asked quietly when she couldn't stand his silence a minute longer.

He cocked an eyebrow at her. "What could you have done?" He laughed shortly.

"You're so quiet…" she murmured.

He took a draw from the cigarette and blew it out, controlling the powerful sports car with the same deft hands he'd used to control Abby last night. "I'm working out that White case in my mind, honey," he said after a minute.

"Are you sure?" Her eyes were more revealing than she

knew, wide and green and faintly apprehensive as they met his across the short distance that separated them.

"I'm sure." He winked at her, and she relaxed a little. She settled down in her seat with a long sigh. Everything would be all right now.

The morning was hectic, and Abby felt as if she were being torn in two by the pressure of clients and a phone that wouldn't stop ringing, and by McCallum's growing impatience.

She eased into his office with a file he'd demanded ten minutes earlier, to find him glaring down at a scatter of notes and documents on his desk. His jacket was off, his tie loosened, his sleeves rolled up over muscular tanned forearms sprinkled with dark hairs. Abby stood there for a long minute just looking at the broad, hard face she'd begun to love so dearly.

He looked up, anger glittering in his unblinking silver gaze. "I asked for that over fifteen minutes ago," he said shortly.

"And you'd have gotten it if the phone hadn't decided to ring off the hook, and that woman whose divorce you handled for a favor hadn't called to wail out her problems to me, and Jerry hadn't asked for the file on his divorce case..."

"I don't pay you for excuses," he replied.

He hadn't spoken to her that way since she started to work for him. Perhaps the rough morning had made her sensitive, or their delicate new relationship had left her unprepared for such a flat statement to remind her of her real status in his life. Whatever the reason, tears began to slip hotly down her cheeks.

"Abby!" He threw down the pencil he was jotting notes with and went around the desk.

She tried to back away, but his arms caught her and brought her close to his big, warm body.

"No, don't fight me," he said in a tone that was worlds away from the sharp, hurting one he'd used seconds before.

"I don't understand you," she managed brokenly. She leaned her sodden cheek against his shirt and sighed.

"I don't understand myself when it comes to you," he admitted drily. He folded her closer, until she felt as if they were joined, every inch of the way, up and down. "Oh, Abby, it's been a rough morning, hasn't it?" he murmured as he rocked her gently back and forth. "I haven't snapped at you in a long time."

"Not since yesterday," she agreed. A smile peeked through the tears.

He tilted her wet face up to his soft, amused eyes. "You ought to be used to it by now."

"I am. It just stings more than it used to," she said without meaning to.

His long forefinger traced the curve where her lips parted over her pearly teeth. "Does it?" he asked.

She went very still in his arms, amazed at the sensations he could arouse so easily. Only his finger touched her, but she felt the reaction all the way to her toes.

"No one ever affected me the way you do," she said shakily.

He was breathing a little harder, a little faster. "How?"

She caught his free hand and pressed it to the underside of her soft breast, holding it there while she looked up into his eyes.

"Like this," she whispered. "Feel it?"

"Very soft," he whispered back, smiling as his hand took the delicate weight and molded it gently.

"I meant my heartbeat," she murmured unsteadily.

"I'd rather touch your breast," he whispered, bending. He

brushed his mouth over hers slowly, tenderly. "I held you naked in my arms," he breathed, as if he could hardly believe it, "yet this morning you look almost virginal. Are you the same woman who sank her teeth into my shoulder and begged me not to stop?"

She reached up and linked her arms behind his head, going on tiptoe to keep the devastating contact with his teasing mouth. "I never knew it could be that way with a man," she said softly. "It was so beautiful, Grey."

He drew back for an instant and scowled at her. His silver eyes narrowed as he studied her worshipping eyes. "Abby, you're not getting involved, are you?"

She blinked. "Involved?"

"Emotionally." His eyes cut into hers like silver knives. His hands moved up to frame her face and hold it steady under the unblinking appraisal. "Are you?"

She closed her eyes in self-defense. She knew how he felt about that. If she admitted what she was beginning to feel, he'd walk away forever, and she knew that, too.

She laughed nervously. "Do we have to analyze it?" she asked, averting her eyes so that she missed the expression that crossed his face like a shadow.

"No," he said after a minute. "We don't have to analyze it. Kiss me, Abby," he whispered against her mouth. He half lifted her against his powerful body. "Kiss me hard, baby…"

Her nails bit into the nape of his neck as she obeyed him, her mouth opening to his, her tongue touching his, answering its gentle, slow thrust, her thighs lifting, trembling against his. A soft, hungry moan sobbed out of her as he deepened the kiss, his mouth expert, demanding, blotting out everything except the need that flared up like a torch between them.

He let her slide back to the floor, his eyes watching her steadily. "Tonight," he said deeply, "when we get back to the apartment, I'm going to undress you inch by aching inch. I'm going to carry you into my bedroom and kiss you all the way down to your toes before I take you."

The words, and the intensity with which he said them, made her tremble. "McDougal…" she reminded him breathlessly.

A corner of his mouth went up wickedly. "It's her day off, Abby," he whispered. "There won't be anyone to see us, or to interrupt us. And this time…" The nagging buzz of the intercom broke the spell violently. McCallum released Abby with a muttered curse and went to jab his finger at the switch.

"Well?" he growled.

"Uh, Mr. McCallum, it's Mr. Dalton for you on line one," Jan said nervously.

"Tell him I'll only be a minute," he said, cutting off the connection without waiting for a reply. His eyes met Abby's apologetically. "Lunch in twenty minutes, honey," he said with a smile.

She nodded, her eyes full of dreams. She went out and closed the door behind her.

But when lunchtime came, McCallum shot through the door of his office like a cyclone, jerking on his suit coat as he came, his face like a thundercloud. He was on the heels of a frantic telephone call Abby had just put through.

"I'll be at the jail," he told Abby curtly. "White just tried to hang himself." And he was gone.

She barely heard Jan coming down the hall. Surely after all the work they'd done trying to prove that Wilfred White was innocent, he wasn't going to die before it even got to trial?

"Trouble?" Jan asked.

"Big trouble. Wilfred White just tried to hang himself," Abby told her. "Mr. McCallum's on his way to the jail."

"Mr. McCallum?" Jan teased. "Your lipstick's smeared, did you know? Too bad about White," she added with a grimace. "You've put in a lot of time with the boss on this one. That suicide attempt will look bad, too; like an admission of guilt."

"McCallum will find some way to use it to his advantage," Abby said from experience. "You just wait and see."

"It wouldn't surprise me," Jan agreed. "Want to go to lunch with me? I'm not tall and ruggedly handsome and magnificent in court, but I'll buy you a hamburger, just the same."

Abby laughed. "You're on, and after this morning, I won't mind at all if you aren't magnificent in court. It will probably mean that you don't have such a low boiling point!"

McCallum came back two hours later, looking every bit as ill-tempered as he had when he left. "Damned fool," he bit off on the way into his office. "Three days before the trial begins, and he has to do a Greek tragedy in the damned jail!"

"Will it go against him that much?" Abby asked.

"That's a question for the clergy," he snapped. "He's dead."

He went into his office and slammed the door. Abby stared after him. McCallum had grown genuinely fond of the eighteen-year-old boy who was accused of murdering a liquor store owner in the course of a robbery attempt. White had been intelligent and pleasant, not at all the kind of man who'd murder someone. White had seemed rather reserved to her, a gentle sort of person. Of course, the complaint stated that he'd allegedly been on drugs when he went into the liquor store to rob it.

McCallum had put in a lot of hours on the preparation. He thought the boy was innocent, and he was determined to free him. Abby smiled wistfully. He was like that about his clients. He never took a case unless he believed in his client's innocence. And he very rarely lost one. This particular one was going to hurt more than most. White had a wife, a wispy little thing who was five months pregnant.

She left her desk and went into McCallum's office. He was sitting in his big padded chair facing the window, a forgotten cigarette in his hand, his jacket off, his big body faintly slumped as if he was exhausted. He probably was, and hurt, to boot. He could be very human at times, despite that rough exterior. He cared deeply about people, despite his maintained emotional distance from his women.

Abby went around the desk and stood beside him, hesitation keeping the words on her tongue.

He reached out a big hand and caught hers, just holding it while he smoked. "His wife lost the baby this morning," he said blankly. "He was depressed over that, and one of the other prisoners started taunting him about what it was going to be like when they shut him up in a federal prison for the rest of his life." He drew a deep, slow breath. "He was an outdoorsman, you know. He hated closed places. I should have spent more time with him," he ground out, jerking his eyes up to Abby's. "I should have convinced him that we'd win the case."

There was anguish in his eyes, his face. "Grey, all we can do is our best," she said gently. "And you did that. You can't live people's lives for them."

"Is that going to comfort his widow?" he asked curtly.

"No. But I thought it might comfort you," she said gently. "It hurts very badly, doesn't it?"

He drew a sharp breath and pressed her hand. "Yes, Abby. It hurts."

She reached down and gently took the cigarette from the dark hand, crushing it out in the ashtray. Then she eased down into his lap and her fingers smoothed the cool, black hair away from his forehead. Once, she'd never have dared such an intimacy, but it seemed to come naturally now. She bent and kissed him softly, slowly, his forehead, his thick, dark eyebrows, his closed eyelids, his cheeks, his chiseled lips, his chin…she kissed him as if they were both children, lost and hurt and afraid. And he seemed to sense it, because he began to kiss her back the same way, with a tenderness that took her breath.

His hands cupped her face and he looked down at her with darkening eyes. "Abby," he breathed softly. Nothing more, just her name, but the way he said it made her think of an open field of wildflowers, of the wind breaking the treetops.

"Let's go home, Grey," she said gently. "And I'll make you forget it."

He sighed roughly and leaned his forehead against hers. "I'd give five years of my life to do that, to lie down with you and give each other the pleasure we did last night. But I can't, Abby. Dalton's on his way here, and he's having dinner with us tonight, as well. I've got to get this merger out of the way."

She swallowed down her hurt pride. "Oh. I see."

"No, you don't," he said enigmatically. His eyes searched hers. "You never have. But one of these days, Miss Summer, you may take off your dark glasses and see the world."

She studied his tie. "Did you have to invite him for dinner?" she asked.

She felt his powerful thighs stiffen under her, felt the minute contraction of his arms. "No. But I thought it might be a good idea at this point."

Her eyes darted back up to his. "I don't understand."

"What an understatement." He was wearing his poker face now; nothing showed under it. "Hadn't you better get back to your desk?"

"Most employers would give a lot to have me sit on their laps," she informed him, sitting up straight.

"I'll amen that," he agreed. One big hand slid under the

hem of her skirt and up her smooth, lovely thigh, while his eyes traced an appreciative path behind it. "God, I've never seen legs like these before. Long and silky and sexy as hell." He drew her back down against him and kissed her, his mouth hard and hungry, holding the kiss until she moaned and clung to him. He drew back a whisper. "I've got to be sure, Abby, and so have you," he murmured. "It won't hurt either one of us to wait a few more days."

"That wasn't what you said this morning," she managed through lips that still stung from his kiss.

He scowled. "That was before…never mind. Up you go, you sexy creature. We've got work to do."

"Slave driver," she muttered, getting to her feet. She smoothed down her skirt and smiled at him. "Feel better?"

"I ache to the soles of my shoes, if you call that feeling better," he said with dry humor.

"Not my fault, counselor. I offered to do something about it," she reminded him with a demure smile.

He leaned back with a hard sigh. "I want you very badly, Miss Summer," he said bluntly. "But until I get a few things straight in my mind, I think we'd better keep this at a manageable level."

That didn't make sense at all, but she wasn't clear-minded enough at the moment to puzzle it out.

"Whatever you want, Grey," she murmured on her way out.

"Not quite," he said under his breath. "Not yet, anyway. Get me Nicky on the phone, honey."

"Of course."

"What did we interrupt this morning?" Nick asked when Abby reached him, and she could see the wicked grin on his face in her mind.

"Not a thing," she protested.

"Sure," he laughed, "that was why you had pine straw all down your back and Grey was ready to throw a punch at me."

"I fell," she lied through a wistful smile. "And Grey is always grumpy early in the morning."

"You ought to know," Nicky said.

"Anyway," she continued, "your big brother wants to speak to you. Hold on a minute."

She pressed the right button, buzzed McCallum, and then waited for him to answer before she put the receiver down. She hadn't heard the office door open, and her back had been to it. When Robert Dalton suddenly appeared in the threshold, she felt a jolt of surprise.

"Oh, you startled me!" she burst out, breathless,

"I'd like to do a lot more than that, Abby," he teased. "Are you all right?"

She stood up, trying to catch her breath. "I'm not usually this jumpy," she murmured.

He moved closer and caught her by the waist. His smile was full of memories. "You were once. That first time I kissed you, remember? In my office at the shipyards, with workers going back and forth outside the window, and I thought there'd never been anything as sweet as your mouth."

Involuntarily, her eyes went to his lips as she recalled that long-ago day, and the wonder of finding someone to care about who seemed to care as much about her. She smiled wistfully.

"So you do remember," Dalton breathed as he bent and kissed her softly, gently, a salute to something that had passed like a faint sun shadow on the meadow.

She didn't fight him, but her hands went to push gently at his chest—just as the door opened and McCallum came out of the office.

Abby didn't even have to ask what he was thinking. It was obvious. He scowled at both of them, and the look he gave Abby made her want to wither.

She opened her mouth to speak, but Dalton beat her to it. "Reminiscing, Grey," he murmured with a glint in his eyes. "That's all. We were just…reminiscing."

But that wasn't how it sounded, and Abby began to wonder if his apparent surrender to her suggestion that they close the door on the past had been sincere. It looked very much as if he was trying to show McCallum that he was still the man in possession, despite Abby's residence with the younger man.

"If you'll come in, we'll get started," McCallum told him in a cold tone. "Nick will be here in about fifteen minutes. Abby, get us some coffee."

She glared after him, refusing to give him the satisfaction of an argument. Unless she missed her guess, he was going to be spoiling for a fight when they got back to his apartment. She knew that look of his very well.

She took them the coffee, holding back a scathing comment about not being the maid before she swept back out again. It was her break, and she sat down with her legal pad to jot down a fiery argument that said absolutely nothing, but relieved her frustration. Why hadn't she said something? Why hadn't she come right out and told McCallum that Dalton wasn't part of her future?

"Idiot," she muttered.

"Someone call?" Nicky asked from behind her.

"They're both in there," she said, gesturing toward McCallum's door. "Want me to announce you?"

He shook his head, sauntering past her to open the door. "Never give Grey any warning. It's suicide."

She muffled a giggle when the door closed behind him.

It took a little over an hour for the conference to break

up, during which the phone seemed to have a nervous break-down. Abby did little else but answer it and explain why Mr. McCallum couldn't come to the phone right then. It was a relief when the office door opened and the three men came through it.

"We'll meet you at the Rendezvous Lounge at seven," McCallum told Robert Dalton.

"I'll be there. See you later, Abby," Dalton added and paused by her long enough to drop a kiss on her forehead. She stared after him, stunned by the gesture.

"I'll say goodbye, too. I left a client sitting in my office," Nicky murmured. "See you both later."

But neither of them answered him. Abby and McCallum faced each other like championship contenders, wary and taut, while the silence stretched like a Texas highway between them.

CHAPTER NINE

"I vaguely remember telling you that I don't enjoy being made to look like a fool," McCallum told her in his courtroom voice.

She straightened. "And might I ask why you think you do?"

"What the hell kind of games are you playing, Abby?" he growled. "What, exactly, is the relationship between you and 'Grandad'?"

"He's only four years older than you, o ancient one!" she shot back.

"The whole idea of moving in with me was supposed to be keeping him at bay," he reminded her.

"That was when I thought he'd be a threat," she said. "He isn't."

"Of course not. You want him and he wants you. And now that he's separated, the path is clear, isn't it?" He smiled, a cold smile that hurt her.

She started to tell him that it wasn't true, that he was the only man she wanted, or loved. He obviously didn't feel the same way, with all his warnings about getting "involved."

Her pride froze the words in her throat. She couldn't tell him how she really felt.

While she was hesitating, he went back into his office and closed the door.

He didn't speak to her again until they were back in his apartment. They'd both dressed for the evening, McCallum in his dark suit and tie, Abby in a vivid red gown with a handkerchief hem, a nipped waist and a very low neckline.

"How appropriate," he murmured, casting her a cool glance.

She stiffened. "The color?" she asked with an overly sweet smile. "Yes, isn't it? I thought I might open a brothel someday and this is just the dress to drum up business."

"You said it, honey, I didn't," he growled. "It's five-thirty. We'd better be going."

She followed him to the door with an emptiness in her that she'd never expected. Her fingers touched his sleeve lightly, and his big body went taut at the action.

"Let's not argue," she pleaded gently.

His face was still like a block of ice, but he did smile—if it could be called that. "Why not? By all means, let's be civilized. I assume you'll be moving out in the near future?" he added with chilling politeness. "After all, there's hardly any reason left for you to stay, is there?" And he opened the door.

She thought about it all the way to the exclusive downtown restaurant, and by the time they were escorted to Robert Dalton's table, she was in a state of depression that was trancelike. She'd gotten so used to being with McCallum. Having breakfast with him, watching television with him, talking and laughing and making love with him, and how was she going to get used to the idea of being alone again? How was she going to cope with life without McCallum?

Her hungry eyes fastened on his profile as they wound

through the tables, drinking in every line of his dark, broad face. He was the most elegant man she'd ever known, and by far the most masculine. He attracted female eyes without even trying; especially Abby's. She studied his mouth and remembered the way it felt hard against hers. Her eyes slid down the big, hard-muscled frame and she could still feel its warmth and weight in that bed at his mother's house as he taught her all the secret pleasures of lovemaking.

He heard the tiny little sigh and glanced down at her. "Impatient?" he chided coolly.

She wondered miserably what he'd have done if she'd admitted that it was the memory of his ardent lovemaking the night before that had prompted the sound?

"Yes, of course," she replied with practiced unconcern. She didn't look at him again.

Robert Dalton rose as they approached the table. "Good evening," he said formally, smiling at McCallum and treating Abby to a long, appreciative look. "Abby, you look enchanting in that dress."

"I've been told that the color suits me," she murmured as he seated her.

"It does," Dalton murmured. "It's bright and vivid and eye-catching—like you."

"Why, Robert, how very gallant," she sighed. Her angry eyes met McCallum's across the table.

But the taciturn attorney ignored the dig and concentrated on his menu. "What will you have, Abby?" he asked with icy politeness.

She turned her attention to the tempting dishes, and once McCallum had ordered, he dragged Dalton into a discussion about the merger that lasted all the way through the main course of rack of lamb and didn't end until the lemon mousse was being served. It almost seemed to be deliberate, as if McCallum intended to make it impossible for Dalton to say anything to Abby. However, over the dessert, the older man toyed with the long stem of his wineglass. He smiled at Abby and leaned toward her.

"We had lemon mousse that first evening we spent together," he said in a soft, gentle tone. "Remember?"

She smiled back. "It was at the restaurant on the top of the skyscraper," she recalled. "And I wore a business suit while all the other women were dressed in silk and covered with jewelry. I wanted to go through the floor."

He laughed delightedly. "I thought you were the most striking woman there," he reminded her.

"And you were surely the most striking man," she replied with a glance toward McCallum, who was glowering down into his wineglass. She averted her gaze with a secret smile. "We had fun together."

McCallum set the wineglass down with a thud that all but shook the table. "If you two are finished, I've got a brief to work on tonight. I need to get home. Coming, Abby?"

"I'll bring you home if you'd like," Dalton said quickly, his eyes hopeful. "We could go dancing," he added.

Abby smiled demurely. "Why, thank you, Robert, I'd like that."

McCallum shook hands with Dalton and went to pay the check. He left the restaurant without another glance in Abby's direction. Good enough for him, she thought bitterly. The way he'd been behaving, it was a relief not to have to be around him. She told herself that, but his treatment of her had hurt just the same. He'd as well as told her to leave the apartment, to get out of his life. She supposed that he was afraid of any further involvement with her, and that was why he wanted her to leave. But it didn't seem possible that he could care so little after their night together, when he'd been as tender a lover as any woman could want. Surely, a man couldn't be that loving unless he loved…except in Mc-Callum's case, she added silently. He was just an experienced man and she'd been a challenge with her coolness, her poise. He'd wanted to prove that he could get under her guard and he'd done that. How he'd done that!

"I said," Dalton murmured gently, "how would you like to try that new lounge down the street? It's a disco, but I think we can manage to blend in."

She smiled at him halfheartedly. "I'd like that very much. Shall we go?"

The disco was bright and colorful and loud, and Abby drank far more than she should have. She danced uninhibitedly, light on her feet, and closed her eyes as the throbbing music and lights washed her in a loud oblivion. She wasn't drunk when Dalton gently suggested that it was time to leave. But she was on the verge.

"I feel a little fuzzy," she admitted when Dalton pulled up at McCallum's apartment building. "Nice, but blurred around the edges."

Dalton sighed. "Oh, Abby, I had such hopes for tonight," he murmured. "I told Grey that we were…well, that's not important now. You've had him on your mind all night, haven't you? I have to admit that at first I thought you were using him as a cover, to keep me from getting too close. But that's not so, is it? You really care about him."

Even through the blur of the alcohol, that hit home. "Yes," she admitted after a minute. "I care—terribly."

"There's no chance for me?"

She looked at him wistfully. "A year ago, yes. But not now. I'm sorry. I truly am."

"Not half as sorry as I am." He leaned forward and kissed her cheek gently. "I should have let well enough alone. You told me it was over, but I didn't believe you. I hope I haven't messed things up too much for you and Grey."

That remark flew right over her swimming head. "Good night, Robert," she murmured. "Thank you for my evening."

"Thank you for mine. Good night, Abby."

She fumbled with her key once she was at the door of the apartment, and she wondered if McCallum was home. She walked in, closing the door behind her, and found the living room dimly lit, the door to his study closed with a sliver of light showing under it. But there wasn't a sound to be heard.

Abby made her way to her room and stripped off the red dress with a silent vow never to wear it again as she hung it back in the closet.

She studied her slip-clad body in the full-length mirror on the closet door with a critical eye. The low-cut neckline of the lacy apricot slip was enticing, as was the raised hem. With her long blond hair cascading around her shoulders, she wasn't bad-looking at all.

Her lips smiled lazily. Perhaps McCallum had just been jealous of Dalton. That would explain his moodiness, his irritability, his treatment of her. If that was the case, then all she had to do was go and seduce him and everything would be all right. She wouldn't have to leave, they'd live happily-ever-after and Dorothy would indeed get back to Kansas.

It made so much sense that she didn't think any further than that. She opened her door and went across the hall to McCallum's bedroom. But the bed was still made, and the coverlet untouched. He must be in the study.

She wobbled down the hall, convinced that she wasn't even tipsy. She simply felt capable of conquering the world, that was all. And if she could do that, conquering McCallum shouldn't present too large a problem.

Sure enough, Grey was sitting behind his desk. His shirt

was open down the front, his sleeves rolled back. His dark hair was mussed and his face showed every hard line. He looked up at her entrance with eyes so cold they made her shiver.

"Still up?" she teased. She leaned back against the closed door for support. "I thought you'd be in bed by now."

"Thought, or hoped?" he asked carelessly. "I hope you didn't get the idea that I was waiting up for you. I couldn't care less how late you come in."

"Of course not." She smiled woozily. "Jealous, Grey?"

He cocked an eyebrow and laid down his fountain pen. "Of you?"

"You've been furious at me since I went out with Robert the first time," she reminded him.

"Good God, of course I have!" he burst out. "I didn't expect to have you hanging on his sleeve the whole time he was in town. Damn it, hasn't it occurred to you that I'm trying to conduct a million-dollar business deal with him? How in hell can I get his attention when he's lavishing it on you?"

She blinked. "Oh, come on, now," she laughed. "Is that the truth?"

He stood up and came around the desk. "You're drunk," he said with faint contempt.

"I only had four," she muttered.

"Four what? Double Scotches? That's what you look like."

"Do you like the way I look, Grey?" she murmured, moving close. She lifted her hands and slid them inside his unfastened shirt, tangling them in the thick growth of hair over the smooth, hard muscles of his chest and stomach. She went on tiptoe to press her lips slowly, hungrily against his. But there was no response. None at all.

She drew back and frowned up at him. She couldn't read a trace of emotion in those rigid features.

But she wasn't giving up. Not now. With a tiny smile she

slid the straps of her thin slip off her shoulders and let it fall
to the floor. She stood there, nude except for her panties, and
watched his eyes trace a path down the length of her and up
again, lingering on the high swell of her breasts before they
levered back up to meet her eyes. The look on his face made
her want to cringe. It wasn't desire. It was a kind of contempt
that got through the alcoholic haze and made her sick.

"I don't need any leftovers, Abby," he said coolly.

Shocked, humiliated, she pulled the slip back on with a
jerky motion, her face hot and red with embarrassment.

"I…after the…after last night, I thought…" she stammered.

"Did you pretend that I was Dalton, Abby?" he asked carelessly, bending his ruffled head to light a cigarette. His silver
eyes pinned hers. "Was that why you were so loving in my
arms? Didn't Dalton ask you to help 'keep me satisfied' until
this deal was closed?"

"No!" she burst out.

He laughed shortly and turned away. "Perhaps not. But
you're not going to use me to bring him to heel. Pack your
things, Abby. You're leaving here in the morning. You can
move in with Dalton or follow him back to Charleston. And
furthermore, I think it would be in the best interests of both
of us if you started looking for another job. I'll expect you to
work for at least two weeks, but I'll find a replacement within
a couple of days."

She gaped at him. Tears welled behind her eyes. "I wasn't
using you!" she cried. "Grey, I don't want Robert Dalton
anymore, I don't!"

He spared her a glance as he slid down into his desk chair.
"Strange, that isn't what he told me."

So that explained Dalton's strange remark out in the car,
the one that had gone over her head. And McCallum sat there
as unyielding as a boulder, his eyes accusing as they met hers.

He wasn't prepared to believe anything she said. He was convinced that she was still in love with Dalton, and that was the end of it. He didn't want her.

She turned, her posture drooping, and reached for the doorknob. "I'll take the morning off, if you don't mind," she said proudly. "That will give me enough time to get moved and put in my application at an employment agency."

There was a brief hesitation before he spoke. "I suppose I can spare you."

"Jan's roommate is looking for a job," she mentioned, recalling Jan's enthusiastic efforts on her friend's behalf. "You might ask her."

"Abby…"

She bit her lip to keep from crying. She couldn't look at him. "You're right, it's for the best. Damn you, Greyson McCallum. I wish I never had to see you again!" She opened the door and ran all the way to her room.

He was already gone when she went in to breakfast, and it was a blessed relief. Abby hadn't known how she was going to face him after her exhibition last night. Just the memory of it made her face flame with self-contempt. How could she have been so brazen, so blatant? She'd never forgive herself. She should have left well enough alone and gone to bed. As it was, she didn't know how she was ever going to be able to look him in the eye. She didn't want to, she told herself. She'd meant it when she told him she didn't want to see him again. But that wasn't going to be possible. She was going to have to work those two weeks, and she couldn't imagine a purer torment.

How simple everything had seemed when McCallum had suggested that she move in with him. How uncomplicated. Abby had never expected it to wind up in such a tangle.

"Have enough?" Mrs. McDougal asked from the doorway with a smile.

"Plenty, thank you. It was delicious," Abby said automatically, while she felt as if she'd eaten cardboard.

"Then I'll see you this evening. Have a nice day," the housekeeper said pleasantly as she turned back into the kitchen.

Abby could have cried. No, Mrs. McDougal wouldn't see her, not that evening or any other. She wondered if Vinnie Nichols would move in with McCallum now. It seemed likely. She got up from the table, leaving a full cup of coffee untouched.

Her apartment seemed alien now. She missed the big easy chair she'd curled up in while she was staying with McCallum. She missed hearing his voice, his step. She even missed his temper. Life was going to be so lonely now.

She took her time about unpacking, while mentally she thought through her options. She could go back to reporting, of course. She had enough experience to qualify for a copyeditor's job. Or she could find another legal firm to work for. She still had high hopes for the novel she was working on, but that was going to take more time than she had. She couldn't expect to just pop it in the mail and have a check back in two weeks. She was more likely to have a rejection slip in that length of time. First novels were notoriously hard to market, and she had no mistaken ideas that she was a phenomenal talent. The competition was fierce, and Abby was a beginner. Someday she fully expected to break into the market, but she was realistic enough to know that it would take some effort, as well as time.

The immediate thing was to look for another job. She tidied up her apartment and went downtown to the state employment agency. Unemployment was rampant and she had to wait for a long time to see a counselor. But it didn't take a great deal of time to fill out the form and answer the questions.

"You're in luck," the young woman behind the desk told her with a smile. "We've got an attorney looking for a secretary. He's just passed his bar exam and it'll be a one-girl office. Want to try?"

"Oh, yes!" Abby said gratefully.

She was given a name and address and she beat a path to the nearby office building where Elton Pettigrew, Attorney at Law, had just opened his practice.

He was a personable young man with blond hair and green eyes, and he was impressed with Abby's secretarial skills.

"There's only one thing," she said nervously, "I'd just as soon you didn't say anything to my previous employer about my working here. There was a…a personal problem there."

Pettigrew's eyebrows levered up. "McCallum, huh?" he asked with a knowing smile. "I don't know him personally, but I hear he's quite a success with women. Most women," he amended. "Did he make a pass, if you don't mind my asking?"

She looked down at her skirt. "I lived with him," she murmured.

"Oh." He shifted uncomfortably. "Sorry. Of course I won't say anything. It isn't necessary, anyway. When can you start, Abby?" he asked with a smile. He indicated the piled-up desk. "I'm pretty desperate."

Abby's mind was whirling. Did she dare? McCallum would be furious. Jan would inherit all her work until a replacement could be found. But what was she worrying about? There were temporary agencies, weren't there? Surely, one of them could fill in until McCallum got a new secretary. She'd call Jan, swear her to secrecy and apologize. She brightened. She wouldn't have to endure two weeks of watching McCallum in the office and aching for him at home.

"Today," she said firmly. "I can start right now, if you like."

"You angel!" He laughed. "All right, Miss Summer, sit down and let's get cracking. And I swear on my honor McCallum will never hear your whereabouts from me."

Pettigrew was an angel himself, to work for. He didn't yell, lose his temper, or throw things. He was considerate, kind and pleasant—all the things McCallum would never be. It was a pity that Abby had learned to love him, disagreeable traits and all. She felt like a widow away from her volatile boss.

She left an hour early with another new idea in mind. She found an apartment practically next door to Pettigrew's office and paid two weeks' rent in advance. Then she rushed to her own apartment, which was, fortunately, a furnished one, packed all her things—again—and moved out. By midnight she had everything arranged, and all the doors were closed on the past.

She'd forgotten to call Jan. She did that the minute the unpacking was through.

"Were you in bed?" Abby asked when Jan answered drowsily.

"Abby! Where are you, how are you, what—" she began frantically.

"I'm fine," she said gently. "I just got a new job and I'm… I'm not in the city anymore," she lied, hating the necessity of it. "I'm so sorry, Jan, but McCallum and I had a horrible argument, and I just couldn't bear another minute of him. I know you've got more than you can handle…"

"I got an agency girl. Don't worry about that," she muttered. "I'm worried about *you*. Honest to God, Abby, McCallum's been like a wild man today. He called hospitals and even the morgue. Please, let me tell him that you're all right, at least!"

Guilt, she thought miserably. He was remembering what

he'd said last night and feeling miserable because he thought something had happened to her.

"Tell him," she said carelessly, "but I'm not going to tell even you where I am or what I'm doing. Jan, I never want to see him again. Never."

"What did he do?" Jan groaned. "Abby…"

"It's all in the past," came the weary reply. "I'm so tired, Jan. I'd just had all I could take. McCallum told me last night to get out of the apartment and find another job. Well, I did both, and I don't know what he's upset about. He told me to go."

"I don't think he meant to, is the thing," Jan sighed. "Men do strange things when they're in love and jealous."

"Want to hear the truth?" Abby asked. "McCallum let me stay in the apartment to protect me from getting involved with Robert Dalton. I… I knew him from Charleston, you remember."

"I remember. You were in a bad way," Jan said gently.

"I'm in a worse one now." Abby laughed miserably. "Anyway, there was never any real emotion on McCallum's part. He just wanted to keep me on the job. I'd told him I'd quit if I had to see Robert every day."

"And he let you move in just because of that?" Jan asked slyly. "Uh-uh," she murmured. "Not McCallum. He never does anything without a motive. Even Vinnie Nichols has never stayed more than a night at his apartment. Did you know that? I found it out accidentally, and it quite shocked me. He values his privacy more than anything else in life. He wouldn't share it just as a favor."

"So I thought, too, once," Abby said, recalling with painful clarity the offer she'd made McCallum as she shed her slip—an offer he'd refused coldly and contemptuously. "But I was wrong. And so are you, my friend."

"Abby, did Nick ever tell you what McCallum said at the Christmas party? He said he was going to when I talked with him a couple of days ago. Did he ever?"

Abby frowned. "No."

"McCallum told Nick that he'd have given half his practice to kiss you under the mistletoe, but he was afraid that if he did you'd quit, and he'd never have another chance to get close to you."

Abby felt her heart spin around. She drew a steadying breath. Well, McCallum had gotten close, all right, she thought. The problem was, he'd discovered that he didn't like being close to Abby, physically or otherwise. That was why he'd sent her away.

"Did you hear me?" Jan prompted.

"I heard you. But it doesn't matter. Not now."

"Do you love him, Abby?" Jan asked bluntly.

She bit her lip. "Oh, Jan, I do love him so," she whispered. "I tried not to, and leaving him…" She swallowed tears. "It was the hardest thing I've ever done. But he doesn't want me. He sent me away. He hates me…!"

"You're upset. It's my fault. I'm sorry." There was a pause. "Will you do something for me? There's a file at the office that you've written a note about, and I can't make it out—it's on that murder trial coming up, the Harris case—could I call you about ten in the morning? McCallum will be out," she added, "and you can decipher the note and tell me what to do with the things in your desk, where to forward your mail…"

Abby sniffed back the tears. "Okay. I'll give you the number, but you swear that you won't give it to McCallum."

"All right, I swear," Jan said reluctantly.

"Talk to you in the morning, then. Good night, Jan."

"Good night, Abby," came the reply. Now, why did Jan

sound so satisfied? Well, she could tell McCallum to stop worrying, anyway, but he wouldn't know where Abby was. Not a chance.

Abby had a fresh cup of coffee in front of her as she riffled through the papers on her desk. Pettigrew had gone to court, and the office was empty. She'd caught up the correspondence and was working on a divorce petition. It looked like a slow day, so she didn't feel guilty about taking the time to have a second cup of coffee.

The phone rang four times before Abby picked it up breathlessly and gave the name of the law firm.

"Hi, Abby," Jan said with a smile in her voice. "Are you still okay?" she added gently.

"Fine. Just fine. Now read me that note."

"I'll get it right now." There was a long, long pause before Jan came back on the line. "Okay, here it is. Something about calling up Newman…"

"But that was about a case we finished weeks ago," Abby protested. "Are you sure that's the right note?"

"I thought it was…yes, that's the only one in the file. Maybe it was misfiled," Jan stammered.

Abby sighed. It wasn't like Jan to get rattled. "As for my stuff in the desk, just put it in a box and keep it by you. There's bound to be a day when McCallum is out of town and that's when I'll come by to get it."

"I'll do that. You take care of yourself, hear?"

"I will. You, too, my friend. Bye, Jan."

She hung up and stared at the receiver. Tears began to roll down her cheeks. That was that. The last link severed. Now all she had to do was learn to live without Greyson McCallum.

Thirty minutes later she was just finishing the petition

when she heard the office door open. She whirled around to see who it was, and her heart seemed to levitate and hang in midair.

"Hello, Abby," McCallum said quietly from the doorway.

CHAPTER TEN

She stared at him with tear-filled eyes, and hated the weak part of her that wanted to get up and run to him. But pride and hurt kept her seated.

"How did you find me?" she asked shakily.

He shrugged. "I looked up the address in the telephone directory…"

"Jan told you the name of the law firm," she finished for him.

He scowled. "Thank God she did. Do you know I've been all the way to Charleston looking for you? I followed Dalton back there, expecting that I'd find you with him. When he hadn't seen you, I had to assume the worst." He started toward her, his whole stance menacing. The dark brown suit he was wearing made his silver eyes seem even lighter as they glittered down at her. "I called hospitals and funeral homes and the morgue. I called the ambulance service and the police. I gave up at two in the morning and went to bed, and even then I couldn't sleep. When Jan came in this morning and told me you'd called and that you were all right, I damned near got down on my knees to thank God that you weren't lying somewhere dead."

She straightened up from the chair, standing behind it for support. "You don't have to worry. I'm fine. I've got a new job, a new apartment—a new start. I'll be fine."

"No, you won't," he said. He stopped just in front of her, and for once he looked every year of his age. He was absolutely haggard, drawn. "I hurt you. I seem to have done quite a lot of that over the past few days. I came here to ask you if you could forgive me."

Her green eyes widened on his face. She'd never once heard McCallum apologize, not to anyone. It was something he didn't do. But he was apologizing to her, with a humility she'd never expected from him.

She dropped her eyes to the coffee on her desk. "That... that part of my life is over," she told him gently. "I won't hold a grudge. You can't help what you feel, any more than I can."

"Do you hate me, Abby?" he asked roughly.

She shook her head. "I... It's just that I'm so ashamed," she whispered. Her voice broke on the word and she half turned away.

He moved with uncanny speed for a man his size, whirling her around to catch her hard and close in his big arms.

"Ashamed of what?" he ground out. His face was unnervingly close, his pulse as erratic as hers. "Of offering yourself to me that night? I wanted you. Oh, God, I wanted you! But I thought Dalton had turned away from you, and you were looking for a substitute. You were half-stoned..."

"You said you didn't want me." The words came out on broken sobs, and tears streamed down her cheeks.

He held her closer, tilting her mouth up to meet his. "How

could I?" he whispered as his lips slowly, softly, parted her trembling lips. "When all I want in the world, in life, is you?"

His mouth opened against hers, pressing her lips along with it, his tongue tracing first the upper lip, then the lower before it shot into her mouth and took absolute possession. He ground her body into his, moving it silkily in a slow, maddening rhythm that very quickly began to have an unmistakable effect on him.

"Come back to the apartment with me, Abby," he said in a rough whisper over her lips. "I want to show you exactly what I feel for you."

"But...but I'm working..." she protested weakly.

"Put the phones on hold and lock the door. We'll call him later," he said, his eyes eating her.

She was too weak-kneed to argue. She jotted a note telling Pettigrew she'd had an emergency, locked the door and followed McCallum without another word of protest.

He'd barely closed the apartment door and locked it after a brief, silent ride, when he drew Abby's body against his and began to kiss her—long, slow, deep kisses that very quickly made her moan.

"I missed you," he whispered huskily. His hands unzipped her dress and slid it down her body; her slip followed. "I never knew a man could miss a woman so much." He unhooked her bra and drew it sensuously down her arms. His eyes worshipped her high, bare breasts in the aching silence that followed, before he bent and took each taut nipple in his mouth, tantalizing, caressing, until her fingers caught the back of his head and her body arched to give him better access.

"Undress me," he whispered.

Her hands slipped off his jacket and worked the buttons of his shirt with feverish impatience. She eased it off and ran her hands slowly, aggressively against his broad chest, savoring the feel of it.

"Hurry," he murmured. His hands were all over her, touching, teasing, making her tremble with pleasure.

She eased off his trousers and bent to help him out of his shoes and socks. There was only one last garment, and her fingers hesitated only briefly before they tugged at the elastic and drew it down. Following an impulse, her lips traveled from his chest down his flat stomach to his thighs. The reaction she got was completely unexpected. With a harsh, deep groan, he caught her around the waist and eased down onto the thick carpet with her, his hands quickly removing her tiny panties before he covered her body with brief, teasing kisses. She writhed in a torment of pleasure, begging, pleading, until she felt his warm, hard body easing down onto hers.

"Look at me," he ground out as his body slowly merged with hers.

With a gasp, she looked straight up into his eyes, her body involuntarily arching, falling.

"I love you," he said in a voice that trembled with hunger.

"I...love you," she managed.

It was the last intelligible sound she made for a long, long time as he led her into an intensity of sensation that even surpassed the first time with him. She thought that no woman alive had ever been loved as tenderly, as fiercely, as completely, as he loved her on that cool, silky carpet in the middle of the living room.

She could barely breathe at all when he pulled her beside him and lit a cigarette in what seemed like a lifetime later.

He pulled an ashtray down from the end table and propped it up on his sweaty chest, easing up against the end of the sofa for a back support.

"You see what you drive me to?" He chuckled breathlessly. "My God, on the carpet!"

She laughed delightedly, nuzzling her face into his throat. "I love you," she whispered. "I love you, I love you…"

He reached down and kissed her. His lips were cool and he tasted of smoke and tenderness. "I love you," he whispered back. She'd have known without the words. It was in his eyes, in the way he looked at her, touched her. It had been there for a very long time, and she'd never noticed.

"I've worshipped you from afar for months, Miss Summer," he told her gently. "But you were wearing a suit of armor I couldn't get through. I'll always be grateful to Dalton for finding a chink in it for me."

"There hasn't been anything between us, Grey," she said earnestly. "I told him that I loved you."

"He was trying to cause trouble at first, I think," he agreed, "but eventually I worked it out for myself that he was doing the chasing, not you. Abby, I'd give anything to take back what I said and did to you the night I told you to go."

The pain in his eyes hurt her. She reached up and kissed them tenderly, her fingers caressing his broad face. "You just made up for it, counselor," she said with a loving smile.

"Well, just in case there were any doubts left in your mind," he murmured, and his smile teased her.

"I did plan on making it up to you some more—several times," he added, watching her color delightfully. "Just one thing, though, love—I suppose you noticed that I didn't do much protecting."

She looked up into his eyes. "Grey, would it matter terribly if I got pregnant?"

He shook his head. "No, ma'am," he said with a grin. "I think pregnant ladies are sexy as hell. There's just one catch."

"What?" she asked suspiciously. She sat up, unconsciously

graceful, like a Venus kneeling on the rug, and his eyes ate her. "A wife you didn't mention? A shady past? A…"

"You'll have to marry me," he said.

Her eyes searched his. "I'd like that," she said.

"But you don't have to."

"I know. I want to." He finished the cigarette and put it out. "I wanted to six months ago. I never believed in commitment until I met you, honey, but right now all I want is to get you in front of a minister before you change your mind."

"I won't do that," she promised. "But if it's all the same to you, I'd like to put something on before you take me to get the license."

He chuckled, reaching up to her. "Later, baby," he whispered as he lay her down. "I'm not quite through explaining how I feel about you."

She reached up to pull his warm, hair-covered body down against the soft bareness of her own with a worshipful smile.

"Don't let me interrupt you, darling," she whispered against his warm mouth, "but isn't Mrs. McDougal due any minute?"

He poised with his mouth just over hers and checked his watch. "So she is. All right, temptress, come on."

He got up and swung her up in his arms to carry her toward the privacy of his bedroom.

"But, Grey, the clothes…" she protested, looking over his broad, bronzed shoulder at the scatter of them on the rug.

He only laughed, the sound deep and pleasant in the silence of the apartment. "It'll be good practice for McDougal," he replied.

"Practice?"

He looked down at her as he carried her into the bedroom. "I have a feeling that this could be habit-forming, honey," he murmured as he closed the door.

There was a muffled laugh behind it, a deep chuckle…and

then silence. Mrs. McDougal, just opening the apartment door, spotted the clothes, smiled broadly and made a mental note to put dinner back two hours.

★ ★ ★ ★ ★